The woman has approached her and now reaches out, her hand finding Isbe's upper arm. She draws Isbe's hands together, turning her palms up, and then, moments later, presses something into them. Something cool and lightweight, made of crystal or glass. The object is hollow, with a long, narrow opening at the top. One end is pointed, the other round.

A slipper. Just larger than the length of Isbe's hand.

"She left you a . . . shoe?"

"A glass slipper."

WINTER
GLASS

LEXA HILLYER

HARPER TEEN
An Imprint of HarperCollinsPublishers

HarperTeen is an imprint of HarperCollins Publishers.

Winter Glass
Copyright © 2018 by Lexa Hillyer
All rights reserved. Printed in the United States of America.
No part of this book may be used or reproduced in any manner
whatsoever without written permission except in the case of brief quotations
embodied in critical articles and reviews. For information address
HarperCollins Children's Books, a division of HarperCollins Publishers,
195 Broadway, New York, NY 10007.
www.epicreads.com

Library of Congress Control Number: 2017939010
ISBN 978-0-06-244091-4

Typography by Carla Weise
Map by Diana Sousa
18 19 20 21 22   PC/LSCH   10 9 8 7 6 5 4 3 2 1
❖
First paperback edition, 2019

To the memories of George and of Ellen:
may eternal peace
include some great reads

Ice contains no future, just the past, sealed away.
—*Haruki Murakami,* Blind Willow, Sleeping Woman

[The sea] is like what we imagine knowledge to be:
dark, salt, clear, moving, utterly free
—*Elizabeth Bishop, "At the Fishhouses"*

THE MYTH OF THE HART SLAYER

Sing high in the air
For the heart of the deer
Laid bare
By the hunter who roams
The royal forest.

Good king's betrayer:
Hero of the poor,
His name, no one knows,
Whose blood must slay
Man's greatest foe.

Or so cry the future sayers:
For among all men
And across all fae,
No heart can be braver
Than that of the hart slayer.

THE HEART OF THE DEER
LAID BARE

1

Malfleur,
the Last Faerie Queen

Sleep is a vast and dreamless dark.

But then: tiny lights, like seeds, shower across a corner of the black. Something has snagged its claws in the soft flesh of night.

The panther is upon her before the queen has fully awakened: the scent of flowers and meat on its breath, a feral purr rumbling at the base of its throat. The tight leather muzzle Malfleur always keeps chained over the animal's mouth has torn loose.

She does not have time to wonder how the panther—afflicted by the sleeping sickness for many weeks—woke up from its spell. With the speed of thought, her hand has found the letter opener beside her bed and wrapped around its thin handle, just as the animal's fangs tear into her shoulder.

The queen cries out; pain ricochets through her body as she thrusts the letter opener in an arc over her head. It is only meant for hacking open a waxen seal, too dull to cut through the creature's skin, but never mind—its point has found the eye. The panther roars, pulls back and flails, slashing the pillow beside Malfleur's face, sending bloodied feathers into the air. The queen gasps and rolls off her bed as the animal continues to wail—a sound like a rent in a glacier: half scream, half growl.

Dawn's cool light barely illuminates her royal chambers, but it's just enough to catch the glint of her dagger, unsheathed, on the window ledge. She crawls to it, her right arm shaking from the shock of her wound. Clinging to the ledge, she pulls herself up. The panther has noticed her movement. It lunges, a blur of white fur and fangs—the letter opener still jutting out of its face at an angle, like the tusk of the fabled unicorn.

Malfleur sucks in a breath, then strikes with the dagger, which jolts raggedly into the beast's rib cage.

A gargling howl fills the air, seems to swallow up all the light in the room. Time slows. Malfleur sways with the aftershock. The panther's claws catch the skirt of her nightgown as the beast thuds to the floor, forcing the queen down onto her knees.

Still it struggles, legs scrambling, claws scraping stone.

She breathes roughly, leaning over the body as it

continues to writhe for several moments more; her night-dress is torn, covered in blood half the panther's and half her own. She can't feel her shoulder.

Finally the panther goes still, steam rising from its nostrils. The queen's breath begins to calm too as she stares at the majestic creature, who always seemed to her like an incarnation of winter, full of pale fury and long, cold solaces. How ugly it has become now, where once the animal was all grace, its purr deep as a subterranean tremor.

This was her favorite pet—her companion, her *creation*—but it turned on her. Betrayal rings in Malfleur's bones, so familiar by now it has come to feel like a passing season. For a moment, it is not her shoulder wound that aches and pangs but the sudden depth of her loss, echoing through her.

She collects herself, calculating the facts as she staggers slowly to her feet.

There was nothing truly sentient driving the attack, that much is obvious. Malfleur can still sense the animal's panic and hunger lingering in the air like the electricity of a storm. The large white beast—pristine, dangerous, loyal, *trained*—must have forgotten itself while it slept, forgotten the humanity the faerie queen had breathed into its mind, using the powerful magic she has accumulated over the years.

The panther had even warned Malfleur about the sleeping sickness, and the gaping purple flowers surrounding the palace of Deluce, before falling into its own slumber several weeks ago. *Hungry for hungry for*, the cat had said in their last conversation, struggling to isolate the words.

Poor animal. Most humans cannot find words for such things either.

Still, the question that tugs at Malfleur's mind—as she steadies herself to force the dagger from the panther's flesh—is not why her pet attacked her, but why it broke free from its long sleep in the first place.

And how?

She wipes the knife clean. The smell of guts and bile is stifling; it's as though the queen herself has been consumed. She sways, then stumbles to the wall and pushes open her shuttered window.

She heaves a breath of fresh air. The smoky undulations of LaMorte seem, at just that moment, almost peaceful, swept in a morning gauze just shy of blue, no longer silver.

There can only be one answer to her question, she realizes.

The faerie curse has been lifted.

Princess Aurora has awakened.

———

"Happiness is like starlight, my Marigold," Malfleur's father told her one summer evening when she was very little. King Verglas had always enjoyed the sound of his own voice. But Malfleur thought he was right, in a way: we do what is necessary, for our joy in this world is scarce and must be wrestled down from the black vault of all that is random and meaningless.

And so, less than a week after Aurora's awakening and the

panther's attack, the queen and a small retinue of soldiers—using information she gleaned from her squeamish and simpering cousin, Violette—push their way into the royal forest of Deluce, dense with the heady coniferous scent of pine needles and sap. Even in the dead of night, the abandoned cottage isn't hard to find. The breath of memories comes to her, soft and stirring, but she does not let it touch her.

Now Malfleur stands in the doorway of the nursery she once shared with her sister, Belcoeur. There sits the spinning wheel, its gold contours flickering in the light of her torch. The instrument had been a gift to her beloved sister . . . and, later, a symbol of all that had splintered between them. She gazes at the rare, beautiful spindle. She takes her time; imagines threading her desire through the eye of the flyer, then carefully pedaling and pulling, pedaling and pulling, until the cord of revenge grows strong and taut and fine.

Until it shines.

2

Isabelle

Isbe shudders in the cold as she and several royal attendants pick their way across a field at dawn in the unpleasant business of scouring for survivors—and taking account of the lost. She is thankful, just now, for being blind. But then again, she doesn't need to be able to see the sun push up through the fog hanging over the strait in order to know the unflinching cruelty it brings, doesn't have to see the bones of the dead blanching in the grass, either—bodies forever fallen among thorny, shriveled vines, forming miniature castles for sparrows and mice.

It has been a week since the sleeping sickness officially ended, but it has left Deluce in shambles. The moment Aurora shifted, gasped, and grasped her sister's hand, everything changed: the purple flowers along the crenelated palace walls began to wither. Scattered servants and nobles throughout the palace startled into consciousness, though the vast majority remained still, their lungs frozen from the chill of winter, or their throats slit by pillagers. The list of the dead within the castle village has grown by eighty-three since yesterday. That number does not even include the eleven council members who died. The only one who lived is the chief of military, Maximilien.

"Another courtier, Miss Isabelle," says one of the servants in her party. A woman takes her arm and guides her to a body.

Isbe kneels down and feels a sunken rib cage, covered in a surcoat of ermine and velvet. She scrambles for the buttons—something light, like fine gold, and something glossy, perhaps pearl—removing each one expertly with her bare hands. "Add them to our store."

When William first told Isbe that they must scour and save, she scoffed. "Deluce has more gold than any nation in the known world," she told him. "Surely you know that."

"In war, every single jeweled ring in the land may be melted into a metal that could save a man's life. Or a woman's." His comment made her think of the nasty Lord Barnabé—*Binks*—an ostentatious noblefaerie who wears ten ruby rings at once, one for each of his fat fingers.

"My lady." A servant tugs on her sleeve, and Isbe recognizes the kitchen maid's voice, the buttery scent of her hair and clothes.

"Yes, Matilda?" At least it isn't Gertrude, who used to beat Isbe when she stole biscuits. Gertrude, like so many of the others, perished during the sickness. There'd been a rolling pin trapped in her clenched fist when her body was found.

"The prince is asking for you. May I lead you to him?" She sounds a little out of breath.

Isbe hesitates before answering. "Of course." She places her hand on the older woman's weathered wrist and allows Matilda to lead her back across the castle yards.

Early spring has a bite to it. The wind stings and cools Isbe's flushed face as she thinks of the prince. How there had been a miracle, a *yes*, on the tip of her tongue, a gift of a word. A yes that would have allowed her to skip right over a lifetime of no, over the impossibility of being born a bastard and not a princess. A yes that would have made her a queen, that would have made her William's.

The Aubinian prince has left an imprint on Isbe: she keeps replaying the way his words and hands tindered her, how she burned and was left shaking. But then Aurora awoke, and that alive thing—that inner self, that *yes*—withered on Isbe's tongue, dissolved into dust. She feels overcome now with a bashful shame, stunned by the sickening glare of the obvious: Prince William of Aubin was never hers except in that brief instant, in the wine caves, when they felt they were truly at the end of all hope. He is not hers anymore, and she is certainly not his.

But she has her sister back, and that is all that matters.

"You've been avoiding me," William announces quite accurately, as soon as she's deposited in the king's tower meeting room.

"I've been doing exactly what you've asked of me," Isbe replies, keeping her voice calm. She reaches out to steady herself, touching the back of an elaborately carved chair.

"Exactly that and only that," William responds, and she could swear she feels his gaze sweep across her skin, lighting it on fire. He is always so cutting with his words, so frustratingly precise, so pointed—like darts driven into a map to mark a location.

"You've expected more, then."

"Expected. Hoped." He clears his throat. "As you know, there have been clashes in the western villages. Bouleau and Dureté have fallen, and we were unprepared."

We.

"Queen Malfleur may be holding back the extent of her forces for now," he goes on, "but I have persuaded Maximilien that our next step is to shore up our defense along the Vallée de Merle. In the meantime, we are sending scouts into the mountains to assess the cause of Malfleur's delay. I've shown my new bombard design to the forge, and we're moving forward with—"

"William," Isbe inserts. "If I may interrupt."

"You've certainly never asked permission before." There's a familiar amusement in his voice.

It's intolerable! He finds these little ways to insinuate that he knows her intimately, when in fact, as of a month ago, she was hardly aware that a third prince of Aubin existed—and, to be sure, he'd never heard of *her*.

Never mind what had happened between them just seven nights ago, the kisses that left her lips swollen; his fingertips on her shoulders, her neck, her collarbone. . . . Never mind the fact that she too feels the same connectedness—feels that even when he surprises her, he does so in a way that further clarifies and satisfies her sense of his *Williamness*.

"Sarcasm is ill-fitting on you," she says now with a huff. "I don't believe, William, that our problem is one of strategy."

"What do you mean, our *problem*? Our problem is Malfleur."

"*Or* maybe Malfleur is just a symptom."

"That symptom is murdering your people."

"Only those she has not persuaded to her side."

"The sword's blade can be very persuasive," William says dismissively, but she can hear the rhythm of his pacing as he considers what she said. "So too can the bands of thugs doing her dirty work, much like the ones who captured us back in Isolé."

"Perhaps," Isbe admits, remembering how they'd been seized and tied together by the wrists, how certain she'd been that they were going to die. "But what if there's more to it than that? Everyone knows Bouleau and Dureté are the worst villages."

"Worst?"

She cringes. "Poorest, I meant. Unhappiest. I heard a

story about Dureté. That the lord who rules there is a faerie whose tithe is compassion. I heard he lived for years in constant tears, while all those who worked his fields grew angrier and more heartless by the tithe. As he took their compassion, they became hard. Is it any surprise, with such inequities, that they fell to Malfleur? Perhaps our greatest weakness is not a lack of assets or intelligence but an issue of, well, attitude. I can't help but think of the many tales we heard along the Veiled Road. . . ."

The atrocities performed by Malfleur's mercenaries are countless—barons and lords throughout the land brutally murdered and strung up in the village greens, a mockery made of their wealth and power: bodies stripped bare and mutilated (eyes removed, bloody guts leaking out of the M-shaped wounds carved into their exposed fat bellies), their fancy furnishings torn to shreds. Most horrifying of all were the fresh recruits, Delucian peasants dressed in fabrics made from the destroyed possessions of those lords, raiding and torching their manors, or sometimes hundreds of them taking up residence and wreaking havoc, feasting and celebrating while Malfleur's soldiers offered them weapons and promises of liberation.

To anyone who knows anything about Queen Malfleur, those promises should seem thinner than the brittle layer of ice that laces the creek Isbe used to scramble across in winter, delighting in the crackle as it shattered beneath her—yet another one of her dangerously foolish (or if you asked her, fearless) pastimes. So what's making people believe the faerie queen's promises, if not a deep, preexisting anger within them? This, Isbe is convinced, is Malfleur's greatest weapon: a dangerous flame that lives inside all of us, that blooms and burns when stoked.

And there is something worse, Isbe knows, than suffering backbreaking work, a hungry belly, or the burden of enormous levees and taxes, and that is the experience of being treated as though one's life simply does not matter. Isbe knows that feeling.

William has approached her; the velvet swish of his floor-length cloak against the stone floor mirrors the warm rustle of his voice. "I remember the rumors, yes. And everything we witnessed." He pauses.

Isbe is momentarily overcome by the prince's limelike musk—part bitter, part sweet. She now associates that scent with a prickling sensation throughout her body, sort of like pins and needles, but searing as the spray of stray sparks from a forge.

"And I don't disagree with your assessment," he admits. "However, the problem you've identified is one that can only heal over time, with the careful rebuilding of Delucian society. We will lose thousands of lives in the meantime if we are not focused on aggressive tactics, fortifying the biggest and wealthiest fiefdoms first, along with those most exposed to Malfleur's path to the palace. We must stall her advance until we can detect a weakness, which we will then go after with clean, swift, vicious action."

Clean. Swift. Vicious.

Isbe moves toward the draft from a nearby window and slides her finger along the cold glass. *William is like a windowpane*, she thinks, most of his story withheld, his surface a distraction from the landscape she cannot see. She isn't sure yet what she thinks of the prince as a military mind, or how to balance what she knows of him already—his alacrity and efficiency, his sometimes overly serious nature, his righteousness, which borders on passion—with the qualities that are still in a state of emergence, like waves of reinforcements arriving from distant lands.

"If you're not interested in my opinion, why did you seek me out today?" she asks, a mixture of impatience and curiosity coursing through her. The truth is, she hasn't yet figured out her part in this war. Not that she'd admit that to William. When it comes down to it, she's just the untrained bastard daughter of a dead king, the product of a meaningless and thwarted affair, the victim of an unjust faerie tithing.

"I *am* interested. How would you have me respond, though? What would you have me do?" William touches her arm lightly, and she pulls away.

The answer has already been sitting in the room, of course, staring at her like a pig's head on a platter, an apple stuffed in its jaw, big, obvious, and somehow unappetizing. She turns back toward his voice. "You must marry Aurora, like we planned."

Not more than a month ago, it had been presumed his eldest brother, Philip, would wed Aurora, and little thought was given to the fates of Philip's younger brothers, Edward and William. But then Philip and Edward were both murdered on their way to Deluce by Malfleur's forces, and the alliance relied on Isbe convincing the last remaining Aubinian prince—William—to awaken Aurora and marry her. Only somewhere along the way, William began to doubt his commitment to that plan. He even proposed to Isabelle instead—not once, but twice!

But then Aurora woke up, before Isbe could say yes. And ever since, the prince has been awkward around Isabelle. He has been visiting Aurora's bedside every day to make sure she's recovering from her long sleep, and though he hasn't spoken of a wedding, Isbe figures there is no reason to keep stalling.

The prince releases a breath. "And *this* will fix Deluce's 'attitude problem,' as you call it."

She bristles. "Not *fix*, no. But perhaps it will dull the spike of fear that has them turning against their own land. The people need to feel safe, they need to perceive that we are doubling in size and force."

"Aren't you worried a wedding could give the opposite impression—that we're celebrating instead of strategizing against a common enemy?"

She nods. He has a point, and it's one she has already been turning over in her mind. "The ceremony should be brief, only a few key witnesses, minimal fanfare. Just enough to make it look optimistic."

"You don't *sound* optimistic," William says.

Isbe huffs. "What do you want from me, William?" Does he really want her to say the unsayable? Confess to her dreams at night, in which his hands continue to trace patterns on her skin, his breath to dance along her neck, his words to twirl through her veins like silk ribbons, finding their way into her heart, waking something in her? *No.*

"What do my *feelings* about this wedding matter?" she presses on, ignoring the tiny break in her voice. "I never suggested anything to you but that you marry my sister in the interest of both our kingdoms." Her ears burn in anger, in frustration, in all the wanting that she has been pushing down inside her. "Yet you continually question me, challenge me, protest, and put it off. But tell me, is there any good reason to delay further what could be done and over with by week's end?"

"Over with?" His voice, usually soft, grows hard. "Last I heard, marriage is for life."

"You know what I mean." She puts her hands on her hips to still their trembling.

There's a pause and she hears him sigh. "Then no," he finally answers, so faintly she's forced to sway slightly closer to comprehend him. "I see no reason to delay."

She knows she has no right to let his response—so definitive—disappoint her. It's what she wanted to hear, what she forced him to say.

Isbe swallows. "Good. Now if you don't mind, I'll speak to my sister and begin readying the staff."

He clears his throat. "Wonderful."

She pauses, waiting—unable to leave. He's still standing so near she could reach out and touch him, pull him toward her.

But if he was going to make one last effort, going to beg her to reconsider the proposal he made to her in the wine caves, insist that it is Isabelle and no other woman he will marry, that moment has passed.

She straightens her shoulders. "Excellent."

She storms off, letting the door gape behind her like an open mouth.

⸻

Isbe flies through the stone corridors, dimly aware that only action—violent, halting—will keep her from falling apart, from allowing a scream to erupt, or worse, tears.

By the time she reaches the library, her temper has simmered only a little. Aurora is in her favorite chair, but not reading. Isbe knows this because of the rapid whisper of vellum pages, suggesting her sister is thumbing through them impatiently.

Isbe is not the only one who has changed since the sleeping sickness. Aurora has grown distant or, rather, gathered into herself. Her lack of voice now has a weight to it, the way the soundlessness of being underwater seems to press in on you, *enter* you and echo, making you less aware of your surroundings and more aware of yourself.

The fluttering stops.

"We must do better," Isbe tells her sister. She squares her shoulders. "We have to be strong now, for Deluce."

Aurora stands up, a tiny stir in the stillness of the room. And then she is beside Isbe, pulling her into the room, her delicate fingers pressing words into her sister's palms.

But how can I be strong for Deluce, when I know that Sommeil needs me too? My heart is in two places, sister, and I cannot bring its other half back.

"Whether it's split in two places or a dozen doesn't matter. You must move forward with the half you still possess. Or whatever portion."

You've never been terribly good with math, Aurora teases, and Isbe laughs.

"I've never been good at much, really." She forces the next part out. "I'm quite sure I won't be any good at all when it comes to planning your wedding, either."

Aurora's hand twitches in hers. *So there is no way to stall further?*

Isbe sighs and hugs her sister. "For what?" she whispers. "Heath?"

Aurora pulls away.

When she first awoke, she and Isabelle had spent hours relaying what had happened to each of them since Isbe ran from the palace. Isbe was shocked to learn that Aurora too had experienced an unbelievable journey. That she'd not just been sleeping, but somehow, another part of her—a part of her that remained awake—had been transported to a land called Sommeil, a world constructed out of dreams by the once-thought-dead Night Faerie, Belcoeur. In Sommeil, Aurora had come close to falling for a hunter named Heath, but she hadn't had the time to find out if it would blossom into true love, because Sommeil itself was in distress. . . .

Is in distress *still*. When Aurora awoke, she left Sommeil in flames, and she has pleaded with Isbe since, begging to return. *I'll bring a small brigade of soldiers with me this time*, Aurora insisted. *We'll find a way for everyone to be safe.*

But it's not that easy. They don't know for sure if it's even possible to return, or to bring others. And can Deluce really spare a legion to stage a rescue in a nebulous dream world?

There's a settee in front of the hearth. Isbe flops down onto it. "Aurora. True love—it's a trick." She hates the way the truth abrades her throat. "The language of the curse? It was all a terrible lie, a puzzle. The fae are notorious for their deceit. We know this."

Aurora comes back to her, pushing Isbe's feet off one end of the settee so she can sit beside her. *Maybe so. But that should have been for me to discover, for me to feel. And now I'll never know for sure.*

Isbe is doing everything she can to control her frustration, but the fact is that Aurora's romantic notions have no place here anymore. They're no longer little girls. She has realized something in the last few weeks: at birth, we receive our share. Though we don't always know it, our hand has been dealt. Our lives will have their demands, their inevitabilities—and what we *want* will have very little to do with it.

She thinks suddenly of the way she and her lifelong

friend, Gilbert, came together urgently in the slippery, salt-sprayed chaos of the whaling ship and kissed just once before the sailors wrenched them apart. And then, the same way the stench of the injured narwhal's blood seemed to permeate her hands and hair and the whole ocean, her separation from Gil infused everything that came after: Her desperate arrival at the Aubinian palace. Her bargain with Prince William, Deluce's oil for use of Aubin's weapons. And of course the other trade: Deluce's princess—and her nation's gold as dowry—for Aubin's military alliance.

Isbe picks at a loose thread in the upholstery to keep herself from shaking her sister into reason. "I'm convinced now," she says, "that love and pain are two sides of a coin, and you would be blessed to be spared both. Besides—" She pauses, the thought coming to her in a sudden, unwanted burst. "There's no reason to think that, over time, you might not fall in love with William. There are many things to admire in him. He is not as serious as he seems. He has a mind like fire. He—"

Isbe stops, feeling heat rush to her cheeks. She hasn't brought herself to tell Aurora *everything*. She can't—the secret of what happened between her and William is something that even she can't quite believe, let alone admit aloud. It was wrong; wonderful and wrong. And yet she cannot find a way to feel ashamed of it, which terrifies her more than anything else. She clears her throat. "And anyway, what matters is that we have a duty to our kingdom. We have lives to save, people to rally."

But the people of Sommeil are real too. What about their kingdom? What about their lives?

Isbe leans back, facing the hearth, listening to the morning fire crackle and pop. All this talk of love and war is overwhelming. She feels like a loose carriage wheel about to come undone, on the verge of dropping her cargo, of letting everyone down, and still so far from their destination. "I can't tell you which lives to save—or if we can save any at all." *Even our own*, she thinks. "All I can say is that we need you here. *I* need you."

Aurora stands up then, and pulls on Isbe's hand. *Well, let's go to the gardens, then.*

"Why?" Isbe allows her sister to take her by the arm and lead her out the library door.

Because, Aurora taps, *something must be in bloom even now. Maybe the crocuses. And I can't get married without proper table bouquets, now can I?*

3

Belcoeur,
the Night Faerie

Fire, like the open throat of the death faerie—his ash breath.

Sommeil burns.

Servants scream, fleeing the castle amid the acrid scent of smoldering clothes and flesh. Belcoeur crawls out of the rubble, toward the flaming Borderlands. In her palm: a charred thread. Huddled into herself, she pulls. She unravels. Her fingers move deftly, taking the threads of her own dress and rebraiding them, weaving the chaos of her heart by hand until there is no more gown, until she is exposed, nearly naked, skeletal. Old. Dying. This is the true Belcoeur. The world of lies—*dreams*—that sheltered her softly, like a spider's web, is coming down in a tremulous haze.

But even in ruin, hope blooms. There—moving toward her—something white. Something gold.

Belcoeur gasps, letting the threads drop from her hands. "You came."

———

There is such a thing as wanting something too much—waiting so long and so fiercely for it that when it finally arrives, it cannot satisfy the hole its absence created.

She stares. There is no rush of joy in Malfleur's return; instead, Belcoeur feels only the halo of loss surrounding her sister, the unfillable gap between wish and reality. She is newly conscious of her own aged body—its protruding bones, covered in a thin layer of underclothing and lace. Her knobby shoulders and hunched back. The unraveled, ashen dress strewn around her on the ground. All lives, Belcoeur realizes—faerie or mortal, long or short—are but an unspooling of the inevitable.

"Sister," Malfleur whispers, kneeling before her.

And still, hope flutters and starts. "Sister," Belcoeur chokes out. Fresh tears form at the corners of her eyes. "Will you help me?"

Malfleur seems to take in the disaster around them for the first time—the raging fire, the trapped people, the falling trees and crumbling towers. "I need to know something first," she says calmly. Her eyes gleam black and cold. Belcoeur remembers, quite suddenly, that her sister does not dream—has never dreamed. Her eyes contain that dreamlessness. It is not a lack, but a gift, a form of power. "What did you do with the child?" Malfleur asks.

"The child," Belcoeur repeats. *The child. The child.* Thorns prickle up around her heart, vines squeezing in on her lungs. She tries to breathe, but the smoke has gotten denser, the sky darker. "I don't . . . I don't know. I can't remember."

"Yes," Malfleur seems to hiss. "You must."

"Please," Belcoeur whimpers.

"What happened to the child?"

"I . . . she . . . I left her. Left her there. Tucked her into bed one last time. I kissed her good-bye. She looked so cold. So cold."

"You *left* her," Malfleur repeats slowly.

Belcoeur nods, the memory sapping all that remains of her strength. Her head is too heavy to hold up any longer. Her arms start to give, and she lowers herself onto the ground, one cheek in the dirt. How foolish, to think her sister had come in time to save her.

She has only come in time to see her die.

"Yes, I left her. My baby. Frozen forever . . ." A sob chokes back the rest.

"Wake up, Daisy," Malfleur snaps, and for a second, the old nickname shoots one last frantic fumble of hope through Belcoeur's veins. "You didn't bring your daughter into Sommeil. You left her behind. And did she live?"

But that was more than a century ago now. And there are some things we cannot have, no matter how badly we wish for them.

Belcoeur shakes her head against the ground. "She died."

And then Malfleur's icy fingertips have grasped the back of her neck.

Suddenly Belcoeur begins to cough and sputter. "What . . . what are you doing?" she asks desperately, struggling now, fighting against whatever is happening to her, as an incredible pain sweeps through her bones.

"It's called *transference*, my dear Daisy," Malfleur says. "And I've been perfecting it for many years. It won't take long now, and then . . ."

But the physical torment is so great, Belcoeur can no longer follow the words. She scrabbles against the grit and grass, tearing open the skin of her palms.

"Your magic," her sister is saying. And then, *"It will be mine."*

A wild agony rips through Belcoeur's flesh, parting her lips in a wail that cuts off abruptly, a snapped string. She is reduced to silence, to the sudden clarity of pure pain. There is no space left for sadness, or loss, or love.

With her last breath, the queen of Sommeil turns up her bleeding hand; the blood sizzles, becoming smoke. *Transference.*

4

Aurora

There's a knocking at the gate. Aurora sits upright in
bed. Her first thought is that the war has arrived, just
outside her door. Malfleur and her army of Vultures. Some
shadowed, hidden part of her almost yearns for it—for an
escape from this new prison. When she woke from Sommeil,
her sense of touch and her voice had vanished, just as she'd
feared and knew they would. Now this tower, this castle,
this *life* is slowly burying her alive, eating away at her like the
moths and termites that destroyed Queen Belcoeur's tower,
turning it into a crumbling relic she could never leave. The
waking world hardly resembles the one she left behind. The
roar of waves against Deluce's cliffs sounds alien to her now,
full of an anger she never noticed before. It's the *not knowing*

that tortures her the most—what happened to Heath, and Wren, and Belcoeur, and little Flea. *Were they even real?* Was what she *felt* real? And was that love?

The knocking again.

Aurora flips back the coverlet and hurries to her window, but the crisp night brings nothing other than the distant scent of woods . . . and ash. A strange burning scent that brings back, with a flash of horror, the memory of her last moments in Sommeil, and the fire that ravaged the castle, the Borderlands, the whole world, it had seemed.

Thud, thud, thud. The iron locks of the front gate rattle in their sockets. The pounding is inside her, a rhythm to her racing heart.

She lets go of the window curtain and moves toward her door, inviting the escape from her chambers. Tomorrow she will wed Prince William of Aubin, and she'll finally be crowned queen, a notion too massive and tangled to give her peace. Sure, she knew she'd be crowned when she came of age, shortly following her sixteenth birthday, so long as she agreed to marry the prince—but that doesn't stop her from dreading both.

It's not that there's anything wrong with the prince. No, the problem most certainly lies with *her*. There's a restless animal caged in her chest, clawing to get out. She's afraid if she sets it free, it will destroy her, destroy them all.

She steps into her night shoes and slips into the corridor, then makes her way down the winding stairs, where torch-light plays against stone.

The knocking grows more urgent—a powerful drumming of blunt fists against the wood. There are shouts from outside.

Aurora reaches the receiving hall just as Isbe bursts in from the doors to the opposite wing, in a nightgown just like Aurora's, her short-cut hair tied back in a dark tangle at the nape of her neck. Isbe collides with Prince William of Aubin—Aurora can still only think of him by his formal title, not the more intimate term "husband," though that is what he will be to her by the time the sun sets tomorrow. The prince is wearing just a pair of loose-fitting pants, and Aurora notices the strength of his bare chest and shoulders, the gleam of his dark skin in the flickering light, the way he grasps Isbe's arms to steady her, his hands lingering a moment more than needed.

Servants have clustered into the hall too, and Maximilien appears, looking unusually ruffled. "What's the meaning of the commotion?" he demands, though clearly no one knows. "Unbolt the doors."

Four soldiers pull open the grate.

Aurora's chest tightens, and her skin grows cold. What if it *is* an envoy of Malfleur's, a brigade of her deadliest mercenaries?

But into the hall stumbles a ragtag group of peasants: two men carrying an injured woman, plus one other man and woman following just behind, restrained by a pair of castle guards. Soot dusts their skin, as though they've been spit out by one of the great southern volcanoes Aurora has

29

read about. One of the men is wounded in the leg—Aurora's gaze sweeps to the bloody mud that he has tracked inside. The injured woman groans. Her taut, rounded belly rises and falls with her heaving breath.

Aurora is suddenly reminded of Helen, one of the daughters of Greta from Sommeil, the mistress of the kitchens at Blackthorn. Helen had been just a few years older than Aurora, and with child.

"They've no weapons," a guard announces.

"We seek conference with Aurora, crown princess of Deluce," one of the men asserts. Oddly, she can picture him gathering hay at dawn. *In Sommeil.* But that's not possible.

All heads turn toward her, and heat rises from her neck to her face.

"We must know your business first," Prince William says, at the same time that Maximilien asserts, "Absolutely not."

The councilman and the prince look at each other for a moment, and then Aurora steps between them. It isn't their decision to make.

Just then, a girl pushes her way through the men. "You!" she cries out.

Aurora swivels at the sound of the voice, and her jaw drops open in shock. She recognizes the servant girl immediately, even in her disarray: the ears ever so slightly outturned like a fox's; skin that reminds Aurora of the sandy beach of Cape Baille, where she once traveled with her father and mother; hair blacker than Isbe's and straight as the fall from the Delucian cliffs. The girl was a close friend of Heath's—perhaps more than a friend, though Aurora was never sure. And now her face is arranged in an image of agony—no, *anger*.

Wren.

The girl lurches toward her. "Aurora," she says. There's an ugliness to her tone, as though Aurora's name tastes sour on her tongue. "This is *your* fault." There are tears streaking the mud on Wren's face.

Aurora is so startled she backs up nearly into William's and Isbe's arms.

"Stand back," Maximilien demands.

A burly guard grabs Wren, pulling her away from the princess. "I *told* you to leave it alone, but you couldn't, could you?" She struggles against the guard.

"Where is it that you come from, in such haste, and at such a late hour?" William interrupts.

Another castle guard clears his throat. "They been talking nonsense about another world—"

Isbe scoffs, cutting off the guard. "Isn't it obvious? There's been a fire!"

"We come from . . . Sommeil," one of the men says. "Kingdom of the Night Faerie, Belcoeur."

"Destroyed now, because of you!" Wren says, before the guard holding her throws a thick hand around her mouth, shutting her up. She writhes against him.

The injured woman, still held in the two men's arms, whimpers. Aurora gestures urgently to a few of the palace servants. The woman moans again, and Aurora rushes toward her. She doesn't just look like Helen, Aurora realizes with a silent gasp. She *is* Helen.

Maximilien nods his permission. "Medical supplies."

Several of them hurry away down the east wing, and she hopes they'll return quickly with bandages and salves. She's still reeling, though. Wren. Helen. The other servants from Blackthorn, in Sommeil. *They're all here.*

"Your Highness," one of the men says. "We need your help."

But . . . how? Aurora's hands tremble.

"I don't understand it myself," the man—*Jack*, she remembers—explains. "One moment we were fleeing the flames in Sommeil, and the next, we heard the high wail of the queen. Belcouer . . . she's, she's *dead*. And then . . ." He trails off, clearly registering what must be a look of unfathomable shock on Aurora's face.

Everyone else in the room is staring at her, and Isbe has her head cocked at an angle, just as puzzled as the others.

"Are you all right, Princess?" Prince William asks, leaving Isbe's side and striding toward her.

I'm fine, she thinks. *Just completely confused.*

"We're as confused as you are," Jack responds easily, as though he has heard Aurora's thoughts.

But that's impossible. Aurora brings her fingers to her lips, which, she's surprised to realize, are moving automatically with her thoughts. *No one can hear me.*

Now it's Jack's turn to look bewildered. "Why not?"

Because I have no . . .

She stops.

"What's going on?" Isbe demands.

Maximilien's face is pale with suspicion.

But exhilaration is beating through Aurora's chest. It's as though someone has punctured a hole through the top of the invisible coffin she'd been thrown into before, and with it pours in light, and air, and the possibility of *escape*.

Everything happens in a flurry of activity then. Prince William tries to get more answers out of the newcomers, but Aurora is quick to grab Isbe's hand and inform her that she knows these people, that she must learn more about the collapse of their world. She commands that they free Wren, and the guard, begrudgingly, lets her go.

Wren practically collapses onto the ground from weakness, and Aurora runs to her, helping her to stand.

Wren pushes her away. It's not the force that startles Aurora but the coldness of Wren's hands, the bruised feeling in her chest where the girl made contact with her. *Touch.*

"Please," Aurora mouths, testing her voice. None of the others—Isbe, William, Maximilien, or the servants—seems to notice, but Wren turns to her. "Please, Wren. I'm sorry. I want to help."

"We've had enough of your help," she practically spits.

The irony stings. Something has obviously happened to Sommeil—the fire there has leached into *this* world and freed its inhabitants—but they can still understand Aurora. It's as though the faerie tithes on her have no effect among those from the dream world, even here. But Wren resents her, blames her, maybe even hates her. She could have been a friend, *should* have been, might be one of the few people with whom Aurora can freely *speak*. But Aurora ruined everything, allowed her home to be destroyed.

"Please, let me talk to you. Let me understand what has happened," she insists. She turns again to Isbe, tapping so rapidly her fingers nearly seize.

Isbe relays her thoughts to the prince, who agrees to let Wren and Aurora speak privately. "My future wife," he says to the rest, "must be trusted to conduct her own business. And if she trusts these people, then I do too." The word "wife" sends an unpleasant zing through Aurora.

Meanwhile, servants return with medical care for the injured. The men are found rooms; Helen is given a guest bedroom in the west wing and a nursemaid to tend to her. Soldiers are immediately sent out to investigate the fire in the royal forest, and Aurora has half a mind to join them, but she hangs back, eager to speak with Wren, to convince her she's on her side.

Back in her room, she hastily clears all the scattered wedding wreaths and garlands—they seem but the playthings of a child now—while a servant draws Wren a bath behind a folding screen.

Once the girl has been fed and bathed and has borrowed a sleeping robe, Aurora runs her eyes over Wren, taking in her slightly shaking hands. Her bottom lip has a tiny cut, beginning to scab. Aurora can see the fear in her eyes, the emotion welling up. She looks like she hasn't slept in days. Aurora is eager to talk to her—to talk again, period. But Wren lets out a trembling cough. She's so frail.

I think, Aurora starts, *that you should rest*. She forces herself not to touch her own lips again as she speaks, but it's clear Wren has heard her. She gestures to her bed.

Wren flushes. "This is *your* room? I couldn't. I won't. I'd rather sleep outside on the grass."

Behind the fierce stubbornness of her words, the girl is shaking. She looks so weak, but her anger burns bright.

"I won't sleep tonight anyway," Aurora insists. The questions feel like they are going to burst out of her skin, tearing her flesh apart.

"Neither will I. Who is your head of military? I must speak to him. Whoever is in charge. They have to fix this, they have to—" Here she collapses onto the bed, her face in her hands, trembling, though with tears of fear or sadness or fury Aurora isn't sure. Maybe all three.

Aurora sits beside Wren on the bed and puts her arm around her, feeling the way Wren vibrates with emotion. It radiates out to her, until she too feels upset and distraught. Wren doesn't shake her off.

Though she didn't have a long time to get to know Wren in Sommeil, the girl had been tender and, Aurora thought, trustworthy. Where Heath had welcomed Aurora with a curious fervor—and argued with her with the same heat— Wren had been cautious, careful, and above all, kind. It made Aurora feel even worse about what she'd done . . . that kiss with Heath, raindrops still clinging to her eyelashes and the stubble along his square jaw—both of them panting, angry, yet drawn to each other. Wren had caught them in the moment, and instantly Aurora had sensed how it bothered the girl. She must have been jealous, must have wanted Heath for herself, and Aurora had been ashamed at the idea that she might have come between them.

Now Wren pulls away from her. She curls her legs up onto the bed, tucking the borrowed robe more tightly about her thin frame, then leans against one of the tall, elegant bedposts and stares at the window.

"Our whole world has become dust," she says.

Aurora follows her gaze, then rushes to close the shutters, noticing how freezing it is in her room, worried the chill will bother Wren, whose washed hair hangs wet around her shoulders, black and sleek as an otter's back.

"The Borderlands closed in on us," the girl is saying as Aurora returns to her. Her voice is tremulous. "The wall fell; I couldn't believe it. The trees, still burning, flickered and traded places until I thought I had become as unhinged as the queen."

Aurora sits down beside her on the bed again. Wren's eyes flick toward her and away.

"But then, just as suddenly, they were still. Only they weren't the same trees—not slender and trimmed like the ones in Sommeil, but big and lush, taller than three men. That's when I knew we were *somewhere else*. The fire raged on, and it was so hard to see, to breathe. And there were just so many of them. . . ."

"So many?" Aurora asks, still warming again to the sound of her own voice, like a whisper spoken through a thin wall. She has the bizarre sense that she must stop talking in order to hear herself. It feels *wrong* somehow—forbidden—to speak here, in her real life, in her home. Deliciously wrong.

"Soldiers," Wren explains. "All with the same thorny crest on their shields."

"Malfleur!"

Wren remains staring at the closed window, like it pains her to look at Aurora. She takes a deep breath. "I saw so many die. So many of us." She stops and wipes away a streak of tears. "Those who tried to escape were rounded up on carts. Heath—"

Aurora's own breath hitches. "Is he . . ."

Wren finally faces Aurora. "He went with the white-faced queen. Malfleur. She took him, and cartfuls of others too—mostly men. Back to her own kingdom."

"LaMorte. Recruits for her army, no doubt," Aurora says, remembering Isabelle's account of the evil faerie queen terrorizing peasants throughout the land, her mercenaries demanding they either join her cause or die.

"Heath and some of the others seemed to think she was heroic, that she had saved us from Sommeil, freed us—they were chanting, rallying, but . . ." Wren's eyes search Aurora's face. "You told us Malfleur and Belcoeur were sisters."

"Yes."

Wren shakes her head. "No matter how evil we may have once thought Belcoeur, I can't see myself trusting another faerie queen who's willing to murder her own blood."

"No," Aurora agrees. "Queen Malfleur is not to be trusted. She . . ." Aurora takes a breath. "She propagates lies, tithes the youth of all the women in her territories, performs strange experiments with animals—I used to think it was all just rumors, but I've seen evidence of her dark magic."

The words "dark magic" rush across her lips as she remembers the talking starling at her window, and a new idea tickles across her mind like a spring wind stirring through trees. "Now," Aurora adds, "Malfleur is preparing to march against Deluce, and we will be at war."

Wren's eyes blacken. "But Heath . . . we can't leave him in her clutches."

Her memory of Heath, her longing to see him again—his grin, his mussed wild hair, his enthusiasms and despairs—leaps and gutters like a candle in wind.

Aurora shakes her head. "I am supposed to marry the prince of Aubin. Tomorrow."

Wren recoils. "*Marry?* You can think of marrying a prince at a time like this?"

"I have no choice!" Aurora says, surprised to find she is shouting, shaking.

"But *you* were the one who opened the floodgates, you were the one who showed up and spoke of another world, who stoked the flames in Heath's heart and made him want this, want freedom, and now look what's happened. All our best men gone. We have no place to go. We have *nothing*." Wren is staring at her with a presence so powerful Aurora feels something tightly wound inside herself come loose.

"I didn't know, Wren. I was only trying to help. You couldn't have survived much longer there anyway, you *know* that."

Wren lays her hands on Aurora's shoulders. Aurora draws in a quick breath, the rush of touch like a flock of swallows startled into flight.

"I will hear no further argument from a spoiled, clueless princess who cares more about her wedding garments," Wren says, with a nod to the wreaths and garlands stacked on a chair, "than the well-being of her people—or ours."

Though the girl is only a maid by station, she has a strength of conviction many nobles lack. She reminds Aurora of Isbe in that way. But her accusation sounds a lot like the ones Heath hurled at her in Sommeil.

Aurora's sick of everyone doubting her. "If that's what you really think, fine," she says, struggling to keep her voice steady. "I will handle things my way, and you may handle them yours."

———

She leaves Wren in her room. She walks through the darkness with no torch, feeling both the helpless clumsiness of her body in the cool, ambivalent night, and the creeping numbness, the solitude, of having just stormed away from one of the only people in the world who can communicate with her.

She walks down the long, wide corridor that leads to Prince William's visiting chambers, thinking of rousting him again, of seeking his help in rectifying the dire circumstances of the Sommeilians. But as she approaches the closed door to the guest wing, she already knows what the prince's answer will be: Heath is a recruit of the enemy. Deluce's duty is to defend its own citizens first.

She makes her way outside instead, moving among the still gardens, which glisten with dew in the moonlight. Thinking. Simmering. Who will help them? How can she possibly prove to Wren that she's wrong about Aurora, that Heath was wrong too, that they all were? That her rank doesn't determine her role. That she can be strong too, just like Isbe.

Aurora had been the one who drew out Queen Belcoeur, after all, the one who got her to reveal the truth at last. Belcoeur had told them that Malfleur killed Charles Blackthorn—cut off his head and sent it to her in a treasure chest along with a cruel note that said "Everyone deserves true love." Malfleur did it because she felt betrayed that Charles had chosen her twin sister over her.

But there is still something missing to the story, Aurora senses, something that has been troubling her ever since she put on Charles Blackthorn's *True Love* crown and woke herself up. Of course she doesn't know Malfleur beyond the stories that have become more myth than history. But still, she just can't quite believe that Malfleur, evil as she may be, would go to such lengths to make Belcoeur suffer over the love of a man. The fae can be petty, certainly. But to get so upset, *just* over a man, a mere mortal? It's only a hunch, but Aurora suspects there's more to it than that.

That there's something else Malfleur was really bitter about. If Aurora had to guess what's always been most important to the evil queen, it would be power. Magic.

Aurora pushes back inside the palace, past the guards, who only eye her noncommittally, and remembers how she dragged that heavy ax through Blackthorn Castle in Sommeil, lifted its weight over her head, and smashed down the door to the hall of tapestries, working away at the illusion, even as her arms throbbed with exhaustion. Hacking at the wood again, and again, and again, until finally it splintered and started to give. . . .

Let the prince and Isbe wage a war. Aurora will seek out the evil faerie queen herself.

———

The idea isn't precise in her mind, not yet. It is still coming into itself, just as the fog over the strait shifts and morphs into the mold of the cliffs, holding their shape for moments at a time. And yet the rightness of what she must do sends a tingling, burning heat through Aurora's whole body.

She must travel to LaMorte and confront Malfleur. Demand the safety of her captives. Offer her something she cannot refuse in return.

And what's the one thing Malfleur can't refuse?

Careful not to wake Wren, whose long hair still smells of smoldering cinders even after being washed, Aurora tiptoes through her room, bending to select a wreath of half-opened crocuses from a tufted bench. Next, a piece of vellum and an ink-dipped pen. When she is ready, she pushes aside a heavy tapestry on her wall and enters the secret passageway to Isabelle's room.

She moves through the long, narrow passage, running her hands along its stone walls but feeling nothing. And that dull silence only reinforces what she must do.

When she enters Isbe's room, quiet as a cat, her sister does not stir. Aurora moves closer, gazing at Isbe's sleeping form—one bare leg kicked out from underneath the covers, her short hair curled into cursive patterns across the pillow, making it look as though she is somehow in motion.

That is how Aurora thinks of Isbe—continuously moving, running when she should be careful, reaching out to meet the world with the ends of her fingers, always alert and listening and alive to sensations. Unafraid.

She's struck by the memory of one of their early adventures at the edges of the castle grounds—Aurora must have been around seven, Isbe nine. They raced, tripping and laughing, to the cliffs. Aurora was certain Isbe wasn't going to stop in time, would simply run straight into the open air and float across the fog. She cried out silently in a blend of terror and elation—had her sister simply flown,

Aurora would not have been surprised. Isabelle was magic, she thought. Invincible.

Aurora stands over her sister now, frozen with the certainty that she will lose Isbe. That she cannot stop her—has never had the power to stop her—from throwing herself headlong into her future. The truth of it pounds against her chest like the Delucian surf, hard and drenching. But she will not cry.

She must go where she can be heard. Where she is *truly* needed.

Besides. Prince William will look out for Isabelle, Aurora knows. She has seen the way his eyes travel over her face, the way his arms reach out almost instinctively to keep her from harm, the way he speaks to her with a bluntness that betrays a keen trust. Aurora may not know the prince well, but he is a good man, she can see. Kind and smart.

Aurora can't be certain what will come next, only that this feels painfully, beautifully right.

She sets her letter, and the wedding wreath, on top of a bureau before she leaves.

———

When she is back in her own room, Wren shifts, fluttering open her eyes. Aurora stands hovering near her, and Wren startles slightly. "What are you doing?" she whispers.

"I need your cloak," Aurora whispers back, packing, hurrying.

"What? Why?" Wren asks, sitting up.

"I am going to save Heath," Aurora says. The promise

arrives with a surge of determination. "And all of you."

Already Wren is up and out of the bed. "I'm coming with you."

Another feeling comes back to Aurora now: the moment when the wooden door to the hall of tapestries wobbled, cracked, and her ax, at last, broke through.

5

Isabelle

"This is your fault," Isbe tells William.

"*My* fault your sister and her maidservant friend have vanished with the dawn?"

"Shh," she hisses, pulling him from the doorway, where murmurs echo against damp limestone as the bustle of guests fills the courtyard. Canopies billow in the crisp spring wind. Garlands of hawthorn and fern hang from lattice archways, their musky scent permeating the fog. Banners bob and dip, thwack and clap. She can hear the harsh cries of a few children tossing acorns—the ten-year-old phantoms of herself and Gilbert and Roul.

Isbe folds and unfolds the letter in her hands. In it, Aurora stated that she abdicates the throne in order to be free to marry whomever she chooses. And, as Isabelle is already of age and the only other daughter of the deceased king, Aurora has officially named *her* queen, upon marriage to William of Aubin.

Sister. I want to go back to Sommeil, Aurora had said, a whisper of urgency in the cadence of her fingers. *But I don't want to leave you again.*

And yet you have, Isabelle thinks. *For the impossible dream of an unfinished romance*. Aurora has clearly gone off to find the hunter she met in Sommeil. Heath.

Isabelle and the prince follow the corridor farther away from the inner bailey, toward a quiet alcove near one of the northeast stairwells. "Obviously, no one can know about this letter," she says now, trying to swallow back the tremor in her voice. "The people will revolt if they think she has abandoned us on the day of her coronation. We need to go after her and Wren."

"They can't have gone far," William offers. "I'm sure the guards will locate them before nightfall."

He is probably right—after a frantic search of the palace, the royal carriage was discovered missing about an hour ago. Even if they got a head start by leaving in the dark, everyone knows that the spring mud makes travel by carriage cumbersome. Still, this is the second time Aurora has strayed from the confines of the castle grounds in her entire life, and Isbe knows all too well what happened last time.

"How can you be so dismissive?" Isbe grabs his arm, forcing him to stop pacing. She feels him turn to her, the dark heat of his defensiveness. "Your bride ran off on the morning of your wedding! Don't you realize how damaging this could be if the guests find out? And what do we even know about the girl with ash in her hair?"

"We know," William says quietly, "only what the travelers told us last night—that Malfleur rallied, pressured, or possibly imprisoned many of the survivors of the fire. If your sister has indeed fled straight into the jaws of the enemy with the notion of finding one man, then she has done something both valiant and excessively reckless. I can't say that either quality surprises me," he adds, a bitter quirk to his voice.

"What do you mean?"

"I mean . . . ," he replies, then quiets for a moment as a pair of servants rushes past them, carrying clattering trays. Once they are at a safe distance, he continues, "I mean that you and Aurora are not so unalike, after all."

"It seems a particularly bad time to throw around accusations of rash behavior," Isbe snaps, "or any insult, for that matter. Your tone is not befitting of a prince—or a bridegroom. Certainly not a king." However, his point has given Isbe a new thought. "Now if you'd be so kind as to indulge another *reckless* decision, please call a servant to escort me to the stables at once."

The prince lets out a breath too forceful to be considered a sigh. "I suppose you plan to go after her, despite the fact that we've already sent our best men."

"Our best men," she says, "may not prove as useful in

anticipating my sister's next *reckless* move."

"I said *valiant* and reckless," he corrects.

She shrugs, dismissing the half compliment.

"Isabelle," he says more determinedly. Instead of calling for a servant, he leads her past their alcove and into the solitude of a stairwell, where his breath suddenly turns louder, heavier. "Don't."

Silence.

"Don't go after her. Stay."

Still she can't respond, afraid any words would be sand against her throat.

"Stay and marry me in her place." There they are. The words she wanted him to say before, has been waiting for him to say. His lips are close to her ear; his body hovers in front of hers, his cloak almost enclosing them both.

She takes a step backward, but her shoulders hit the curved wall beside the steps. He has her hands in his now. He tugs on them, ever so lightly, but it sends a tingling current through her.

"Don't you see?" he says. "Your sister never even wanted this marriage. Why won't you just marry me?"

The memories rush at her: the heat between them, the way his lips lingered on her skin that night in the wine caves. His hands, his words, soft and pressing. How close she felt to him then. How beautiful, powerful, changed.

"Please, Isabelle. I ask you a third time, and I don't think I can ask you again."

Devastation brings its own brand of heat to her cheeks.

"We can't just pick up where we left off, William. You know as well as I do. Aurora woke up, and you were perfectly willing to throw away what we had in order to wed her—"

"Which had been *our plan* and *what you wanted*!" he protests, pulling away. "And listen: Your sister clearly *didn't choose me*."

"But *you*," Isbe counters, turning her face high, feeling bold with the truth of it. "*You* didn't choose *me*."

"Yes, Isabelle. I did. I chose you, and I choose you again."

She folds her arms over her chest, maybe to keep from falling over, or falling into him, or falling completely away from herself. She doesn't know.

Except she *does* know. "You only chose me when there wasn't a choice at all."

He can't deny that, and he doesn't.

But she won't linger in his silence, won't wallow in the truth he likes to distort in order to satisfy whatever whim of feeling passes through him at the time. Just like a man, to want what he wants only when he wants it.

And she doesn't need an escort, either—she can find her way to the stables on her own. After all, she has been running there—running from the palace, from its rules and its cruelties—all her life.

———

Her fury and confusion are muffled by the life's worth of memories brought on as soon as she steps into the barn. She has not been here since escaping with Gilbert the night before the council intended to send her to the convent in Isolé for good.

The barn scents overwhelm her with their familiarity: equine sweat and sweet feed, worn leather and hay dust and dank wood. The horses snuffle quietly. Those that survived the Sleeping Sickness were left wary, restless. She has the urge to soothe them but knows they must sense the unease in her own heart.

She passes Freckles's empty stall, and stops. For a moment, she thinks she can hear her favorite mare nicker softly. Her throat tightens and she reaches between the bars, but no velvety nose nudges her hand.

She clicks her tongue anyway. *Tss tss tss.*

There is no shuffling of hooves or flick of a mane. Silence.

She leans her forehead against the stall door, breathing deeply, letting the pressure in her chest rise and fall, rise and fall. But it does not lessen.

She knows she must accept that Freckles is dead, and so, truly, is the young girl who used to ride her, the king's wild bastard daughter. The king is dead too—has been for years now. And Gilbert?

She has heard nothing of his fate, though she did send a messenger to Roul's village. He has not seen his brother. No one has. It can only mean one thing, yet Isbe refuses to believe it. She *feels* that Gilbert is alive—can nearly hear his easy laughter in the distance. Then again, she feels like she can hear Freckles whinnying in the far fields too—wants to believe the mare has simply sneaked away, breaking from her stall as she's done so many times in the past. But that is an illusion, a wish.

No good ever came from wishing.

Isbe has always resisted the temptation to wish for things she knows she cannot have, because she fears the disappointment will break her. But it's more than that: even the beginning of a wish taking shape in her heart hurts—sends an actual physical pang through her body, a kind of vibration that scares her, like a bolt of painful lightning running straight through her chest. Like a curse.

She takes a deep breath, trying to settle herself.

When Isbe first lost her sight, she began to feel that the world was made mostly of a darkness—and that this darkness was itself a kind of material, a fabric that contorted into shape and meaning only by necessity. Until a person heaved a breath or spoke, or ruffled the air around her, that person had not yet existed. Things and people alike would disappear back into that amorphous fabric just as easily as they came. But gradually Isbe grew to believe in the world she could not see, to have faith in it.

She reminds herself to have faith in it still.

She selects a different horse and begins readying the saddle, losing herself in the tightening of buckles and the smoothing of the stallion's coat. It takes a moment for her to sense the presence of another person.

Isbe freezes.

Whoever has arrived just now is definitely not a stable hand, whose footfalls would be easy and confident, perhaps accompanied by a low hum or whistle. The person who has entered the stables is shadowed, movements muted in a way that makes him or her seem larger and more fearful. Or perhaps she only thinks so because of the mingled sounds arising around her, of snorts, huffs, stamping hooves.

A woman clears her throat. "How delightful," she says, in a voice like a cannonball's slow roll down the bore. Loaded.

Isabelle turns. "Mother."

Reverend Mother Hildegarde is as large of body as she is of spirit, Isbe recalls, having first met her at the convent of Isolé, where she and the prince took refuge on their grueling journey from his palace in Aubin to her home in Deluce.

"I suppose you know why I've come," the woman says calmly.

Isbe flushes, remembering how she had wondered if Hildegarde might turn out to be her own mother—though the hope hadn't been all that unreasonable. After all, Hildegarde indicated she'd been stationed at the palace for many years prior to Isabelle's birth, and in fact had struck a deal for Isbe's safety, though that had apparently been contingent on a payment that the convent never received.

That's right. The money.

Isbe bristles, tightening her grip on the leather reins in her hand. "You have a funny way of bargaining."

"I'm not bargaining, my dear," Hildegarde replies. "I'm simply here to ask for what is fairly due me and my own.

Now that the sleeping sickness seems to have fled the land, I thought it might be the safest time to come and see you."

"You've come to persuade me to forgive you." Isbe did not think it possible to feel more divided. On the one hand, her awe for Hildegarde's bravery is whole and unmatched. But then again, she can hardly forget, let alone forgive, the fact that Hildegarde sold her out to Malfleur's mercenaries, who cornered her and the prince in the village not more than two miles from the convent, from whence they intended to escort them all the way to LaMorte, perhaps to become lunch for Malfleur's Vultures—or leverage.

If it hadn't been for the bravery of Sister Genevieve and Sister Katherine, well . . . Isbe can't think about that right now.

"No. I do not ask for forgiveness. Forgiveness is, like the word indicates, something that must by its very nature be *given*, not sought. It belongs to the will of the giver."

"You risked our lives for your own gain," Isbe says, feeling both disgusted and torn. "Fortunately for you," she adds, turning back to her horse and tightening the stirrups, "I have more important concerns right now than retribution. I have a princess to rescue."

Hildegarde has the gall to snort.

Isbe drops the leather strap. "What was that?"

"Noble. Very noble of you," the woman replies, shifting her massive weight with the faintest of creaks in the wooden planks.

Isbe turns back to the horse once again but remains still,

regretting the way the reverend mother's voice holds sway over her, makes her want to hear more.

"It is a worthy cause to save the life of a princess, especially a beloved sister," Hildegarde admits. "But is it not worthier to save the lives of twenty peasants, or a hundred, or possibly thousands?"

Isbe steps out of the stall and faces the woman—they cannot be more than thirty or forty paces apart. "It is neither my right nor yours to value one life over another. I only seek to help where my efforts may be of real use."

"Well, it is certainly too late for Josette," Hildegarde says harshly.

No. Not her, too. Isbe recalls the young girl who suffered from pneumonia at the convent.

The nun betrays no emotion about the death of the little girl, but her voice is low and determined as thunder. "However, you could be of use to me."

"I suppose I could plead your case to the council," Isbe says slowly, thinking of Maximilien, the only one left. Would he care? She might find a way of persuading him. "Perhaps I could get you your gold, if I wanted to . . . but how am I to know you won't return to your ruthless ways?"

"I don't consider arming a house of women with both education and weapons ruthless. I consider it a means of survival. And besides . . ."

Hildegarde leaves a heavy silence that makes Isbe fidget.

"It's what your mother would have wanted."

"My . . ." Isbe's mind has suddenly gone blank, and

she's tempted to swing her arm forward into thin air, seeking something solid.

"She was—well, let's say that I admired her greatly. At first, anyway."

"At first?" Isbe is still stunned . . . and suspicious. Why should she trust Hildegarde after she's already lied once?

"Cassandra was so much better than the king she settled for." Hildegarde's voice holds a sneer. "She came from peasantry but abandoned her roots. She folded her past life away when she moved into the palace, like a secret into a seashell."

"Her past life . . ." A wash of dread moves through Isabelle, leaving her fingers tingling.

"I had my suspicions about her. King Henri, he had no idea who she really was. Your father wasn't the brightest, I'm afraid. He let his appetites make his decisions—"

"Stop." Isbe feels a wave of revulsion. "I don't want to hear this. I'll get you your funds. . . . Just please, leave me now."

"After all these years, you aren't interested in knowing the truth about your mother?"

The stallion shuffles beside Isbe, letting out a huff. It nudges her as if to agree.

Of course she wants to know. She's desperate to know. But she is gripped too, with a complete and overwhelming fear. "Just tell me this. Do you know what happened to her? After . . ."

The reverend mother steps closer to her with a rustle of her musty robes. Her voice is much softer as she replies.

"Your mother always loved the sea. When the king banished her, I believe Cassandra set sail across the strait, maybe to one of the small islands in the north. I never heard from her."

Isbe's ears ring.

"However," Hildegarde adds. "She left me this."

The woman has approached her and now reaches out, her hand finding Isbe's upper arm. She draws Isbe's hands together, turning her palms up, and then, moments later, presses something into them. Something cool and light-weight, made of crystal or glass. The object is hollow, with a long, narrow opening at the top. One end is pointed, the other round.

A slipper. Just larger than the length of Isbe's hand.

"She left you a . . . shoe?"

"A glass slipper," the nun corrects.

"But why?"

"It was her most precious possession, that is all she told me. Something given to her by her own mother. She was cautioned never to lose it, but she said nothing of its true meaning or import. She wanted me to give it to you. However, I too was sent away soon after, and felt it would be safer in my possession than yours."

Now it's Isbe's turn to snort. "You stole it."

Hildegarde sighs. "Isabelle. I see you hold an unflattering impression of me, but I only want what is best for this kingdom, and I believe we are alike in that. It takes great bravery to travel in secret through the countryside, harboring a fugitive prince. Your mother would have been proud."

At this, Isbe takes a step backward, her throat seizing up tight. It's too much. This is all too much. She wants to throw the glass slipper and run—but she's overcome with the wild impression that if she lets go of it, she'll never possess it again. Not that it will shatter, but that it will simply vanish in the air.

"Isabelle." Now the reverend mother has grown to the size of three men on the backs of three horses, and Isbe is certain she will be stampeded by the woman's words, by her intensity. She is a storm cloud ready to break open and send down a torrent that will erode everything Isbe knows to be true. "I did not just come here for money."

Isbe clears her throat, determined to stand strong, even as her world mudslides. "You came for *me*." It is a statement, not a question.

"I came to *galvanize* you. I thought the slipper would inspire you."

"Inspire me to what?"

"To lead."

6

Binks,

a Male Faerie of Modest Nobility,
Who Still *May or May Not Be Important to This Tale,*
Except That He Once Again Happens to Be
in the Right Place at the Right Time

He wouldn't have believed it if it weren't for a lack of jam.

He approaches the swollen corpse with caution, glancing over his shoulder to make certain the town green is clear.

Surely there can be no other reason for Claudine's brash escape from the relative protection of her manor, can be no other justification for the violet smears staining her mouth and face. She was fascinated with the vines, spoke often of their virulence—many of her maids could attest to this. And yet apparently she ate the purple flowers anyway, driven by, one can only imagine, a deep and unappeasable hunger.

Maybe if the roads hadn't been closed, if trade hadn't halted . . .

Maybe if there'd been just a little more jam to go around . . .

Claudine's deep pockets have already been picked, Binks is disappointed to discover—even the collar of her heavy coat crudely shaved off by what can't have been a very good blade. He is already wary of getting too close to this . . . this rotting, bloating flesh hill, its dance of maggots, its terrible reminder that even the fae must perish like the rest. He has begun to think better of his own sojourn to the village, and curses the bad gamble that lost him his preferred driver as well as three of his best mounts. He would have demanded his own butler drive him into town, but the man began to sob wretchedly, talking of plagues and soldiers, of lords with bloody sockets where their eyes should have been.

Binks is not usually one for mass hysteria, as the timid make terrible game mates. He is not too proud, however, to admit that perhaps his manservant was right: these are dangerous and unpleasant times.

He is in fact about to turn back when he spots a scroll balled in Claudine's fist. Her fat fingers, nearly as blue as her lips are purple, curl tightly around the vellum. It is not easy to wrench it free. *Perhaps a love letter*, he thinks, or a tally of debts paid and owed. Perhaps a list of items for a maid to procure from market. But no. Claudine must have grown desperate if she had left the safety of her manor to seek out a courier on her own.

Binks has always had a nose for other people's business.

Information can prove more valuable than even the best of latterlu hands.

He wrenches the note free at last, and sees that it has been addressed to the Faerie Duchess Violette. He averts his eyes from Claudine's purple-smeared mouth as he breaks the letter's seal with one of his carefully filed fingernails. His pulse leaps, like it does in response to a marked card, a twisted lip, or a sleight of play.

The message says only this:

V:
IT IS TIME.
IT MAY IN FACT ALREADY BE TOO LATE.
MALFLEUR MUST BE STOPPED.
OUR ONLY HOPE IS TO FIND THE HART
SLAYER.
—C

7

Isabelle

The wreath Aurora left on her bureau whispers to Isbe when she returns to her room from the stables, and she wonders how she didn't notice it earlier: *crocus*, its scent says, and *spring, hope, sisterhood, promise*. It slips easily onto Isabelle's head.

Matilda's hands tremble as she pins up Isbe's short hair neatly and affixes a long veil. The kitchen wench is one of the few servants she can trust with this task.

Isbe was a little too narrow and a little too tall for Aurora's gown, but with the help of a tailor they managed to make a few necessary adjustments, and now the heavy layers of silk sway against Isbe's body, the fine boning tightens around her torso, stiff with formality.

Isbe is shaking too, as Hildegarde's words still reverberate through her. She offered the nun a place to stay and make herself comfortable for the duration of the festivities, but Hildegarde had refused—she took her money and set off immediately to Isolé.

When Isabelle had first heard Aurora's letter read aloud this morning, she was in shock. Her reaction was reflexive and immediate: *Bring Aurora back. This is all a mistake.* She hardly even listened to the response of the remaining council or what William thought. But after Hildegarde placed the glass slipper in her hands, something shifted. Shock began to give way to realization.

She had built her whole life until now on the idea that the alliance was contingent on Aurora marrying William. That had been the entire point of her journey to find the prince and compel him to return to Deluce with her in the first place. It never occurred to her that there could be another way. That Aurora could simply and willingly relinquish her title. Isbe never thought one's identity could radically change overnight.

But it's as if Aurora has stepped out of her own storybook and into a completely new one.

And now Isabelle has been handed a chance to be queen in her place. She's worried desperately about her sister's safety—but what kind of person would she be to receive this opportunity and say no?

Still, the decision was made in such a whirlwind, she's

not completely sure whether she's doing the right thing. It feels like she's snipping a thread that once tethered her to Aurora, and to her old life; like she is once again flying backward off a boat and into the roiling arms of the sea.

Meanwhile, the prince waits at the altar in the courtyard. He has been told only that his bride has been found and is even now being dressed for the wedding.

When Isbe descends the stairs, one hand trailing lightly along the rail, three servants lifting the train of her gown, she is convinced that in a matter of mere hours she has become someone else. Not Aurora, exactly, but a princess from one of Aurora's stories—a vision of regality and romance. Gone is the girl who loved a stable hand, who once kissed him in the rush and gurgle of a spring stream. Gilbert's grip on her shoulders as their vessel swayed, the salt sting on her cheeks—of tears or seawater—his lips against her mouth, his fingers tracing her jaw . . . these sensations live on in her memory, but faintly, like the wash of a distant tide seeping through the sand.

She moves slowly, every step bringing her closer to the choice that will change her life forever. But soon enough she is led through the arched south entrance to the bailey, then down a path of pebbles and strewn petals. The guests' stares are as tangible as the heat thrown from a hearth fire. None of them yet know the truth.

"Princess." William's voice floats above the muffled din of the crowd as she approaches him. She hears a question in his voice, and wonders if he can guess at her identity through the veil.

Her hands are placed in his, which are solid and strong. These are the hands that have spent hours carving fine miniature cannons, knights, and warships out of marble—the hands that have held her in the intense and heady silence of the hearse they shared, in the steam chamber beneath Almandine's estate, and in the wine caves. These are the hands of her husband. In his wrist pulses the soul to which she's going to bind her own.

During the ceremony, she is not expected to respond to the priest—after all, ostensibly, she is Aurora, and cannot speak. It is only toward the end of the vows that the priest pulls out the letter Isabelle gave him and begins to read aloud.

A confused murmuring spreads through the crowd.

It's then that Isbe lifts her veil.

Gasps ring out. But it is too late for anyone to protest.

The priest lowers something onto Isbe's head. It's the same crown her stepmother wore for years, the one that would have gone to Aurora had she not left this strange and hasty letter—had she not formally abdicated. The crown is not heavy, but Isbe can feel its cool weight pressing down on her temples.

"Yes," she says quietly when the priest asks if she accepts this responsibility, accepts the title of queen.

And then, in a blur of intoned prayers and carefully

pronounced vows, she answers again, "Yes."

Then "Yes."

Then "Yes."

———

The feast and celebration are a somber affair—full of worried whispers Isbe is certain are meant to be overheard. She can hardly stomach her serving of roasted boar decorated in caramelized pomegranate seeds. She takes a big gulp of spiced wine instead, letting its heat shiver down through her chest and limbs.

Thankfully, no one stops the prince from leading her away before the dessert course is served.

———

As soon as they step into the royal bedchambers—newly appointed and prepared for them, having remained empty since the death of King Henri and Queen Amélie—William gently unpins the veil from her hair.

She breathes a sigh of relief.

"What changed your mind?" he asks quietly. They have not had a moment alone until now to speak of it. And yet she finds she is still nervous, that she doesn't know how to answer.

What *did* change her mind? *A nun*, she thinks. God, perhaps—a distant figure to whom she's given little thought before now.

Or maybe . . . her mother. Her heart. A tiny shoe made entirely of glass.

Or maybe she hadn't fully made up her mind until she stepped into her room to find the wreath Aurora had left behind, and was flooded with the sudden understanding of what her sister wanted. She wanted her own chance at love.

And she wanted Isabelle to have the same.

I realized I couldn't lose you too, she is tempted to answer, which is also true.

But the truest reason Isbe changed her mind is not because it was what William said he wanted, or what, deep down, she wanted, or what *anyone* wanted, for that matter. It was because Hildegarde was right: Deluce needs Isbe. Not just a bride, not just an alliance, but *her*.

"I couldn't let this dress go to waste," is all she says, tilting her face up toward William's.

"No. With everything at stake, we wouldn't want that." His finger traces the line of her jaw, and all the humor that welled up in her explodes into nervousness, the full tilt of what she has done registering abruptly, like when Freckles used to spook, leaping into the unknown with Isbe desperately clinging to the reins. She holds on now to the prince's doublet, flat against his firm chest.

His hands wrap around her waist, pulling her against him. His lips meet her temple and linger there, then drift to her cheekbone. He kisses the corner of her mouth. She parts her lips, inhaling. But this kiss remains incomplete—his breathing has altered, just subtly—he leans in and lifts her up, carrying her backward across the room, and she's half tempted to push him away, to say what a terrible, doomed idea this is, after all.

He sits her at the edge of the bed.

"I've been thinking," she says now. "That I can help."

"I'm listening." He takes her hand and kisses the inside of her wrist.

"If Malfleur can convince so many men to join her ranks, why can't we do the same? While you advance the army, I can recruit. Increase our numbers—"

He stops her with a kiss. "Yes," he says. Then he kneels before her, his hands on her knees. "I wish." He sighs. "I wish it wasn't like this. That we didn't have to speak of war. That I didn't have to leave tomorrow."

She knows he must ride to meet with a new brigade of soldiers tomorrow—that she may not see him again for at least a fortnight. There's so much to be done, but it all feels impossibly far away.

"Nothing ever comes of—"

"Wishing," he fills in. "So you've said many times. And still I do."

His words feel too heavy for this moment, especially when her heart feels so eager, so alive it might burst from her chest like a spring bulb finally breaking through frozen soil. "We have tonight, at least," she reminds him, touching his face—the strong jaw, the serious mouth, the small knitted scar.

"What shall we do with it?" He turns her hand over and

kisses her knuckles, his patience a form of torture.

It suddenly occurs to Isabelle that she has been waiting for this—waiting and dreading and wanting and then pressing that want back down within her—ever since that night in the caves, the air pulsating with the cool memory of merlot. "I'm sure we can think of something," she says.

Then his hands have found the border of her skirts, have shifted them, ever so gently, have found their way under all the layers of fabric and ribbon and fuss, have discovered her legs, bare beneath the silk. He pulls back the dress, revealing only her left knee. He kisses the tender spot just to the inner side of it. Isbe flushes, heat coursing up her leg and through her whole body.

Then he whispers against her skin, so softly she hardly hears the words, though she can feel their tickle across her thigh. "Yes. I'm sure we can."

———

In the morning, he is gone. The dress was, thankfully, designed for only a single use, and it now lies half in shreds somewhere on the cold floor, along with the wreath and the veil.

She wants to reach over and find the prince there beside her; she wraps her arms around herself instead. Last night was . . . there are no words for last night. But now is the dawn of a new time, and a new Isabelle.

She is *married*. The word seems odd to her, delicate and yet binding, like the soft click of a lock.

She floats somewhere between before and after—she's

gone ethereal, and might in fact no longer exist. She should be afraid, but she is not. Already another idea is forming. Her mind skims through the sheets and the sensations and the sighs, and travels back to the one thing that now tethers her to the present . . . packed safely in a velvet-padded box beneath her bed, the tiny gift of her mother's— heartbreakingly fragile, yet sharper and more real than anything. The strange, the beautiful: the slipper of glass.

PART

II

WHOSE BLOOD MUST SLAY

8

Wren,

Formerly a Maiden of Sommeil,
Indentured to the Mad Queen Belcoeur

Wren has never liked secrets. She imagines them as smooth, invisible stones that fit inside your palm— at first, they give you a sense of importance, of meaning. But then you learn that you can never put them down. They startle you awake at night with their clumsiness. In the water of dreams, they pull you under.

Some secrets are given to you without your having any say in the matter. They become worn and polished inside your hand. You begin to forget their heaviness. You begin to lose track of where your skin ends and the stone begins.

———

It is late. Wren leaves the small campsite where Aurora lies sleeping and moves through low trees toward the soft babble of a nearby creek. Kneeling in the damp moss, she collects a pool of silt-laden water in her hands and splashes her face. Again. Again. She looks up at the watery clouds, smears of darkness against the greater black. She heaves in a breath, willing herself to be calm.

But she knows she cannot remain calm. Not when she is holding the weight of a terrible secret.

Not when she knows she must be dying.

Wren searches for her reflection but finds only fractured images in the rippling stream: eyes that don't align, a mouth that wavers and splits, skin that is at turns moonlit and shadowed. There's no evidence of her concealments in those features, but they haunt her nonetheless.

The first is one she has trouble giving a name to. It is a fine layer of feeling, chiffonlike and subtle, that invades her senses whenever the princess speaks, or moves, or lies close to her in the bleakness of the evening. She does not know the true meaning of this sensitivity, only that it runs against the grain of her bitterness. She doesn't know *what* to think of Aurora. She'd resisted Aurora's half-cooked plan at first, then finally insisted on being a part of it, if only to make sure Aurora was true to her word—if only to be reconnected to others from her world.

If only to save herself.

But the second secret burns clear and bright behind her eyelids whenever she closes them, draws chills through her limbs when she sleeps, ravages her breathing with quick gasps and shudders she pretends come from the bitter wind rather than the truth within. It is the reason she knows they must hurry.

It has been several days since they abandoned the royal carriage. Neither Wren nor Aurora could really figure out how to drive it, a terrible harbinger of the journey to come, and Wren knew it. Besides, the road itself was temperamental at best, nonexistent at worst. And of course, there was the fact that the carriage's royal insignia was practically a call-out to bandits and thieves. The last thing they wanted was to travel to LaMorte conspicuously.

It was this last thought that had given Aurora an idea: What if they made themselves *as conspicuous as possible*? She ripped the thin black underlining from the carriage seat cushions and dismantled the harnesses from the carriage rod, then insisted Wren help her topple the carriage into a ditch by the woods and release the horses, sending them galloping riderless back to the palace.

The princess then draped the torn black fabric over her own head like a long veil and tied a rein to her wrist, holding out the other end to Wren.

Now as they passed through woods and villages, following the direction of the sun's movement, Wren led Aurora like a condemned prisoner. They no longer had to fear widespread apprehension—in fact, Aurora had been banking on it. And Wren had to admit her idea was working. Whenever they confronted a distrustful traveler on the road, Wren would recite the lines Aurora told her: "My ward is a survivor of the sleeping sickness. I've been charged with taking her to quarantine in the Vallée de Merle—have you not heard of it? No one else was willing to do the job." If probed with further questions, she began to plead for assistance, confessing that she could not look the prisoner in the face as the disease had so mangled the woman's appearance as to make the sight almost unbearable.

So far, at the mere hint of contagion, people have offered the two journeyers a wide berth. No one has lingered long enough to question their story. No one knows enough to contradict it—for of course there is no quarantine in the valley that separates Deluce from LaMorte.

No one has guessed that the woman beneath the veil is the princess of Deluce herself.

At night, the two women have made camp on the outskirts of farms, in goat pens and chicken coops and sometimes, when the weather has allowed, right out in the open, beneath a wintry sky alive with starlight.

And this has all been enough, almost enough, to quell the pull of the inevitable—the monster Wren had thought to outrun, to outlive, but which has caught up to her at last. Wren once told Aurora that she never wanted to leave Sommeil, that a whole new life outside of it would only serve to diminish everything that had come before. But she was lying. Of course she wanted to believe in it—to maybe one day see with her own eyes the waking world of which Heath so often spoke in animated whispers. But even Heath didn't know it, the beautiful, simple irony, formed like a crystal with perfectly equal sides.

How Aurora's curse undone would activate an even older curse—the one on *her*.

It was for this reason, more than any other, that Wren ought to hate Aurora. But she doesn't. Not exactly. Not when Aurora seems to be the only person willing to take up her cause.

Still, she doesn't trust her. Wren doesn't trust *anyone* easily. After all, she's never had to. The people she grew up with in Sommeil were ones she saw every single day of her life. There had never been a stranger to meet until Aurora. And no matter the princess's intentions, she has unwittingly ruined Wren's life, destroyed a world of people she swore to help, and set in motion an old curse Wren had always hoped was just a myth.

Now, in the thin, wavering light reflected by the creek, Wren pulls her knees into her chest and carefully rolls back her skirt. She removes her shoe to expose her ankle bone, a miniature planet in the expanse of darkness. She rubs the inside of her foot, feeling the divot between bone and tendon, and swallows back her dread. *The curse is real*.

It's just as she expected. A stretch of skin there, about the width of three fingers, is cold and firm as marble, as solid and inanimate as stone—*is* stone.

9

Aurora

Aurora never knew how vast Deluce's countryside was until now, as she allows herself to be tugged along dirt roads, across muddy pastures, and through woods dense with the crackle of pine needles and half-thawed tarns. With the dark veil over her head, her breathing feels forced, her sight limited to stray chances of light and shadow. Her stomach grows hollowed and hard. Her feet bleed. She does not know it. She hopes, at least, that this is enough to show Wren she's serious. Nothing has *ever* felt this serious.

The idea of Malfleur sitting high in her castle in LaMorte, training the refugees of Sommeil to become her newest soldiers—perhaps even poisoning them with her own brand of sinister magic, casting spells over them to hold them under her command—drives Aurora forward, making her more determined than ever that her plan must work.

She must convince Malfleur to let the Sommeilians go. She must free Heath.

Even if it comes at an unthinkable cost.

"What can you possibly offer Malfleur in exchange for helping us?" Wren keeps asking, and each time, Aurora tells her only that she knows what to do, and that Wren should trust her.

But Wren does not. And Aurora knows that if she reveals her plan to Wren, the girl may try and stop her.

Of course, Wren is not the only one. Aurora's certain that William and Isabelle will try to stop her too. Which is why, when she gets the opportunity, Aurora pens a letter to send back home, in her steadiest and most convincing script. In it, she writes the story she wishes were true, the story that ends in her finding Heath, healthy and alive. The story that ends in true love.

Wren gives the letter to a courier on the outskirts of Bouleau, and then they trudge onward.

———

At dusk and dawn each day, Wren and Aurora forage vainly for food, both of them growing thinner, subsisting mainly on leaves and berries and even, on one cold night, bits of beetle-filled dirt that make Aurora retch. One evening, she spots a lone doe in the woods. It stares at her with glossy eyes, and her whole being cries out with the agony of her hunger.

After that, Wren begins to open up a tiny bit, to lift the stormy silence she's been holding for long stretches at a time. Even if she still blames Aurora for the destruction of Sommeil, her anger seems to be softening, and this lets in a tiny hint of hope. Wren tells her stories from her childhood, tells her about how she used to follow Heath into the Borderlands to watch him hunt. The awe with which she saw his mind funnel into focus, his arm muscles going taut as he raised his bow and arrow and aimed. The gasping thrill as an arrow found its mark.

But the stories of Heath bring a new kind of agony to Aurora, ushering a return of her guilt—after all, Wren was in love with Heath before Aurora arrived—as well as a resurgence of all the emotions he awakened in Aurora when she first arrived in Sommeil: the terror when he held the tip of a knife to her neck at the cottage, the intrigue when he relented and helped her. How he guided her across the meadow when she injured her ankle, then tended to her in her room, his hands fumbling but gentle. How he caressed her cheek, brushed her hair out of her face before she pulled away, stunned and overwhelmed and inflamed. She longs to see him again. To finally put a name to all that remains unfinished between them.

And to tell him that it was never meant to be. He was not, and is not, hers to fall in love with. If they had both stayed in Sommeil, perhaps she would never have realized this. But now it seems clearer than ever. Her desire for true love had been like a lit spark that, in his presence, flamed and grew. He was the first person to really touch her. Of course she wanted it to be him—wanted that first touch to be the beginning of their love story.

But as she's lying beside Wren in the night's long hours of darkness and breath and rustling wind, she finds herself seeking out any excuse to be touched, to be reminded of its possibility. She begins to wonder whether it was really Heath at all that she'd been drawn to in Sommeil, or just what he represented: a whole new world of sensation. Had she confused the longing to be touched with the yearning to be loved?

Now, even the way the horse rein wraps her wrist during the days, rubbing the skin raw, means something. She feels connected to herself, to her body, and, increasingly, even to Wren.

Which perhaps explains what happened the other night.

It had been rainy, near midnight, and they were asleep in a barn when a farmer, reeking of alcohol, stumbled inside, muttering that he'd seen trespassers and that they'd better show themselves if they didn't want to be killed. Aurora and Wren were lying side by side for warmth, hidden in the upper floor behind large bales of hay. They froze, and Aurora automatically clutched Wren's hands, both of them holding their breath until the farmer at last gave up his fumbling, drunken search and left.

When they were sure he'd gone, they finally exhaled, gasping with stifled, relieved laughter. "That was close," Wren whispered, letting go of her hands and grabbing

Aurora's arms instead. The marvel of it—of being held—rushed through Aurora, signaled a change in her. She felt awake and alive with it. She wanted more of it.

Wren's face, outlined in faint light, was so near to Aurora's that she might have inched just a little to the left and kissed her. The thought came to Aurora with a surprising smoothness, as though it had been waiting there in her mind for some time. In the moonlight piercing through the dripping rafters, Wren's lips looked like a miniature bow, curved and taut.

Wren let go of Aurora just as suddenly and rolled onto her back, blinking up at the ceiling.

"Yes," Aurora whispered then. "That *was* close."

In the morning, as she had done every morning of their journey, Aurora held out her wrists for Wren to bind them.

———

In this way they manage to cross weeks' worth of land, moving slowly but steadily westward, passing undetected even through the lush Vallée de Merle, where a falcon eyes them from above, steering at a slant through the sapphire mist.

The border along the river should have been fortified by the Delucian army, but instead they see only razed villages, huts leveled into the mud. Abandoned roads and empty barns that bring back eerie visions of Sommeil itself—a crumbling, desiccated land, left by an unfit ruler to rot.

And always, in the distance: steam clouds, cradling Mount Briar and snaking throughout the territories.

In LaMorte, the terrain becomes increasingly rocky and

steep as they make their way up a narrow mountain pass. The pass is deserted, and they've given up their plague ruse by now. Wren carries the loose rein in her pack, and Aurora has flung the black fabric from her head, tucking it into her belt so that she can breathe and see, though the higher they climb, the thinner the air becomes, and the heavier Aurora's heart grows, pumping urgency through her chest. It's hard to breathe, hard to think. They have not eaten in three days.

So when she smells the faint, distant scent of smoked meat, something in her lurches, desperate. She begins to run, jaggedly, uphill.

"Aurora," Wren calls out, trying to follow her. "We don't know where it's coming from; we can't just—"

But an eager, wild hunger leaps in Aurora's veins, pushing her ahead, toward the wisp of smoke in the trees. . . .

As she runs, she sways, dizzy with the desire that has awakened like a beast inside her. She holds out her arm and can see the blue veins rising underneath her skin. She staggers over to a scrawny birch tree and leans against it to catch her breath, and her balance. The sky spins. She blinks rapidly.

Wren finally catches up, her voice hoarse with exhaustion. "We're not three days' from Blackthorn now. We can't risk getting caught. It's not worth it, Princess."

"But—"

Her vision goes hazy at the periphery. Wren's face swims in and out of focus, her concerned dark eyes, her gaunt cheekbones, her hands shaking as they reach for Aurora. . . .

We are going to die out here, Aurora realizes. The thought is sharp as an arrow, cold and hard as ice. It hits her square in the chest.

Breathless, she falls.

———

When Aurora comes to, the thick scent of smoke and river trout fills her nostrils. She gags, and then convulses from the pain in her empty stomach. Wren hovers nearby, and an old woman with long gray hair is ladling thin broth into a rough clay mug. There's a blanket draped over Wren's shoulders, and one covering Aurora too. Thick pine needles surround Wren, and for a moment Aurora is sure the girl has somehow become a bird, alighting in a tree.

Aurora sits up slowly. She blinks at the steaming mug in the elderly woman's hands. It cannot be true. They haven't seen a hot meal in weeks. Without thinking, Aurora takes the mug and unself-consciously dives into her broth, gulping it down, hardly noticing the flies that dart in and out, vying for a drop of its warmth.

And then a little boy clambers to her side, crying, "She's awake!"

"Flea?" Mud streaks the boy's face, soot in his light hair, and Aurora almost sobs in response to his wide, crooked-toothed smile. It *is* Flea. "But how?" she whispers.

"Survivors. We found them," Wren says. There are tears in her eyes, tracks through the dirt on her cheeks. Guilt, as dizzying as her hunger, moves through Aurora. "Or rather, they found *us*. They escaped Malfleur's army and have been camping out here, in hiding," she explains, gesturing around them at what Aurora can now see is a rudimentary camp sprung up literally among tree branches. Haphazardly hewn boards crisscross the tree branches to form platforms connected by planks, like forts built by children playing make-believe.

But that is where the innocence of the scenery ends. There are *hundreds* of Sommeilians, Aurora can now see, huddled in crowded clumps half covered by makeshift tents, dirty sheets, and clothes hanging off the branches, drenched in the smell of sweat and waste. There are tiny blackened areas both in the trees and on the ground from small, cautious, hastily blotted-out fires. And the flies—they're everywhere, clustered on the arms of sleeping children, drawn to the filth . . . and worse. The broth turns in her stomach. Aurora is sure she can smell, can *feel*, death in the air. These people are dying—of hunger, of cold, of sicknesses they were never exposed to in Sommeil. Their whole *world* has been decimated, gone up in a magical and lethal smoke.

She feels a gush of protectiveness and despair. These are her people—she vowed to help them. And, she realizes as she looks around her, they are all women and children.

"Apparently they've been depending on a few kind locals for help and shelter," Wren goes on to explain. "People like Constance," she says, gesturing to the old woman, who is, even now, putting an arm behind Aurora's back to steady her.

"Thank you," Aurora says. Constance doesn't seem to

hear her, but she smiles, the wrinkles around her eyes deepening. "I will get stronger. I will help. I will—"

"They've been watching Malfleur for weeks now," Wren says.

At the mention of Malfleur, her whole body goes alert. "And?"

Wren shakes her head, gently pushing Aurora back to a resting position. "When you're rested," Wren says, "we'll talk with the others."

But the warmth of the broth has spread through her belly, and Aurora is beginning to feel more alert. "No," she says, touching Wren's hand and removing it from her shoulder. "We'll speak to them *now*."

They make their way through the maze of branches and planks and platforms—Aurora awed by the ease with which some of the others move about, adapted already to this half-life.

In a crowded tent, Aurora listens to horrifying tales of the faerie queen whose storm of evil makes Belcoeur's actions seem like a weak breeze in comparison. How Malfleur and her vultures dragged their men away in chains. How she has sapped the youth from nearly all the women in her territory. Aurora has heard the rumors but has never seen evidence of them before. Now she stares in wonder at Constance, who looks as though she may keel over in a matter of months—her gray hair frayed, her face loose, and her skin dappled with age. She is, in fact, Aurora learns, only fourteen years old. One of the many orphans of LaMorte, her youth—her *life*—stolen from her.

The thought sickens Aurora.

"We must stop Malfleur. I have a plan, but I need to get into the castle. I need to gain access to her." The truth, the determination of it, is like a javelin driving through her, trim and sharp and deadly. She grips the floorboards beneath her, as though to keep herself from springing out of the tent and racing the rest of the way to Blackthorn.

"Our scouts have been watching the castle all day every day," one middle-aged woman is saying. Her fingernails are cracked and black with mud. "We've not seen the queen depart the gates once."

"But," inserts another, as old-looking as Constance—and possibly just as young, "there have been back-to-back attacks in Rocheux and Rigide." She extracts a drawing that Aurora recognizes as a rudimentary map of the LaMorte territories.

"An' the queen spotted at both." The first woman gestures to two places on the map. "Workin' a kind a' fire what could eat right through a man's sword. Fae work, to be sure."

The others nod solemnly, fear in their eyes.

Aurora studies the markings on the map. The villages of Rocheux and Rigide lie on opposite sides of the third-largest peak, which means it would be seemingly impossible for the queen to appear in both locations within a day of one another . . . and certainly not without ever leaving the castle.

Aurora doesn't doubt that Malfleur's power is great. But the accounts of the Sommeilian scouts stretch the limits of possibility. Disappearing and reappearing, phantomlike and at whim . . . these are abilities Aurora has never read about in *any* of the faerie histories. And she has read them all.

And fire that can melt a sword in battle? Great magic, dark magic, always comes at a price, even—or especially—for the fae.

What price did Malfleur pay for such power?

A chill moves through her. If their stories are true, then Aurora, along with all of Deluce, is up against someone far more capable—and more sinister—than anyone realized.

She looks around at the other women in the tent, their bodies weak, their eyes fatigued but fierce. "We must prepare," she says.

———

A light rain falls for several days as Aurora and Wren recuperate, hiding out with the scouts on a perch overlooking Blackthorn from morning 'til night, watching soldiers come and go, with no sign of Malfleur. Aurora's arms and legs have taken on new contours from navigating the treetop campsite and climbing steep terrain. Her body has grown tenser, tauter, stronger, even as her determination has done the same.

All the while, the dampness seeps into her worn clothes and deepens the ache and cold in her bones.

This evening, there's agitation among the group. There was another raid yesterday, at the foot of the mountains, not far from their camp, and the queen was spotted riding her silver-haired stallion through the wreckage, her cloak billowing in the thick smoke as fires raged and people screamed.

The Sommeilians argue late into the night about whether the risk of relocating outweighs the risk of staying. Most don't want to leave: they've learned the landscape here, the hospitable areas where the soil is fertile. They've identified which leaves can be ground into powder for broth, which acorns can be broken open to produce sweet nut meat, and which wild things ought to be avoided at all cost, like the fork-tongued salamanders said to be venomous and the flying squirrels that carry disease in their fangs.

To avoid the mounting tensions, Aurora splinters off with Wren at sunset to forage. She has come to like these moments, when the world appears charred and quiet. She has been getting used to the thin mountain air too, pine filled and smoky, to the constant chill, the fear that radiates out along the branches of their camp like a contagion.

Still, tonight she's agitated. If only she had her palace library at her fingertips. She'd be able to flip through all the histories of the fae in search of a clue that might help explain how Malfleur's powers have grown so mighty, how she's able to leap from place to place around the territories without ever seeming to leave her own front door. Even in the time of the great winged faeries, nearly a thousand years ago or more, there were no stories of disappearing and reappearing, of traveling like a phantom throughout the land. Could it be a combination of flight and invisibility? Could Malfleur have produced doubles—replicas of herself scattered in key areas of tension all over LaMorte? Could she be creating elaborate spells of illusion, sort of like the enchantments Belcoeur inflicted on the castle in Sommeil?

The rain won't let up, even as Wren and Aurora wind their way deeper into the forest, filling their baskets with mushrooms to bring back to Constance, who will sort them into two groups according to type—one for eating, and one for poisoning the darts. The later it gets, and the farther they go into the dense woods, the richer the undergrowth they find, littered with jewellike fungi that seem to glow in the final embers of daylight.

"I'm so hungry I think I might risk death for this one," Aurora says, holding up a toadstool the size of her palm, its speckled top the lush red of an apple.

"Then I suppose I better keep a more careful eye on you," Wren replies. As though Aurora was just a little girl who needed to be watched at all times.

Her words tickle an awareness at the edge of Aurora's mind. "You still don't trust me," she says, turning to look at Wren plainly.

Wren shifts her basket. "And why should I?"

"Why *wouldn't* you? After everything we've gone through to get this far . . ." Now that she's gotten physically stronger, all the feelings she's been pushing down for weeks rise back up, even stronger. "What must I do to prove to you that I'm sorry, that I want to make things right, that I *will* make things right?"

"It isn't your intention that I doubt," Wren says,

unmoving. Her heart-shaped face looks innocent, somehow, in the darkness. Her damp hair clings to her cheeks.

"Then what?" Aurora moves closer to her, sensing there is something, some secret Wren has been keeping from her. "Why can't we be *friends*, Wren? You were so kind to me once. I want you to trust me. I want . . ." She doesn't know what else she wants, only that Wren's resistance lights a fire in her, and at the same time, she feels a powerful need to break through that resistance, to shatter it like glass.

But Wren simply shakes her head and begins to turn away. "I don't want your friendship, Princess," she mutters quietly.

Aurora goes after her, grabs her arm. Wren gasps in surprise and turns back toward her again. "This is because of Heath, isn't it?" Heat floods through her, but she can't stop. They must speak of it. "That day in the gallery . . . when you found us . . . when you saw us—"

"Kissing."

Aurora blushes furiously. "You were upset," she insists. "I remember it vividly. You wouldn't speak to me. I thought—"

"That I was envious. I know," Wren says. Her eyes are impossible to read in the gathering darkness. Rain is still coming down and hovering, misting around them like a cold breath, making Aurora's skin prickle and Wren's glisten. "You said as much to the mad queen, but you were as wrong about me as you were about her."

"What do you mean?" How is it possible, Aurora wonders, that the longer she knows Wren, the greater a mystery the girl becomes? "You loved him, didn't you?"

Wren sighs and nods. "As a brother, Aurora."

"A . . . *brother*," Aurora repeats.

Wren squares her shoulders. "He *is* my brother, in every manner but birth. He took care of me for my whole life, practically raised me. I loved him, love him still, the way you love Isabelle."

"But you tried to prevent us . . . you told me not to break his heart."

Wren just looks at her. Finally she lifts the basket of mushrooms higher in her arms. "Love is like these, Aurora. There are all types. They may look the same to someone who doesn't know the difference, but some kinds can heal, some can nourish, and others can kill."

"But . . . I still don't understand. Please, Wren, just give me a chance. We could die tomorrow. Malfleur's soldiers have detected our camp. There may not be much time left and we are on the same side, don't you see that? Don't you feel that? That's why I'm even *here*."

Wren steps toward her—so close Aurora could swear she's going to reach out for her hands. Wren's lips part, and she pauses, as though holding back what she really wants to say. Her mouth waits like that, open just slightly, and Aurora feels overcome with the need to touch her.

"We are on the same side," Wren says finally, softly; Aurora has to lean toward her to hear it. "But we are far apart, you and I. You're a princess, I'm a servant."

"But surely—"

Wren raises a hand, and the protestations die in Aurora's throat. "I've already said, you don't understand, and you can't possibly. The best you can do is keep your distance until we reach Malfleur. *If* we reach her."

And then she vanishes into the dense woods, leaving Aurora alone.

The silence when she's gone seems to vibrate the mist, making the tiny hairs on Aurora's arms stand on end. Aurora finds she is shaking, and not just from the cold.

She had thought Wren was beginning to warm to her. She had thought, if not a true friendship, then *some* sort of bond had started to develop between them. But now she feels slapped in the face—her cheeks sting with the humiliation of it, the frustration. She feels more certain than ever that Wren is hiding something, has been hiding something for a while now. Perhaps since before their journey even began. Here they are, both risking their lives, not just for Heath but for all the Sommeilians, and for Delucians too. Why should Wren keep secrets? And how dare she withhold her trust, when it's the one and only thing Aurora has asked of her?

Isbe's admonishing, joking voice comes to her now. *Go after her, then.*

She does.

But evening has given way to night. The woods are thick with tangled branches, and though the pine needles above seem to soften the rain, the air is damp and heavy. Her heartbeat stutters. She can't find her way.

"Wren?" Her voice thins in the fog, and she wonders if anyone can hear it. Every time Wren leaves her side, she remembers just how precious her voice is.

Perhaps it isn't fair that she associates Wren now with the incredible feeling of having her voice and sense of touch back—the freedom and elation of it—but it's the truth. And because of that, there are things she longs to tell Wren, things she has never told anyone. How sometimes the chance brush of Wren's fingers along her arm sends a thrill through her that shocks her—different, and perhaps better, than how she felt when Heath touched her. How sometimes she senses a sadness in Wren's eyes that makes her own heart ache and thump. How she wants to be *let in*, wants *more* than just her trust. She wants to be heard. To be touched.

To be understood.

Maybe, even, to be loved.

Somewhere along the way, she has stopped wanting Heath's love with the same fierceness she'd once felt. Could it be she's started wanting Wren's instead? The idea of it is uncanny, unexpected, effortless. And unlike anything she's ever read in one of her storybooks.

"Wren?" she calls out again, breaking into a run.

———

Aurora searches deeper into the woods than she meant to go. She is lost; she can see that now. It is too late, too dark, too cold, and she is too alone. Leaves hiss in the wind. The earth, sodden and spongy, seems to want to swallow her. Seems to throb, as though it's alive. In fact, she could swear the ground beneath her has a heartbeat of its own, a quiet, rhythmic boom. She can't really *feel* it, of course, and yet she can sense it, perhaps even *hear* it.

She stops running and takes a breath, trying to gather her focus. A line of white mist snakes before her like a path, and the ground beneath it hums and pulses. Either she's hallucinating, or there is something beneath the mist, something forming it, she realizes. *Is the earth warmer there?* She bends down on her hands and knees, trying to feel the strange heartbeat of the moss and dirt. She doesn't understand it.

But she follows it.

Soon she has made her way to an impassible stretch of vertical rock. At its base is a pile of mossy stones and boulders, and between these, a thick steam emanates from the cracks. Fixated, curious, Aurora throws her weight into one of the stones, trying to push it aside. Though she's not strong enough to roll it out of the way, she manages to nudge it slightly, and she gasps. A faint gleam of light comes through the crack, and a tiny burst of heat hisses out. There is a *hole*—a path to someplace else. Something underground.

She puts her face to the stones, peering between them, then jolts back again. Movement. Shadows and light. She presses her face to the crack again, and now she can definitely see movement, and in fact can hear a banging, puffing sound. The heartbeat she'd heard before, but it had been muffled by the undergrowth.

Now she's surer than ever that something is going on *beneath the ground*. And these stones are blocking an entrance.

Terrified, she turns around, attempting to find her way back to the camp.

And that's when she remembers.

It's something she'd read long ago in her faerie histories, but hadn't thought much about at the time, as it was mostly rumor—a theory about how Malfleur was able to miraculously transform the once practically barren territories into a fertile place for crops. Underground furnaces. She wonders now if that theory is true. These might need to be lit and traversed for maintenance.

And then another thing occurs to her: if there are heat tunnels throughout the kingdom, creating pathways of steam to warm the soil, perhaps some of them are connected. And perhaps they are not only connected to one another, but connected to the castle—because surely the castle and its grounds would be heated.

Aurora suddenly knows *exactly* how Malfleur has been getting around the territories without ever appearing to leave Blackthorn.

The underground tunnels.

And if there's an alternate way *out* of the castle . . . then there's also a way in.

10

Isabelle

"Together"—Isabelle tilts her chin up, letting her voice rise on the wind—"we are . . ."

The waiting crowd collectively inhales as she lifts the war hammer over her head, then slams it down before her. There's a dull, thudding echo.

She lifts the velvet sack from the platform in front of her and pulls out the glass slipper—perfectly intact.

"Unbreakable."

She holds up the shoe.

The spring wind rushes around her, fluttering her cloak.

Gasps. Murmurs. A wild cheer rippling outward.

A smile pulls across Isbe's face; triumph fills her chest. She is standing on a stage, but even without it she feels taller than ever, visible in a way she hasn't felt before—like a beacon. She never knew what that word meant . . . "beacon." And now she has become one.

Based on the volume of the crowd's cheers today, she guesses they'll have a hearty list of names to add to their growing ranks, and she's relieved. Already, in just two short weeks, Isbe has registered nearly a full battalion's worth of soldiers for the Delucian army, with just her speeches. But it hasn't been easy.

Some towns have refused to let her speak; some crowds have thrown rotten potatoes and eggs at her carriage and called her the Bastard Queen. News of Aurora's abdication has by now spread to much of the land, and not every Delucian citizen is happy about it. Rumors abound: that Aurora never woke at all, that William and Isabelle conspired to kill her in her sleep, that this is all a plot on the part of Queen Malfleur to undermine Deluce's legitimacy.

The slipper has helped combat these rumors somewhat—it has, in fact, taken on a life of its own. At rallies, in town squares across the land, Isbe has exhibited the dainty object—too small for her own foot—and proclaimed that she knows what it is like to be small, to be stepped on. She has worn their shoes. Her mother was a peasant, like them. She should have grown up in poverty; it was only a feint of hand by the fates that landed her in the palace instead. But she has known what it is like to be *unlucky* too.

Every time she gets to this part in her speech, she can

feel the way the breath catches in her lungs. *Gil*. He bargained away his luck for her safety.

She has heard the memory of his voice in the many gathered crowds, has felt his absence everywhere. She imagines he'd be proud of her now.

Or maybe he wouldn't. Maybe he'd see through the words, to the terrified, exhausted girl behind them, the one who's been playing queen one moment and people's voice the next. And he'd be right to cast his doubts. He'd be right to hate her, even. She has betrayed every sentiment she once vowed to uphold—her disdain for all things royal. She has married a prince.

And she loves William, loves everything about him: his mind, his passion for ideas, the way his voice moves against her skin in the dark. Even thinking of him sends a shiver of excitement through her body, and she longs to see him again.

Just married, and two weeks apart—it's excruciating.

And yet. The decision to marry William, to bind her life and soul to his, has changed her irrevocably—the knowledge of it coats every inch of her and inhabits her senses, a heady perfume she once admired but now cannot wash off, even as it intoxicates her still.

And there is a thorn in the side of her love. Though she has never stopped sending out inquiries, has even ordered a royal investigation into the fate of the whaling ship where she lost Gil, the mystery of their parting still haunts her, a dark reverberation of the mystery within the mystery: the meaning of his kiss, of the intensity in Gil's words and hands during that moment in the storm. What might have happened next had it not been their last?

She steps down from the stage, ushered by several guards in full livery. They take her to the royal carriage and stow her safely inside. Then she's jolted against the back of her seat as the horses are whipped into motion.

These long, confining carriage rides drive her mad with anxiety and impatience. They leave far too much room for her thoughts to consume her. And she's painfully aware of the guards—no fewer than six—who accompany her journey, which only adds to the on-edge feeling. She aches for an unbridled courser and an open field.

She removes her gloves to finger the cool surface of the slipper, both transfixed and frustrated. The slipper has given her a kind of influence she never expected . . . and yet its meaning eludes her.

So her mother grew up a peasant.

So she possessed an article of clothing, constructed out of the least likely material: glass.

And the fact that the slipper is unbreakable has now become the touchstone of her campaign. It won't shatter, no matter how hard Isbe has tried—a feature she was shocked to discover when an angry rioter tried to steal it.

But *why?*

There is a story in this shoe and its strange magic. Isbe longs to understand it. However, there is one person in her life who knows stories like no other, and that is Aurora, and she is gone, to find her own happily-ever-after. Isabelle received a single letter from her sister, sent via messenger from some point south of the royal road where the river forks in the Vallée de Merle. It said only that Aurora was alive, and all right, and not to come after her. That she has found Heath and they are making a life together in obscurity, safe from the violence of the war.

Isbe knows she should be happy for Aurora—and she is—but she wonders miserably if everyone she loves will fly from her the moment they have a chance. Her mother, who she cannot remember. Gilbert. Aurora.

Will William be next?

She pushes the thought from her mind as the carriage comes to a halt.

Byrne, Isbe's driver, offers her an arm. "Highness." The title still makes her slightly sick. "Boar's Neck Inn tonight," he whispers.

She has come to depend on him to orient her at each of their stops along the royal road, as well as the many winding offshoots into various villages, some so small she has not even heard of them despite their being within a few days' ride of the palace.

"Boar's Neck? How inviting."

"At least 'tisn't another part o' the boar, Highness."

"Please, Byrne, I've asked you before."

"Yes, sorry, Your High—Miss Isabelle."

"Thank you. That's much better." She climbs out of

the carriage. The afternoon air has gone crisp with the hint of evening. *"Boar's Neck . . ."* she repeats. The name seems dimly familiar. "Byrne, can you tell me what land this is?"

"County of Chasseur, Miss Isabelle."

Her pulse quickens. *Chasseur.*

The guards have already moved loudly ahead, entering and slamming the front doors of the noisy tavern attached to the inn. She can smell cooking meat and the sour scent of old ale. Normally she'd dine with them, demanding a tally of their latest recruits or finding someone who could pen a letter for her to send to William. It had made her heart race with pride two nights ago, when she was able to report more than three hundred recruits in a single village—made her feel certain she *is* helping Deluce. And it made her feel closer than ever to William, despite their being apart.

"Actually, Byrne, there's a detour to be made."

He pauses. "Yes, miss?"

"Are the others . . . dispatched for now?"

"Indeed, all of them inside the tavern, awaiting you any moment."

"Good," she says, stepping back up into the carriage. "Because they can't know. You'll have to tell them I've gone to bed early without any supper. Now let's hurry."

"Without your guard, Highness? It would be unsafe to—" he protests.

"Nonsense. You must do as I ask. And Byrne?" she calls in a whisper.

"Yes, Miss Isabelle?" He leans his head through the carriage door.

"Your discretion will be required."

———

It will be dark soon and the roads unsafe to travel, even in a royal carriage—or especially so. But Isbe doesn't care. She races down the lane toward Gilbert's older brother's cottage, her gloved hand trailing the fence for guidance, her heart leaping several steps ahead, her thoughts chasing one another in circles. What will Roul think of her now? Has he any news? How can she ever truly apologize for what she has allowed to happen? Was it a mistake to keep this visit a secret from the guards?

Surely Prince William would understand her concern for the man who had tried to help her seal Deluce's alliance and who sacrificed both his luck and, probably, his life, to the effort. But a hidden part of her knows she can't tell William about Gilbert. There is something too precious there, in her past, to share. Something that was unfinished, forever left open, unresolved. She loves William—she has given him her body, her soul, her independence, everything she knows of herself. But she can't give him this too.

It is six-year-old Piers who spots her first, racing out into the yard, whistling and hollering and throwing his arms around her.

"Isabelle," Roul says, coming up behind the boy. Emotion clots his throat.

Aalis's mix of babble and whining follows closely. She is

likely in the baby sack tied to Roul's back, from the sounds of it, and Isbe realizes the little girl may not even remember her—it has been no more than a couple of months, but the memory of a toddler is fickle.

Roul wraps his arms around Isbe and she hugs him back, hard, as a desperate, wrenching wave unfurls in her chest, carrying mixed feelings she had hardly even realized were there: sadness and longing and guilt and hope.

"Oh." Roul suddenly pulls away. There's an awkward pause, and Isbe is unsure what's happening. Then she realizes. Roul is bowing down before her.

Humiliation knots in her stomach, and her cheeks continue to burn even after Roul invites her inside his cottage, which feels somehow smaller than it did this winter when she first came here with Gil.

"We had not thought to see you under these . . . circumstances. Are you lodging close by?" he asks her, a faint formality entering his voice.

"Actually, I was hoping I might . . . stay here tonight," she says, the admission painful to her own ears. She can't safely return to the inn tonight, not without her guard—and not when she can never quite tell if she's in hostile or welcoming territory.

But it's more than that. She wants things to be the way they were, just for one night.

He is silent for a moment before replying, "It would be our honor, of course. Please, make yourself . . . well . . . comfortable."

"Here, let me at least . . ." She ruffles Aalis's hair, and picks the girl up, then allows Piers to pull her over to the rickety table, where she plops down, taking in the smells of filth and farm animal, which are far preferable to the putrid stench of the Boar's Neck tavern creeping into the inn's rooms.

"We been heard all kinds a talk about ya, Isbe!" Piers declares, clambering loudly onto a stool. "Maribelle, she says ya gone ta give all us magic powers what like the fae got."

"Well, I don't know about *that*—"

"Yeah, she says you got a magic shoe." *Magic.* Isbe smiles at the word, then realizes that he is not wrong. Though she'd thought about it before, it only now begins to sink in that the slipper *has* to have been touched by the fae at some point. So how did her mother come to possess it?

Piers is rocking back and forth on his stool, clattering its legs excitedly as he goes on. "An', an', an' she says ole queen Maffer shoots fire outta 'er mouth like a dragon. But Jacques, he says Maffer gone ta make us knights in 'er army!"

"That's enough, Piers," Roul says, setting down a small, rough portion of lamb's meat and bread for them both, and gruel for the children.

Isbe shivers. *The knights of LaMorte.* The idea that Malfleur will make all her soldiers into knights with special privileges is a claim Isbe has heard chanted in many of the villages in southern Deluce. It still shocks and scares her how easily so many peasants have been swayed to believe stories just as outlandish as the ones Piers is spouting—how many truly seem to think joining up with Malfleur's army is their best bet, and are either oblivious to her evil or willing to overlook it in exchange for power, weapons, the dream of being treated as important. She hopes she has managed to persuade at least some of them that they are wrong, that the faerie queen will never reward any of them. That they'd only be enslaving themselves to a despot.

That they *are* important.

She hopes that will be enough.

Because if Deluce remains this divided, it will fall.

"So . . . have you still had no word?" she asks Roul. She can't bring herself to say Gilbert's name aloud.

"No," he whispers. "Nothing."

Even though it's what she expected, disappointment floods her, makes it difficult for her to swallow her food. "I would understand it if you hate me," she whispers.

"Isabelle—"

"It's my fault," she rushes on, the confession pushing at her lungs, begging to come out. Guilt that she's even here, when the prince has no idea. Guilt that she didn't come sooner.

"He didn't want to go," she says. "He thought it was a terrible idea. He tried to talk me out of it. If I had listened . . ." Her thoughts have traveled down this road often enough. But she can't finish her sentence, because it's impossible to say how different things might be now. The only certainty is that Gil would be alive. He would be *here*.

"Isbe, you can't think that way. You must know," Roul says quietly.

"Know what?"

He puts down his spoon. "Gil would have followed you anywhere."

———

She jolts awake to the sound of Aalis crying. It's the middle of the night. Isabelle must have been muttering in her sleep again and awakened the little girl. She hurries over to the tiny pile of straw close to the now-cold hearth and picks up the crying girl, swaying her in her arms, holding her young warm body against her own.

"*Shhh,*" she says, as the child begins to quiet. She breathes in the smell of her wispy, unwashed hair and thinks of the fact that Aalis's mother died only a few months ago. She wonders what Aalis remembers of her. The girl settles into Isbe's arms with the comfort of a little hedgehog burrowing into its home.

Isbe can tell by the weakness of light through the window that it's not yet dawn. Roul will want at least another hour or two of sleep before the next hard day of labor.

"One night so mild, before break of morn . . ." She begins to sing the lullaby that always calmed her sister when they were young. Aalis's sniffles seem to lessen, so Isbe continues, substituting the lyrics from her mother dreams, repeating the phrases until her throat aches.

At some point, she notices Aalis has fallen back to sleep.

She lays her down on her pallet and tucks herself back into her own bed.

But as she drifts off again, she senses another presence in the room, in the doorway.

"*Gil?*" she whispers.

"I heard Aalis cry. Is everything all right?" he asks, stepping softly into the room.

She turns toward his voice. "Gil, is that you?"

"Of course it's me."

She feels confused, her head full of cotton. She gestures to Aalis, who is snoring softly, then whispers, "Let's talk out there."

She walks through the doorway and feels as though she is following a ghost.

He is silent, and she begins to doubt whether he's really there.

"Gil?"

"Yes." His voice reaches her, but she can't tell where he's standing.

Suddenly, she feels hot, confused, shaky. *Gil is here.*
Gil is here.

How can this be?

She is shivering uncontrollably, torn between racing into him and cowering. She turns away from his voice, overwhelmed, and feels her way around the kitchen automatically, relieved to discover the bucket from the well still has some water in it.

"What are you doing?" Gil asks.

"Heating the water, of course," she answers, moving about in a numb fog. She locates the tinder and flint stacked four paces from the hearth, as Roul had shown her, and begins to light a fire, the flick and slash of stone on metal cutting through the stiffness of her thoughts. Still, her hands shake.

"But why?"

She's confused by his question. "It's the least I can do to help."

The fire finally crackles to life, and she stands, remaining by the hearth to allow her legs to warm up and her head to clear. *Think. Think.*

She can feel Gil's warmth and closeness when he comes up behind her. For a moment, it seems like he is going to touch her, but he doesn't.

"I'm afraid this life is harder on you than either of us knew it would be," he says quietly.

A protest forms on her lips. "No," she whispers, turning to face him at last.

"Isbe." His voice has gone low and wavering. She is terrified by what he might say next, and by what her own face must show. Gil is here. He is here. Unthinkably, impossibly.

He takes her hands in his, and the touch sends another shudder through her. He traces a finger along her cheek like he did on the boat, just before they were separated. "Isbe," he repeats. "Isbe."

<hr />

"Isbe." Roul's voice shakes her out of the heaviness of sleep. She is freezing cold, her blanket and cloak cast somewhere off to the side.

And then she knows.

She wants to cry, openly and plainly, as Aalis did.

Because Gilbert is dead. He *must* be. Drowned out there in the open sea. She failed to find him, failed to save him. Instead she has gone on to fall in love with, and marry, a prince. And yet what she can't admit to William is that she fears her questions about Gil will haunt her forever. She fears that their unfinished love will flutter like a moth in the secret closet of her heart, slowly eating away at the silks and fabrics of her memories, until one day it is the only thing left.

———

Back at the Boar's Neck Inn, her guards are gathered in the courtyard yelling at Byrne, who is helplessly defending himself. "'Twas by her own orders I left her there!"

"It's true," she announces loudly. She can sense their attention turning to her, hear their surprised murmurs. "I specifically told Byrne to drop me off at a farm where I have distant family. I sent him home, figuring it would be less dangerous than returning in the dark."

Isabelle can't help but grin as the men fumble over themselves to either scold or apologize. She knows she must look ridiculous, with mud nearly up to her knees from the lengthy morning's walk down the village lane to the tavern. But the walk rejuvenated her, brought her out of the murk of sadness and guilt and missing Gil. With a tall gnarled stick in her hand to use as a walking staff, and the spring sun bright on her cheeks and forehead, she'd felt more alive than she has in days.

In fact, she was reminded of something on this walk. Several things, really. One of which is the importance of having a plan.

Gil would have followed you anywhere.

No matter how he might reprimand or even resent her if he were here, she knows more than anything else that Gil would want her to go on. To prove everyone else in the world wrong.

To win.

As her guards scramble to give her further instruction, she holds up a hand. "Fetch me a lady's maid," she tells them. "At once."

"But—"

"Have her prepare the finest dress she can find in my trunks."

"But—"

"And obviously . . ." She smiles, nodding down toward her ripped and ragged clothes. "I will need a bath."

———

A few hours later, Isbe steps out of her carriage wearing the fanciest, flounciest gown she could find on such short notice, follows the steep path up a hill, and raps on Lord Barnabé's front door. During her walk, she had remembered

111

that Binks lives within a short distance of Roul's home—and that he trades in all kinds of things, but most of all luck, money, wine, and *information*.

As she waits for someone to answer, she recalls how she'd been scandalized that wagons full of Binks's furniture were being carted off the last time she was here. Now the private road is silent, save for the stray, halting call of a mistle thrush.

So perhaps it is not surprising that Binks himself is the one to slide open the door's viewing panel.

"You," he says in a not-exactly-friendly tone. She'd recognize his high, pinched voice anywhere, and can't help but picture him wearing a high, pinched ruffled collar to match.

She tries to control her annoyance with this nasty speck of vanity, this faerie who not only cheated her and Gilbert but whose tithe of luck led, however indirectly, to Gil's fate. "Indeed, Lord Barnabé. That *is* the correct pronoun, though not the official title by which I prefer to be addressed."

"Hmph," Binks manages in response.

A silence follows, and Isbe can feel his suspicion through the thick, heavily bolted door. She imagines his eyes flicking between her and the royal carriage.

"Back for more stories, then?" he asks but immediately slams closed the panel's metal grate before she can respond.

A moment later, he swings open the door itself with a *whoosh* and a *creak*.

Without waiting for an invitation, Isbe pushes past him into the airy foyer. "I take it your servants have fled."

Binks bristles, causing some sort of large necklace—hideously gaudy, no doubt—to jangle about his neck. "Not all of them. My tailors are very loyal."

"A shame your tailors won't stoop to answering your door for you."

"I—"

"Lord Binks, I'm not here to discuss the status of your household affairs."

"What business have you—"

"Please, shall we make our way to your offices?" It is clearly not a question.

Binks doesn't offer her a guiding arm, simply marches ahead, leaving her to follow merely by the clop of his too-high heels. Isbe's not offended. Her anger plays into determination, even pleasure. She clutches the small satchel that carries her glass slipper, tied tightly to her belt, and savors the way her expensive gown swishes across the slick marble floors, sending a quiet message of status. She knows he knows: he is outranked and has no choice but to entertain her. She is the queen of Deluce—and what good is the title if she can't use it to get her way now and then?

She sits down in his plush, silencing study, in the same chair Gilbert sat in to play heart of harts with Binks, a game that he lost because Binks marked the queen card. Resentment and disgust bubble up in her chest, and it's all she can do not to launch into a thousand insults.

"I need some information," she explains. "A census of the living fae, and in particular those who still possess large

113

swathes of land and control." She could swear she can hear him lift an eyebrow, and her hand moves again to the pouch at her waist, feeling for the slipper without thinking. "The palace library contains many histories of the fae, but no current census," she adds.

And besides, she can't very well read them. None of the servants can read them. William could, but she can't ask him to do that, not when he's at this very moment staging a battle outside of the hills of Nuage in southern Deluce.

"What makes you think I even possess such a thing?" Binks sits back in his pillowed seat with a muffled squeak.

"Just a hunch," she replies calmly. A man who devotes his life to gambling—trading in goods, gold, luck, and secrets—is one who likely keeps tidy records of who owes him what.

"What might you need this information for?"

"What I need, sir, are their men. As many as I can get. You may have heard there's a war on."

A pause. And then: "What happened to your hair?"

It's an obvious attempt to unnerve her. She reaches up to touch her hair, which has been gathered neatly at the base of her neck. He can't possibly tell how short it is, save for one stray lock, which she quickly brushes behind her ear. He has, she's sure, simply heard the rumors: the foreign prince's wild, short-haired bride. The king's bastard daughter taking to the campaign trail to rally the peasantry.

"What happened to your *staff*?" she counters.

He grumbles. "Say I have what interests you. . . . What

will you give me in return? I've heard you possess something of interest to me."

Isabelle tenses. "Do I?" He can't be asking for her luck, can he?

"The stories have preceded you. Of a certain unbreakable slipper. I might find quite a value in this special token of yours. I might even throw in a tailor or two—you know a man who's good with a needle could certainly help improve the look of those military uniforms."

Isabelle scoffs. "You would trade your own men for a symbolic shoe?"

She hears the soft sigh of his chair as he shifts and seems to reconsider. "Perhaps not," he says slowly. "I would need to see it first."

Her hand moves to the pouch tied to her belt protectively. "Lord Barnabé . . . Binks. I don't have time to bargain with you. You may have noticed that I am now officially your queen. Decisions about the fate of this kingdom's nobility are mine to make. What I can offer you is that I won't have you executed at my earliest convenience."

He guffaws, but she raises her hand. *"Or,"* she adds, "worse, have you publicly stripped of your title and prominence, what remains of your wealth and"—she gestures—"frippery."

This seems to shut him up . . . for a moment.

Then he shoves his chair back. "I won't stand for these empty threats and insults."

"I assure you," she says calmly, "they aren't empty, but

your coffers will be. I'll give you some time to collect the information I have requested, and will expect the names delivered to the palace by special messenger." At this she can practically hear him cringe, thinking of the expense of a courier in times of war. "In one week's time."

"But—"

"One week, Binks."

She waits until she has made it all the way out of his mansion and into her waiting carriage before she allows herself to smile.

11

Aurora

The underground tunnels of LaMorte are lined with iron torches holding a kind of moss that burns all day without fading, even in the close, oppressive heat. Steam swirls, beckons, melts. Through it, a greenish glow glances against the rocks and dirt walls, making them seem to undulate. *Like lungs*, Aurora thinks.

Once, a plague physician visited the palace in Deluce, and tried to explain to Aurora how the disease had come to infect her mother's lungs, described them as soft passages that inflate and deflate with breath, vulnerable to invasion. Though she'd been banned from Queen Amelié's chambers, Aurora sneaked into her mother's rooms and crept to her bed, hoping for a word, a sign of life. Maybe the queen would bestow a last wish, she'd imagined, or at least a harried maternal warning. Perhaps there'd be a cool, dry kiss pressed against her forehead, a bony hand clasped around her own. A gaze that showed what her mother had never actually, in so many words, said. Not just that Aurora was pretty or that Aurora was good. But that Amelié loved her.

All she'd seen, though, was the queen's porcelain skin, her cheekbones cutting like blades into the dusty air of the heavily boarded bedchamber, her closed eyes, her stillness. A whisper of pained breath. A droplet of blood at the corner of her lips.

Aurora keeps thinking of that cold and dreadful morning—her mother's last—as she moves through the tunnels underneath the mountains.

She leads the refugees of Sommeil and LaMorte, a brigade of women armed with anything they could find—clubs, anvils, pickaxes, and sticks—through the mountains' lungs, realizing *they* are like a sickness, spreading, taking hold, approaching the heart.

Her discovery has made her stronger, braver. She'd been right—she'd found the heating channels connecting the furnaces. The next morning, she led the women away from the camp, back to the stones, and pried them apart.

And then they were inside.

Even as she wipes perspiration from the back of her neck, Aurora feels another kind of certainty flowering within her: she's convinced now that true love is something subtler and more complicated than she used to believe.

Wren has been keeping her distance. She never explained why she stalked off in the woods the other night after their argument. She hasn't said why she doesn't want to be friends, and Aurora has respected her distance. She knows how to be patient. She has spent her whole childhood that way: waiting, silent, while others lived. This was why she'd had to go. To leave not only the palace, but everything it contained. Even Isbe.

It's hard, and confusing, this growing awareness . . . that she can love her sister more than anything, yet that she must be apart from her in order to know, and perhaps one day, love herself.

The map of the territories, tucked inside her dress, rustles against her chest, and she tries her best to gauge their direction, stopping to make a mark on the map whenever the tunnels fork, so she can chart which way they've gone. She can only hope she's leading them the right way, and not to their deaths . . . though she knows that she could very easily be doing both at the same time.

The trapped air smells of bodies, of sweat and earth and roots and heat. And too, the vinegary scent of fear. Murmured commands and hissed warnings travel through the pack as the women move in a tight, tangled mass of limbs and skirts, hair and torch and weapon. Aurora can hardly tell where she ends and the rest of her makeshift army begins. They are one.

Finally, after the better part of a day, the tunnel narrows like a constricted throat, and then they are hit with a burst of cool, musty air as it opens wide into a vast underground dungeon.

Blackthorn.

They did it. A sudden euphoria washes through her. They are in the nadir of the castle.

Quickly her excitement mellows into caution. This is Malfleur's dungeon. From the stale stench of human waste and standing water, and the faint groan of rusty voices, Aurora can guess at the state of the prisoners even before she sees them. She pulls her arm across her mouth to keep from gagging as she scans the cavernous room, squinting through the thick air.

There are several aisles of cells, all in a row like horse stalls; hay covers the ground, black with mold and rot. People who hardly resemble humans are locked behind iron bars, and in the dim sphere of her torch's light, the white-gray bones of skeletons cast sharp shadows along the floor. A collection of the dead and nearly dead. The embodiment of disease, abuse, cruelty.

The living are mostly too weak, too faded, even to beg for help. Some hardly seem to notice the sudden entrance of all these women. One prisoner cries out quietly, urgently, "The beast! The beast is back to feed!"

Another moans, "Take me next!"—his voice hardly more than a breath.

Aurora shudders, ashamed at her own revulsion. Is Heath among them? Panic races through her chest. She hopes they're not too late. It's only after she has hurried from cage to cage that she runs into Wren again, and they grasp each other's arms, and she knows that they have both come to the same discovery: Heath is not here. He is not one of the prisoners. She heaves a sigh of relief; can see it too in Wren, who does not pull away. No news of him is better than bad news.

"They aren't from Sommeil, but we must save them," Wren says, looking around her at the wretched prisoners.

The other women have crowded into the cavern, pushing through the filth, searching for the entrance into the castle proper—obviously impatient, nervous, desperate. They are so close now, they can't afford a wrong move.

"We will," Aurora vows with a bravery, and a certainty, that are not quite her own. "We will find the keys and set them all free."

"Look," Wren says. She gestures to where a large group of women have gathered at the mouth of a small, dark stairwell, and are pushing one another to get through.

"Wait," Aurora warns, her heart pounding hard in her chest. Nearly all of them, at least, can hear her voice. This is something she can't take for granted. At least not now. Not yet.

But if her idea works . . .

She goes over the plan and the formations. The fastest and lithest women—the ones carrying pouches of poisoned darts and finely whittled flutes—must lead the pack, disabling as many soldiers as they can. Next come the largest and strongest women, those with heavy, blunt weapons, who will push back the remaining opposition and create space for combat. The fiercest among them will follow at the tail end—those who are not afraid to shed blood, to kill by any means.

Aurora and Wren will lead the first wave. The satchel of poisoned darts trembles in Aurora's fist. She slides one out and slips it inside her wooden flute, smooth and solid against her palm. She has practiced the way to purse her lips, covering the playing holes and blowing air through the flute in a hard tuft to shoot the dart at her opponent. She's tempted to trace her finger along the dart's tip, knowing that even a faint nick could be enough to undo her. As she pushes her way up the winding stone stairs, she is *almost* amused to think of what happened last time she pricked a finger.

———

Their skirmish, if you could even call it that, does not go as planned.

A surge of soldiers greets them at the other side of the bolted door, and Aurora is hardly able to take in her surroundings—a wide storage cellar, lit with dripping wrought-iron chandeliers, and hordes of men in terrifying, curve-beaked masks—before she is shoved violently to the side, dropping her flute and cracking her head against a wall. A spray of blood—someone else's—strikes the stone beside her, painting her fingers in it, making them slippery.

Even as she clambers back up to fight, the chaos has multiplied itself. It seems the women were anticipated. Armored men are bludgeoning the invaders, pulling them back by the hair, stepping on their skirts, holding them down with their knees. The sounds of women screaming echo in the chamber, and Aurora barely manages to shove a soldier, grinning savagely beneath his mask, away from Wren, driving one of her darts into his neck by hand.

She gasps and staggers backward as she sees his grin become a grimace and his eyes roll back. He falls to his knees and collapses. She cannot feel the shock of his death, of what she's just done—*her first kill*—because no sooner has he crumpled to the floor than three more appear where he had been. Vultures, everywhere.

And their eyes—the way they blaze behind those black masks. It suddenly becomes obvious to Aurora that they are more than mere soldiers. They are under the spell of some unfathomable magic.

She is surrounded too quickly; the tide of the battle has crashed epically and too soon. She has led all of these women, whom she pledged to help, into certain death. Panic, thick and ugly as tar, stops her throat—she is panting and heaving as she lunges at one of her attackers, unable to best him. She is forced to her knees and looks up just as a metal-coated knee is thrust up into her chin. Her jaw rattles as blood fills her mouth, sparks swarming her vision, followed by a swift and heady blackness.

————

When Aurora comes to, she is chained to a chair, her head slumped onto her shoulder. She glances up blearily, her vision swimming. The room spins. The person across from her flickers like a candlelit dream.

Pale face, ravaged by a wide, rippled scar.

Aurora blinks.

Beautiful lips.

Dark, piercing, depthless eyes.

A crown of unmistakable iron thorns.

The opening notes of the rose lullaby trickle into Aurora's mind: *One night reviled* . . .

She swallows and blinks again, her vision finally coming into focus.

Before her sits the faerie queen, Malfleur.

———

There's something wrong with Aurora's face. It must be puffy; one eye is so swollen she can barely see out of it. She licks her lips and tastes blood. She tries to concentrate, but her thoughts dance into the shadows.

A cynical part of her, a part she hardly knew 'til now, wants to laugh at what a fool she is. How she imagined storming the throne room and bargaining with Queen Malfleur like an equal. How stupidly, naively unafraid she'd been.

She squints and looks at the queen.

Malfleur's smile stretches across her face as though pulled that way by invisible strings.

Where are they, where is Wren— She cuts off. Her voice is gone again, she realizes. The effort to speak singes her throat, coming out as a rattling gasp. She struggles against the shackles binding her wrists.

"I find it almost enchanting," Queen Malfleur says

calmly, then takes a sip from a goblet of something dark. Aurora wonders if it's blood. "Your arrival. An unexpected gift."

Malfleur's grin is a sickle, carving into Aurora's heart. She clenches her muscles and tugs against the chains again, to no avail.

"I nearly didn't recognize you," the faerie queen goes on, her eyes scanning Aurora from her tangled blond hair to her ragged garments.

She must not, she realizes, look anything like she once did. Aurora grits her teeth.

"But your friend—Wren, is it?—was crying out your name over and over."

What did you do to her? . . . Once again, the words die in Aurora's mouth, and her chest clenches from the pain of it. She's voiceless.

"What I found most intriguing," Malfleur adds, "was that you murmured a reply, which the girl seemed to hear, though I could not." She pauses, eyeing Aurora as though awaiting a response. "It got me thinking, of course. You must know my sister was very powerful once."

Was.

Malfleur purses her lips. Aurora stares at her. She had believed Wren when she'd told her that Malfleur entered Sommeil and murdered Belcoeur, but the coldness of Malfleur's demeanor still comes as a shock.

"It seems my sister's world," the queen says, rising from her chair, "and by extension, those who were raised there, have a sort of immunity to the work of the other fae." She begins to pace, her long dark gown spilling across stone like black oil. "Like an invisible shield. Thus the tithes taken from you appear to be nonexistent among her people."

Aurora takes in her surroundings as the queen paces. It's a small room, more of a cell, really, and six walled. Judging by the light, high up. Probably in a tower. There are no furnishings other than the two chairs. There are, however, two doors. Malfleur comes to one of the doors, pauses, and turns to catch Aurora's gaze.

"Belcoeur could outpower the rest of them, perhaps. Unfortunately for her, though, she could not outdo me."

The queen's words send a chill through Aurora as she wrenches open the door. Through it lies an even smaller adjoining cell, dark and windowless—and in the center sits Wren, hunched on the floor, tied up and whimpering faintly. A rag is stuffed in her mouth.

Malfleur picks up Wren by the elbow and drags her into Aurora's chamber. She yanks the rag from Wren's mouth, and Aurora winces as the girl lets out a choking sob. The rag is covered in blood and dirt.

Aurora's arms strain against the chains. "Let her go!" she commands, thrilled at the rush of her voice's return, which brings with it a surge of anger. Now that Wren is here, Aurora can speak—though only Wren can hear it.

"Now, Aurora." Malfleur smiles and retakes her seat, shoving Wren to her knees at the foot of her chair like a dog. "Tell me. What brings you to Blackthorn?"

Aurora struggles and pulls but cannot free her hands. "Let her go and I'll tell you."

Malfleur stares at her blankly. Obviously she can't understand, can't hear. Then she gazes down at Wren and grabs her by the chin, tilting her face up. "Please ask the princess why she has come to my palace."

"Stop! I—I came for you," Aurora says.

Wren, shaking, meets the queen's eyes. She clears her throat. "She came for you," she whispers.

"What a lovely surprise. And we hadn't even prepared for guests," Malfleur replies with a smirk. "Perhaps I should rephrase. What is it exactly that the princess wants from me?"

Wren practically snarls. "To demand the freedom of my people."

Malfleur backhands her across the face with such force that Wren cries out, falling to her elbows on the stone floor. Aurora gasps.

"I didn't ask you for your *own* answer, my dear." The queen looks to Aurora, studying her face for a moment in silence. Aurora tries to keep from trembling. "I imagine, to have come all this way," Malfleur goes on, "the princess must have been seeking something very important— something important to *her*."

A gust of wind blows through the unboarded window, cut high into the walls above their heads. Leaves blast through its bars and swirl in the room. The heat of anger in Aurora's gut twists into icy fear. Malfleur's eyes seem to bore through her, pinning her even more strongly than the shackles.

"What did you *really* want in coming here?"

Aurora shivers. "I—I wanted—I want—" *To free Wren's people. To convince you to stop this war. To save Heath. To . . .*

All of these responses are at the tip of her tongue, but something stops her from answering. She thinks, as she often has these past weeks, of the starling that spoke from her bedroom window, taunting her, on the eve of her birthday.

She pushes on, forcing herself to be brave, to stick to her plan. "I've come to bargain with you."

Wren looks at her, a flash of uncertainty in her eyes, before she turns to Malfleur. "She has come to bargain with you."

"Go on," the queen says, and Aurora wonders if it's just her imagination or if Malfleur has leaned in toward her, ever so slightly. She wants to cry out with the sudden power and pleasure of it.

She clears her throat. "I would like you to hold back your forces . . ."

Wren repeats her words to the queen.

"And free your prisoners, returning them to Deluce . . ."

Again, Wren translates.

"And in exchange, I'll offer you . . ."

Malfleur waits. Wren watches her cautiously.

Once again the starling flutters through her mind. If the queen can give voice to animals, what else might she be able to give voice to? Aurora feels the crudeness of her wish, the baseness and selfishness of it, thrusting up inside her in a nauseous wave.

"Myself."

"What? Aurora, no!" Wren's face has gone pale as a grave.

"Tell her," Aurora insists. "Tell her that I give her myself."

"Aurora," Wren protests again, but turns to the queen. "She has offered up . . . herself."

Malfleur raises an eyebrow. "And what could I possibly want with you?"

"An experiment." Aurora swallows. "You have great power, so you've said. Maybe the greatest there is. You could make an example of me. Return my voice to me."

Wren repeats, and the queen, to her surprise, barks out a laugh. "I must say I'm impressed. I have heard of you, you see. The princess whose hand is sought the world over. Whose beauty inspires poetry. Whose gentle kindness is enough to melt the hearts of men. A princess whose demure silence makes all those who come to her feel heard and seen." She says all of these things as if they are insults, points of shame. "So I'm delighted to see the feistier side of you. You've come here out of self-interest."

"But it isn't for myself," Aurora insists. "It's for *us both*." Really, it's not for either of them. Aurora doesn't need her voice back—she just needs Malfleur to be tempted. Faeries love making deals, Aurora knows. But can one as intelligent at Malfleur be outwitted?

Aurora holds Malfleur's gaze as Wren translates. "I know what it is to have everything, and yet to want more."

It's not entirely a lie. She didn't do all this—come all this way, risk all these lives—just for her own voice. She'd be happy to never speak again if it meant saving Heath, freeing the others, and putting a peaceful end to the war. But that doesn't mean she doesn't yearn for things she can never have.

She thinks of Isbe—of the years of abuse she suffered at the hands of the palace staff in Deluce. At the hand, even, of Aurora's own mother, and their father. Even still, despite Isbe's insistence that she was the one forced into the shadows while Aurora had all the light, still, *still*, Aurora would, sometimes, in her heart of hearts, yearn for what Isbe had. Freedom.

"Tell me," Aurora goes on, feeling more confident in her plan as Malfleur takes her in unwaveringly, hardly glancing at Wren for her translation. "What would make a better pet than a mortal princess you've magically cured? Who would not bow to the miracle of it? There's time enough to conquer land, but why not finish what you've started, and lure the world to your side instead, bend it to your will?"

She feels as though she has tucked a lit flint beside a pile of dry twigs—at any moment, it will catch fire. Which is both the most dangerous and the most thrilling thing she has ever done. She has, after all, stoked the engine that scares her even more than Malfleur's military: her power of persuasion.

Isbe told her the way whole villages in Deluce have given themselves over to the queen, given up their liberty for a taste of violence and power, willing to turn on their own people if it means seeing the Delucian aristocracy, who have for so long thrived on the thankless labor of the masses, finally fall. She wonders what those same people would think if they learned that Malfleur had taken Aurora in as her own. It might seem a kind of alliance. Would such a pairing undermine the faerie queen's stance, or turn the tides in her favor?

Aurora shudders. She is terrified by what she's about to say—but she knows that Malfleur is only going to keep killing unless Aurora does something to make her change tactics. "Besides," Aurora adds slowly, "I can convince Deluce *and* Aubin to come under your rule. Peacefully."

"My dear," Malfleur says now. "Might I remind you that you are already my prisoner. I may do with you whatever I like."

"I will only make the offer once," Aurora says, trying to keep from shaking. "What is your answer?"

Malfleur looks at Wren and then back at Aurora. Her eyes narrow; her mouth pulls again into that terrifying smile. "My answer . . ."

Aurora feels her decision like a knee to the gut before she even says it.

". . . is no."

———

Aurora has lost count of the days she's been in her cell.

The first few days, she occupied herself with studying

the locks on the doors, analyzing their mechanisms, trying to divine a clever way to undo them, succeeding only in undoing her own composure and crying out in silent anger. She chased the moving patch of pale spring light through the high window, curling up in it, crying until she was too exhausted to cry, or to feel. She pounded over and over again on the side door connecting her cell to Wren's, but got only a dull, repeated thud in response—it was enough to signal that Wren was still alive, but the wood was too thick for Wren's voice to carry.

And because of that, because of her solitude, Aurora finds herself once again voiceless.

Scraps of stale bread and sometimes even the stringy tendons of recently slaughtered meat appear at her door at varying hours, never consistently enough to assuage the panic of starvation, though—the dizzying sensation of disappearing. She is smoke. She is bone. She is thirst. When she rises to stand, the walls tilt, the light sways. The darkness comes, and with it, fuzzy pinpricks behind her eyelids that are crude copies of stars, bursts of unconsciousness. When she dreams, it's of ink bottles full of blood.

She longs to be with Wren, to confess what she feels. To beg forgiveness. She has failed Wren, failed all of the refugees of Sommeil and LaMorte, failed Isbe and William and all of Deluce too. She begins to believe what Malfleur said of her, that she only came here out of self-interest. Not to try and reclaim her voice, which had never been at the very forefront of her wishes—but to prove something to Wren, to everyone. She had wanted desperately to be the kind of person Wren would admire, to be a hero.

But maybe heroes are only for stories.

By the time Malfleur returns to her, silhouetted by a tepid beam of moonlight, Aurora has come to the very brink of loss—has felt everything she knew about herself draped out over the ledge, hooked on by a single finger.

She is, she believes, ready to let go.

———

The queen moves like a piece of darkness. Aurora has the wild fear that if she shifts, even breathes too hard, Malfleur will prove but a phantom, a delirious creation of her mind. And she needs her to be real. She clings to it.

"Shhh," the queen says as she kneels down on the floor in front of Aurora.

It's all Aurora can do not to gasp in surprise—at her closeness, at the shock of seeing the queen bending to her level, like a nursemaid about to comfort a child from a nightmare.

"I have been busy, as you can imagine." Her voice is removed and devoid of pity, her eyes thoughtful as they take in Aurora's decrepit state without reaction.

Aurora's hands shake. She doesn't know what to think, what to feel, what to do. She can only wait, hoping to be put out of her misery one way or another, at last—and yet still, stubbornly, clinging to hope.

"I have not changed my mind . . . ," the queen says slowly. "Entirely. But I *have* been thinking." She works her jaw, and Aurora is struck by the way she can see the bones shifting beneath her pale skin, even through the musty thickness of the moonlit cell. "I *will* give you something."

Aurora hates the way her whole body trembles, the way a sob launches up into the back of her throat, waiting there. How hunger like a sleeping demon uncurls and begins to gnaw . . .

"Not your voice, but . . ."

Water. Ink. Something to eat. Something to bring on sleep, or even death. Anything.

Malfleur's teeth glint in the dark. "Something better."

12

Malfleur,
the Last Faerie Queen

The night forest whistles with the flight of frightened creatures as she charges on horseback into its mist, alive with the need for blood. She must have it. The desire for it is not new, but in recent years it has intensified, provoking her to go to greater lengths to get it—and driving her to greater heights.

To leave the castle undetected, as always, Malfleur moved through the cavernous dungeon, through the crying of its new captives—the countless women who survived her guards only to be locked up, made to share cells with their own rotting dead.

Now, in the fresh night air, Malfleur pulls the vulture mask from her face and dismounts, finding her way to the

135

mountain stream where she has set her trap, wondering what she will have caught tonight, though it doesn't really matter, so long as it is still alive. So long as her killing blade is its first.

Unlike some of the fae, Malfleur does not believe in luck. But tonight she *feels* lucky. After all, she has ensnared the most fascinating creature yet—the pale, trembling beauty, the prize of Deluce.

Beauty like Princess Aurora's is more curse than gift. Malfleur has seen how that kind of beauty acts like an intoxicating drug, how it demands only more of itself. How it begs.

How it withers.

Malfleur and her sister, Belcoeur, should know. Beauty is what killed their mother.

She may have despised the woman—her original tormentor—but Malfleur still relives her mother's suicide every day. Like a meteor shower it ravaged the sky and then was over, leaving a blackness, a blankness. Malfleur knew why her mother did it: she couldn't stand that she'd begun to grow warped and wrinkled with age, that her daughters' looks had surpassed her own.

It happened just before Malfleur had left to study magic all over the world, sending back gifts and discoveries to Belcoeur all the while, even though she didn't want to be near her twin anymore, with those bright eyes, that big hope, that great and tender love. Soft. Suffocating.

Their father, King Verglas, had turned in on himself

already by then, had begun to hoard his tithe, which was knowledge. She couldn't bear to witness that, either. She felt cut off from him more than ever.

So when she discovered that her father had conquered the Îles de Glace in her absence and had remarried the blithering North Faerie, at first the news could hardly touch her. After Belcoeur's betrayal, and after the only response she could find within herself was to kill Charles Blackthorn, Malfleur withdrew to the mountains, unable to face society, the past a terrible riddle that would taunt her, she feared, until she died or went mad like so many other faeries.

Back then, she had felt guilt—and hurt—of a kind that only the deep and stagnant mountain bogs could equal. It had consumed her, had nearly sunk her in its dark, slurping mire. She vowed, at that time, never to kill again.

But as she discovered and began to practice transference, it was like something awoke again—a black-winged bird flew up and out of the swamp her life had been, cawing and crying and carving out a new way forward.

It was Blackthorn himself—young Charles—who had first inspired the idea of transference, though of course it would be many years after his death at her hands that she thought of it again. The elder Blackthorn and Verglas, her father, had arranged another hunting visit, and this time the Blackthorns were guests at the Delucian palace. Things were so different back then, Malfleur recalls: the way the human and fae monarchs socialized as though even the rise of humans to such power could never pose a threat to the fae.

Charles had gone out riding with his father and hers, and returned later with a fox, which she found him skinning in a room off the kitchens. He said he loved to handle all the preparation of the animal himself. Tying up and hanging it by the feet. Brushing the fur clean of burs before making studied, precise cuts around the ankles in order to begin the careful removal of its skin. Once it was separated from the flesh and guts, the meat and the fat had to be scraped away. And then there was the slow stretching, tacking, and drying of the hide.

Charles confessed to her—never taking his eyes away from his meticulous dissection—that he'd always been fascinated with the fae. He had an endless series of questions about magic: what it *felt* like, how it worked, why the system of faerie tithing had even come about. Questions she didn't always know the answer to, but which stirred her own curiosity. It was only the third time she'd seen him since their first meeting and the memorable game of whist. She was now sixteen, he eighteen. She cleaned his knives for him while he worked.

After he was finished with the fox, he washed his hands in a bucket drawn from a well, then retrieved something from a pouch tucked inside his doublet. She didn't say aloud—or even admit silently, to her private self—what she felt when he produced the glistening white pearl she'd given him from her mother's necklace a few years earlier. She didn't want to name it, for that would make the feeling smaller and mundane. She couldn't call it a romance, what was taking seed and spreading its roots through the dark soil of her heart. She couldn't, because that would make it a silly thing, predictable, a story that must demand one of two conclusions, neither of which appealed to her. For as much as everyone lives in fear that he or she might be destined for tragic ends, Malfleur was equally revolted by the idea of a happily ever after. Perhaps because both actually suggested the same thing to her: an ending.

No. Hers would not be a love story—not then, and not ever.

It was during their discussions of faerie magic that day so many years ago now, when he made the suggestion that eventually led to transference, though at the time it struck her as ridiculous. They had left the kitchens and begun to stroll the palace grounds, the brackish sea air blustering off the cliffs and billowing up into the cloudy sky, making the famous Delucian fog writhe and whirl. As they walked, his hair shuffled in the wind, bright and out of place.

In his forthright way, he accused faerie tithing of being outdated and unfair, especially to the human race that now populated the majority of their lands. Malfleur argued that this had always been the relationship of human to fae, though, much like the fox to both. There was, quite simply, a hierarchy in the natural order of things, one that had to be respected in order for each to thrive as they were born to thrive.

He looked at her then, and she felt as studied as the slain fox had been. His eyes took her apart, but so carefully, so gently, and so gradually, that she experienced the confusion and surprise of liking it.

"If I had the power of the fae, I'd use it to tithe away faerie magic from all the others. Bring about a new order, one in which faerie and man are equal," he said.

She scoffed, of course, offended. "You'd have us be just like you, then? What arrogance."

"Is it arrogant to want justice?" His eyes blued, sun passing over water.

Thirst sprang up in her. "It is arrogant," she countered, "to believe you can even know what justice looks like for anyone but yourself."

"You would have us govern without presuming we understand justice as a general principle?"

"Oh, please, Charles," she said with a smile. "I don't pretend that anyone actually rules in the name of justice." She wanted to laugh. "Monarchy does not exist for the sake of fairness."

She didn't know her words would hit him so hard, but he winced as though struck by something small yet infinitely sharp. The truth was like that, she thought. A trim and effective dagger—it fit, well hidden, inside even the daintiest palm.

He turned to face her, forcing her to stop walking. They had passed the gardens and were nearing the top of a squat hill she and her twin had hurtled themselves down countless times as children.

"You have a stark view of the world," he said after a

moment spent staring at her. His breath danced in the cool fog, folding into it, becoming lost.

She wanted to shrug but didn't. She hadn't expected him to make it personal. Instead, she turned to the side, scanning for signs of life over the strait. A stray gull curved through the gray. Closer, a pair of laundresses chased a woman's underclothing that had gotten caught up in the wind's invisible fist.

"It is rarely pleasant to look at things without any of their comfortable disguises," she finally answered.

He touched her scar.

She sucked in a breath but did not push his hand away. It was the first time he seemed to have acknowledged the seared mark on her cheek and brow.

"That's what I like so much about you, Malfleur," he said, so low and so quiet it gave her a shiver. "With you, there can be no disguises. Everything is real. Light becomes anguish."

She turned to face him, then. He was so near. His thumb traced her lower lip.

"And," he whispered, "anguish becomes light."

———

Now, Malfleur traces her fingers along her scar as she nears the trap in the woods. She is still thinking about transference and about the princess's offer. *I give you myself*, she'd said. Malfleur toys with the possibilities. She has already used transference to transcend the old way of tithing senses, instead discovering how to transfer them from one being to another. She has used it on her soldiers, to make them harder and stronger—filling them with the rage and hunger of real vultures.

And now she ponders the possibility of the opposite. If she can tithe magic from the fae, can she also transfer magic *to* another? What might happen to a princess who has been gifted beauty and grace . . . and a piece of Malfleur's own magic? Aurora could be the grandest experiment, the most intriguing pet, the best protégé yet. . . .

Malfleur pushes her way through underbrush and into a clearing. She doesn't believe in luck, but perhaps she ought to.

Because tangled in her trap, still half alive, its front nose and paws clamped down between iron teeth, lies a young fox, twitching, stunned.

She eats it while the blood's still warm.

PART

III

SO CRY THE FUTURE SAYERS

13

Aurora

The hood blocking her eyes is raised. Aurora squints into a vast room, its only light streaming from a hole in the ceiling high above. Her hands are bound by rope. She flexes them, tries to pull. Braces herself.

A figure disappears into the shadows. A door slams. She is alone.

No. Not alone. There's a sound. A shuffling. A fluttering.

Suddenly, heavy iron grates rise all around her. Cranking. Creaking as they're lifted, to reveal bars. Terror races through her. She's caged. Now there's a rustling in the shadows, beyond the bars. Louder. A harsh cry.

Her body clenches, jerks. And yet still she is shocked when a thousand shapes razor out of the black mass.

Wings.

Beaks.

Crows. *Hundreds* of them.

Panic—she can feel it in the way the bodies collide with one another, surging upward and out, pushing through the bars, which are wide enough to let them in but too narrow to let her out. She's surrounded by complete anarchy. She screams but makes no sound.

She struggles against the rope again, unable to free her hands.

The birds swoop and dive. Claws rake across her cheek.

Talons land on the back of her neck, clamping down. She screams again, falling to her knees. They are on her. They are everywhere. A chunk of hair is wrenched from the side of her head. She writhes against the madness. A crow flies at her face. Its eyes gleam like beads. She dodges, collapses forward. Beaks tear at her shoulders.

You will become strong, Malfleur had said.

Talons skewer the rope, ripping into the flesh of her arms. The rope loosens. She tears free. Anger surges through her. Power. She stands. She's up. She swings out, clawing the air with her open hands, her now-ragged nails. The birds launch at her and she defends herself, flinging their bodies aside, her arms as fluid as their wings are frantic. She wrestles one down, but then another is at her throat, its whirl of dark feathers blinding her.

You will become sharp.

146

The blade. The blade. There is a bodkin against her hip—tucked into her suit, which is black and tight, made of leather and buckles, like a full-body muzzle. The hilt slides into her palm, and in a flash of clean movement she has jammed it into the attacker's back. There's a deafening screech as the crow falls from her, tearing flesh away from her clavicle with its beak in a rain of blood.

For a moment, she is frozen in the red spray. She feels no pain, only awe.

Now there are two daggers, fine and slim, one in each fist, and she is all weapon, all movement, a spinning blur of blade and skin. More blood—hers—slashes through the air. Another crow screams, flying straight at one of the moving knives. She becomes the bird now, could swear she is flying.

You will become deadly.

A darkness floods her vision, freezes her blood, blacker than the feathers of these creatures who want to kill her, want to devour her, want to force pain from her. No. She will force pain from *them*. Hunger spikes inside her. Hunger to feel their pain. One knife is in her teeth as she grabs the bars and climbs sideways, scissoring her legs. The crows are furious. She has become the attacker, they the prey, and it feels, *almost*, good. She swings back down, using her momentum to slice the air, slitting the throat of another crow.

It crashes into the floor in a gush, and she slows, staring

down. The ground is a smear of luminous red—her own blood mingled with that of the birds. A littered carpet of black feathers, some of them shredded. Corpses strewn about, claws clutching at air, gone still. It is a horrible, hideous work of art.

She turns to defend herself, but the remaining crows are fleeing the cage, shrieking. Back into the darkness.

Aurora drops her knives. They clang against the floor.

She grabs two of the bars and leans in to them—there is just enough space to push her forehead through. She vomits, her empty stomach releasing bile and acid. Sweat slides down her back and neck, along her cheeks. Wetness streaks her face, but it is not tears. It is her blood, wet and shiny and glorious. She heaves in a shuddering breath, wondering what has just happened. The vile stench of the crows reaches her and makes her wretch again. She is full of disgust at what she has just done. And yet there is another sensation winding up through her as well: the sensation of victory.

———

When the queen had come to Aurora's cell in the dead of night one week before, it was as if she'd offered a dish of cream to a cat. Aurora nodded, doing everything in her power not to sob outright in her weakness. She feared if she did, the cry would split her apart.

The queen's promises—that Aurora would never again have to be seen as a pathetic princess or a damsel in distress—

weren't even necessary. Aurora didn't trust her, and never had, but she would have agreed to anything. Malfleur handed her a scroll and a feather pen saturated in ink.

Aurora saw then, in a flash, that she'd been right to play into Malfleur's pride: the queen craved a new experiment. Aurora would be that experiment.

The document promised Aurora thirty days of training. She'd be pushed to the limit, but given the magical strength to endure it. She'd become a warrior—fearless and merciless. The queen didn't know exactly how the dark magic would affect her—that was the point.

Aurora could not speak, and she did not know what would become of her.

But she thought distantly of the ax she'd dragged through the quiet dawn of Sommeil.

She did not hesitate.

She took the pen, and signed.

———

Aurora's trainer today wears a floor-length cloak and a black mask that covers his head like the other soldiers. She's pretty sure she has a different trainer each day, but they may as well all be one person, since all Vultures look nearly identical.

He drags her from the cage, brings her to a cell where her wounds can be dressed.

She has now been training for eighteen days. Her body has once again morphed into something she doesn't recognize, this time not from hunger but from strength. Her shoulders are rounded with muscle, her back rippled, her calves taut. She moves now like a predator—able to carry stillness in her bones and then spring suddenly. She is alert too; not a fleck of dust can dance in the sunlight without passing detected through the corners of her vision.

And as Aurora gets stronger, her goal gets clearer and clearer, surges within her, waking her earlier and earlier every morning until she soon finds she does not sleep at all. Urgency pumps through her at all hours of the day and night. She feels wild, and hungry—the need to run and to hunt and to kill pulsing in her veins.

And yet a tiny flame deep inside her still sometimes flares bright, making her yearn to speak to Wren, to touch her, to confess everything . . . but then the feeling gutters out, and she is left only with coldness.

She is lucky, one of her trainers told her. The others—all of the soldiers in Malfleur's army—went through a similar initiation, but not all of them were forced to fight off crows. Some had to defend themselves against ravens, some against vultures. Each type has its own lethal fury.

But there are things Aurora can do that the vultures cannot. Malfleur did not just give her a terrifying strength, a sliver of cruelness, but a piece of her own magic. The magic didn't hurt—not that Aurora had expected it to. But when the magical strength and power flooded through her veins, she could swear she felt *something*—a pulse of heat, an electrical jolt, a hardening, as though her blood had become a kind of weapon.

Aurora doesn't know what it all means. She still can't speak, and can't feel. She's human, and not fae, but she senses the way her humanity is shrinking down, day by day, to a tiny burning ember behind her ribs. It's growing fainter, and she has begun to fear that a slight breeze might blow it out. She might not notice at first, and then she'll look for it, and it'll be gone, and then she'll forget what it was she was looking for. And that's when she'll no longer be human at all anymore.

Does it mean she's becoming like the evil queen herself?

She doesn't know. She knows only that she *has* to live, has to hang on to that last shred of herself, because if she can do that, then she can take this curse, or this gift—this power—and use it against Malfleur.

Her trainers tell her that the queen is planning an extravagant event. A grand ball, even in the midst of war. Dignitaries and nobles from across the known world have been invited. Malfleur has a prize to reveal, and Aurora knows that she *is* the prize. The beautiful experiment.

The experiment that will soon turn on its creator.

She longs for the day when the queen's neck will be in her hands, her eyes will blink their last, that sneer will turn to a desperate cry, and Aurora will have her heroism—and her revenge.

Then Aurora can return to Isbe and tell her the truth, tell her all of it.

Wren will be free. Heath too, if they ever find him. And

all the refugees of Sommeil. All the oppressed citizens of LaMorte. All the captured prisoners of war from Deluce. All the unwilling recruits.

Everything rests on the murder of Malfleur.

14

Isabelle

Everything rests on the strength of Deluce's army.

Hooves pound the mud-slick royal road, and a heavy rain rattles the roof of the carriage that carries Isabelle and Byrne out to Verrière and the estate of Viscount Olivier. Isbe worries a worn letter in her hands, every jolt in the road setting her nerves on edge.

So far, the list of names Binks gave her, detailing the fae who have a great deal of land and servants, has proven surprisingly useful. She has managed to grow the army's numbers at an aggressive pace—but has she been aggressive *enough*?

Deluce's best spies have continuously reported Queen Malfleur's lead, not just in men but in arms, just as the

Delucian army rides into battle in La Faim, an area just south of here. This, Isbe knows, is where William hopes to strike back and make a serious dent in Malfleur's forces. The terrain in La Faim is particularly tricky—but Deluce's army has trained on it and will have a strong advantage. It's a last-ditch attempt to drive back the worst of the damage, and Isabelle can't stand how desperate they've become.

She feels so foolish for having thought that with the alliance in place, the war would be a sure thing. Deluce and Aubin combined have more than three times the land mass of LaMorte, after all. But LaMorte has very little industry *other* than its military. *Malfleur has been building up to this moment her whole reign*, Isbe thinks with a chill. Her evil is moving ever closer, like a dark tide, and the resistance only weakens and weakens.

Still, reinforcements are expected any day. William has been perplexed by the delay—the king of Aubin, his father, is perhaps skeptical of William's hasty union with Isabelle. But he wouldn't betray his own son. The Aubinian fleet will come, and when they do, everything will change.

Or so they hope.

Still, Isbe is restless. Her whole body twitches with the need to move. If only this were the type of restlessness that could have been eased by a brisk ride on her favorite mare, seeking out military drills to eavesdrop on, then practicing her stances on Gilbert with sticks instead of swords. It shames her now, the way she used to glamorize war. She spent so much of her youth memorizing the names of every weapon, dreaming up scenarios in which she gallantly saved the day by riding into battle in full armor.

She has survived enough challenges by now to realize the foolhardiness of such a wish. Like so many wishes, nothing good could ever come of it.

"Is something troubling you, Miss Isabelle?" Byrne asks from across the coach.

She startles and then collects herself. "No, Byrne, nothing."

"I see," he says. He's quiet for a moment, but she has begun to learn how to read his silences.

"Well then, what is it you are going to ask?" she pushes.

"Oh, 'tis certain it's none a' my business." He pauses. "I do wonder, though, if there be any other reason you're keen to meet this viscount. You must be—"

"Must be what?"

"Curious, miss. 'Bout the heirloom."

Isbe stiffens. "Byrne, there is a war on, in case you haven't noticed, and men's lives are at stake. This is no fool's errand."

The words, and their falseness, settle in the air between them. Because in her heart of hearts, Isbe knows he's not wrong. She *is* curious. The faerie viscount Olivier is a well-known maker of the kingdom's finest glass. If anyone might have information about her glass slipper, and how Isabelle's real mother came to possess such a thing, it may be him. But she's not going to admit that—not to Byrne or to anyone.

That the slipper seems to sear its way through the velvet

pouch at her hip and into her very bones, that she thinks about it night and day, puzzles over its meaning, longs for answers . . . these things are not important. They are a private matter that she will reconcile one day, perhaps, when peace has returned to the land.

She sighs and, to keep from retorting anything further, toys again with the letter in her hand—it's the latest missive from Aurora. She recalls flushing with something like embarrassment as a servant read it aloud to her this morning. In it, Aurora claims that Heath is everything she dreamed of and more. That they've located a safe house along the southern border of Deluce. Isbe is happy for her sister, but . . . Aurora's happiness feels foreign to her, far off and fictional somehow.

Is it really so hard to imagine Aurora has found true love? Perhaps not. Perhaps what's hard to imagine is that she has found happiness without Isabelle. And perhaps it's not so much that it's hard to imagine but that it's impossible to accept.

But then, hasn't Isabelle gone and done the same, with William? Or *has* she? Isbe never put much stock in true love before, and something about the idea seems almost distasteful to her. Although her blood thrills every time he returns to the palace for even a brief stay—a night here or there— she's not sure she likes what has become of her, now that she's someone's wife. She has gotten too soft, somehow, too blown off course by her emotions, and William is the chief reason for that: the heat of his body alongside hers, the weight of his trust, the enormity of his expectations, the way she still sometimes finds herself floating in his silences like a bird borne on a wind, waiting to see where his thoughts will carry her own.

It's a slow erosion of everything she used to believe was true about herself. She might need other people for things like reading messages and guiding her hand and describing the scenery, but she does not need anyone else in order to feel herself whole. Or at least, she didn't need anyone like that, before William.

She forces down the lump that has suddenly risen in her throat.

She's relieved to know, at least, that her sister is safe. Aurora—*her* Aurora, soft, kind, thoughtful, and always with the best intentions—has found a way to shelter herself from the worst of the war. Isbe can't help but think her sister is kind of like the glass slipper: something to be protected at all costs.

———

The viscount lives in a large manor adjoined to his famous glasshouse, which produces much of the window glass used throughout the kingdom. The estate is surrounded on three sides by a thick forest.

By the time Isabelle arrives, the carriage wheels crunching along a pebbled path, the angry spring rain has let up.

"The trees, Miss Isabelle," Byrne comments, holding her by the elbow as they exit the carriage and pass through the grounds. "Look as though 'ey've got a thousan' hands where 'ey should've a head!"

"Pollarding, it's called," says a polite-sounding manservant who has emerged to meet them on the gravel path. "Master has received your message. He's awaiting your arrival in the glasshouse."

He leads them down a winding path. The scent of the glasshouse greets her before they enter it: charred wood and a lightly floral smoke. The servant leads them inside and gives them a seat in the foyer of the bustling open workroom while he locates his master. Tools and prongs clatter loudly all around them as fires are stoked and wood is axed and materials blown into molds and workers bustle about. The glasshouse hums with production and energy, with movement and heat and flame.

"My new queen," Olivier says, materializing before them, his voice not obsequious but genuine. Isbe is almost taken aback by it. His voice sounds young, especially for one of the fae, and a little feminine. "To what do I owe this visit? Your message was quite mysterious."

"We can't afford the risk of interception. I've come on a matter of some importance," she replies.

After asking Byrne to wait for her, she follows the young viscount through the glasshouse, trying to imagine the high ceilings as he describes them proudly, like in a cathedral, with wooden beams arcing across the top. She tries to imagine too the many earthenware ovens, called beehives for their domed shapes. The tufts and blasts and hisses and clicks of the workroom form a collective buzzing.

"I apologize for the din, but I tend to think it provides

the perfect backdrop for a private conversation," Olivier admits. "One can't be too careful. That is the lesson of the glass, after all."

"The lesson of the glass?"

"Precision. Caution. Care," he answers with a hint of love in his voice.

"We may as well come to the point of my visit," she says, straightening her shoulders. "All of these workers." She gestures at the noises and movement around her. "Surely we could put them to better use."

"Better use?" He balks. "You know, Highness, the recipe for our world-famous forest glass may seem quite simple to the likes of you: just two parts river sand, one part beech ash. However, what it becomes is anything but." He pauses. "There is no art more blessed than to form what is both beautiful and fragile, Highness . . . what could be undone at a whim by the same hands that made it."

"Those hands could learn to hold a poleax in the name of Deluce."

He is silent for a moment. "Do you want to know why I got into this way of life, Highness? It is a faith." He stops and she pauses beside him, surprised. "You see," he explains, "to me, a fresh-blown pane of forest glass is like a new morning. A brief commitment to the possibility of wholeness."

"And do you not see that possibility of wholeness for our kingdom, Viscount?" He doesn't respond, so she goes on. "Deluce is divided. This is not a matter of argument. The question is whether we have a shared faith in uniting once again, in defending ourselves from a much greater foe than that of our differences."

"Differences?" There's a hint of amusement in Olivier's voice. "Is *that* what you call them?"

Isbe feels cold creep along her skin despite the heat of the glasshouse. "What do you mean?"

"You must know of your reputation. Many Delucians do not support your rule. They call you the Bastard Queen, or sometimes, the Imposter."

Isbe tries not to flinch. Of course she knows these things, but hearing the words still hurts. "And is that what you think too?"

"It is not my opinion that matters, but the opinion of the peasantry. They are the majority, after all."

"So they are, and that is why I need them to fight for Deluce. Whether they support me or not, they must understand that their safety and their way of life are at stake."

"You use words well, Highness. I am impressed."

"Does this mean you agree to help me?"

He pauses, as if thinking. "Perhaps I might spare a few men to your cause."

Her chest flutters in triumph. "*Our* cause," she corrects.

"Indeed." He takes her hand to shake it. But as she begins to pull away, he clings to her. "Highness." Suddenly his voice sounds insistent. Alarm rings through her. "If I may . . . I would love to behold the glass slipper. I've heard tell of its incredible durability, and I would like to see it for myself."

She starts to resist. The glass slipper isn't just the last relic of her mother. It has also become a symbol of her campaign—it is special, unusual, and unbreakable. In every town she visits, it seems that everyone, whether they support Isabelle or not, has heard about it. In her speeches, she holds up the slipper and talks about how it belonged to her mother. How she never knew her mother. How her mother was a peasant, just like them. The slipper has become, in a way, a symbol of Isabelle's humanity. A reason the people should trust her.

But then she thinks of William. Everything in her life has come down to numbers: How many more troops can she send his way before the week is out? One hundred? Even three hundred?

"Fine," she says. "You may take a look." Her heart stutters as she removes the slipper from its velvet case and holds it out toward the viscount, noting the softness of his hands—delicate.

One night so mild. The lullaby from her mother dreams sings quietly at the back of her mind.

"So this is the famous item with which you have wooed so many a gullible Delucian peasant. I wonder, though. Can it *really* be unbreakable?" he whispers.

"No amount of pressure seems to shatter it." She shifts uncomfortably.

"The clarity is remarkable, as well," Olivier observes, almost to himself. "It reminds me of something. An old, old tale. Of the Hart Slayer, and his glass arrows."

161

The Hart Slayer. The name stirs a dim memory—she's heard the epic poem before, but doesn't recall anything about him having arrows made of glass. All she knows is that he was supposedly a talented hunter, famous for crossing King Henri by picking off harts in the royal forest, even though the king had made it illegal for anyone to hunt them other than himself. If Aurora were here, she'd surely know about it.

Isabelle is about to ask Olivier more when Byrne clambers over to them, along with a stranger who smells of dust and saddle.

"Tell them what you told me," Byrne demands.

"Many wounded," the man says, breathless. He must be a messenger. "In La Faim. Troops forced to retreat."

Isbe's heart catches in her throat. "William. Is the prince all right? What has happened to the prince?" Sometimes she forgets to call him "king"—*her* king.

"He lives, Highness. But La Faim is the greatest loss we've seen so far. Too many fallen to count—"

He continues talking, but Isbe's ears have begun to burn with panic. "I have to see him," she says. "Take me to William."

"That would not be advised at this—"

"Or I will find my way there myself!" she says, trying to keep her voice steady.

"Your Highness," the viscount chimes in. He takes her hand and places the slipper back into her palm. "Before you go, I must tell you something." His voice drops into a whisper only she can hear. "This isn't made of forest glass at all. If I'm not mistaken, it is made of winter glass."

Her hands shake as she slides the slipper back into its bag and fastens it safely to her belt again. "And what is winter glass?" she snaps impatiently. *William could be injured.* What would this whole trip to Verrière matter then? What do more troops matter if they lose their commander? What does anything matter if she loses him?

But Viscount Olivier seems immune to her urgency. "A misnomer," he answers slowly. She pauses at his curious tone of voice. "Winter glass isn't glass at all," he explains. "It's ice."

15

Aurora

Aurora's blood races through her veins as one of her masked trainers takes her out into the fields. She wonders what her next challenge will be, and shakes with the horror of how much she wants it. Anticipation makes her jaw tense, her teeth tingle. She has already completed a number of challenges, like causing streams to freeze, trees to die at the root, birds to fall midflight from the sky—all by wishing it, by feeling the desire for death move through her and out.

"This will be the true test of how far you've come," her trainer says, dragging her by a leash across the misted, sloping meadows. "Prepare yourself."

His warning rings low in her ears, and she wonders at it. It's unlike the Vultures to caution her. There's something almost protective in this one's voice—almost, *almost* familiar—but when she scans his masked face, his eyes are dark and impenetrable.

At this altitude, the sun sets late—a slow, smeared fall. He pushes her into a copse of trees, the grass dappled in black splashes of shadow like a wildcat's back. Miniature mushrooms and tiny flowers sprout everywhere in the grass, giving her the impression of a quaint picnic scene. He hands her a long sword.

She turns as he leaves her there, watching him retreat, bright lit with the shimmering-rust sun. She has the immediate impulse to run. But surely she'd be caught, or else he wouldn't have left her.

She clutches the sword's hilt. Or maybe he knows. Maybe he knows she will not run. She is tethered here. Not by her magic, but by the cage of her own need: to kill Malfleur.

Then she hears something strange. She swivels back toward the trees, suddenly alert. She scans the shadows and light. Sniffling. A feeble cry. She pushes past the undergrowth, thwacking it back with her sword, and sees . . .

"Wren."

She is tied to one of the trees. Whimpering softly.

No. Aurora's stomach falls, and she nearly sways. *No.* Not Wren.

But it *is* Wren—the tumult of black hair, the trembling chin, the big eyes. The stubborn mouth that Aurora wants, even now, to touch. Pinned and afraid, Wren still somehow exudes pride. Her throat catches a chance of sunlight.

The birds continue their ironic chatter, their song pricking Aurora's mind like tinny darts.

The true test.

She is supposed to kill Wren.

Prepare yourself.

No. She won't do it. She will free her, and they will both run, and—

"Aurora," Wren whispers. She is not looking at the long sword in Aurora's hand, but at her face, and Aurora suddenly wonders what she must look like—with some of her hair pulled out at the side, and claw marks along her cheek and neck and collarbone. Her lip still swollen, one eye still likely black-and-blue with an old bruise. Wren's look of horror says it all. "Don't do this," she says, and Aurora hears it—the fear, not just of Malfleur, or of the situation, but of *her.*

The birdsong above and around them grows wild, becomes a chaotic crying. In the periphery of her vision, Aurora catches movement. She turns, her body at the ready. Squints through the trees. Across the clearing, there is a spot of darkness, a tiny spark in the distance . . . coming toward them at full speed.

It takes a moment for her to make out what it is—low to the ground and gray as a thundercloud. A wolf. Snarling, with spittle flying from the sides of its mouth. Now she understands: it is her or Wren. Even if she freed the girl, the wolf would come for them, and Aurora would not be able to defend them both.

Her mind seems stuck for a moment as she stares at the

wild animal getting closer and closer. She remembers the wolf in Sommeil and wonders if somehow Malfleur has conjured up her fears—or Belcoeur's fears.

But it doesn't matter. The wolf is coming and there's no time and the birds are now cawing frantically and fluttering about in the branches, and Wren is weeping and begging.

Aurora looks at her again as though through warbled glass. She remembers that she might love her, but only dimly, the feeling like a blade that's too blunt to cut.

"I have no choice," she hears herself saying.

Wren shakes her head, writhing violently against her bindings. "Yes, you do, Aurora. You do have a choice. You can—" Fear seems to halt her voice, and she hazards a glance at the wolf, now not more than a few hundred yards away. "You can stop this. This is not who you are."

Aurora is moving slowly—too slow. Still uncertain. She can feel the dark magic leaping in her veins. She steps toward Wren, the sword slippery in her hot hand. She kneels and begins to cut one of Wren's hands loose. Wren lets out a sob. She shakes her arm free and reaches out to touch Aurora's cheek, singeing her with her fingertips.

Aurora lurches back, almost falling. The touch . . . any touch, but especially this. She can't take the intensity of it. It makes Aurora want to burn. It's too sudden and too much, unleashing a tornado of twisting emotions she can't possibly contain. She is terrified, suddenly—afraid of herself, of what she can do and even what she *wants* to do and yet doesn't want to do. She is warring with herself on the inside and doesn't know which side will win, and Wren's crying and the birds' cawing are making her unable to think. She gasps for air, tries to focus, but she's flooded by her senses and overwhelmed and needs it to stop.

The wolf is coming closer.

Wren is still caught, half bound to the tree, struggling with her free hand to undo the knots around her other arm.

Prepare yourself.

Wren is going to escape.

Aurora is going to fail the test. *The true test.*

No.

Aurora pulls out the sword and feels that horrible, feverish need for death surge up in her. She is hot—burning alive—and flying forward. Metal cuts the air.

Her blade slashes the girl's chest—striking stone.

Aurora stares, uncomprehending, at Wren's torn dress. There is stone, actual stone, where her breastbone should be. She looks at Wren's horrified eyes with wonder and confusion. She feels numb.

The wolf is close enough now that she can see the sharpness of its fangs. It is about to lunge. Without thinking, Aurora chops away the ropes that bind Wren's second wrist, then grabs her. Wren is trembling, as though about to break in her hands. Aurora holds her tight, brings her mouth to Wren's cheek, to her neck. Right near the spread of stone, where her throat bobs in fear, Aurora kisses her, softly, with hunger. Then she whispers, *"Run."*

Aurora spins, throws the sword—not at the wolf, but instead at the tree.

She cannot kill anymore.

All her anger and confusion fly with the sword into the tree itself. She feels the magic flood through her again, making her vision burn black.

All the chirping birds go silent . . . and fall from the branches onto the grass in synchronized thumps. Dead.

Aurora collapses to her knees, suddenly weak from the surge of power. She glances up to see the branches, now empty. Then out in the fields, where Wren is racing away—a blur. Then, at the wolf, who has torn through the underbrush into the copse and is ravaging one of the birds.

Aurora breathes heavily. She has inadvertently saved herself. And Wren. Maybe. Nearly.

The wolf is occupied with the feast of fallen flesh—hasn't yet noticed, or smelled, Aurora.

She wants to heave into the grass. She takes in a slow breath instead and rakes her hands through the grass, finding a cluster of flowers and mushrooms. *Some kinds can heal, some can nourish, and others can kill.* Wren had said it both of fungi and forms of love.

Wren, who is now gone, who must now hate her even more than she did before. Wren, whom she has both saved and lost.

Carefully, without making a sound, she plucks a handful of the mushrooms and stuffs them into a pocket. Then slowly—ever so slowly, so as not to draw the animal's attention—Aurora steps backward and away.

Farther and farther, carefully, quietly, with precision, until the wolf is once again a spark—a shifting darkness between the trees, still devouring the bounty of feathered treats. Dusk is coming on.

Aurora begins to breathe.

And then there are hands around her arms.

She turns to face her trainer. Stares at his black mask, at his expectant eyes. And that's when she knows what she has truly done—or almost done.

She would have killed Wren. The girl she is fighting for in the first place. The girl she might have loved—still loves. If love is even possible anymore, and not a decaying, rotten thing in her chest, dead as one of those swallows. She struck Wren . . . with the intention to do harm.

Everything that has just happened finally hits her. Sobs wrack her body. She leans in to her trainer's strength, holding on to his cape and armored chest to keep herself from crumbling to the ground. What has she become?

She would have killed Wren. Would have, had it not been for the strange enchantment of stone on her flesh—a mystery Aurora can't explain to herself. Did she create the stone with her own magic? But it has never worked like that before—her magic has always sought to destroy, not to protect.

She would have killed Wren, but she did not. Instead, she helped Wren escape. Yes, Wren has run free.

But Aurora has lost herself.

The true test.

The trainer, Vulture, leans toward her, and his voice whispers down at her from within the mask. "All is not lost."

Fear and hate shudder through her.

"You feel remorse," he says, "which means you are not gone." No Vulture has ever broken from his stoicism.

She looks up into his eyes and gasps.

She could swear she knows him.

But he blinks, and the impression is gone.

16

Wren,

Formerly a Maiden of Sommeil,
Indentured to the Mad Queen Belcoeur

She cannot help the others until she helps herself. She cannot help them if she is dead. That is the mantra Wren repeats in her mind as she flies from the mountains and across dew-stung forests, ravaged by the cold winds and aware only that she cannot allow heartbreak to catch up to her.

She saw what Aurora has become, and though she didn't understand it exactly, she sensed something terrible—something inhuman—had happened to her. It sickened and scared Wren beyond anything—even beyond the burning of Sommeil, her home, her world. In another life, she might have wanted Aurora to be her home, but in this life, she sees now, the barriers are greater than status, greater than shame, greater than the curse of a jealous faerie. A dark magic has come between them.

And it doesn't matter anyway, because whether Aurora had succeeded with her sword or not, Wren was going to die. Wren *is* dying. She has been turning to stone, gradually but certainly. It began at her ankle and spread up along one calf. Then sprouted behind an ear, traveling downward toward her chest. Soon it will be evident where others can see it: on her face, and hands. And then in her heart and lungs, stopping their beat and breath.

That is the secret Aurora could not know. That Wren is cursed too. But Aurora undid her curse—she woke up. And Wren has tried so hard over these past weeks to salvage hope for herself too. Maybe there's some way to undo it.

But she's running out of time.

She was very little when her aunt first told her of the stone curse. Wren recalls sitting on the floor before a warm hearth, smoke curling up beside them as she learned the tale of the curse that had supposedly been passed down in her family from generation to generation, but had never been tested or proven. It seemed more like myth to her then—a mere bedtime story meant to reassure her of her rightful place in Sommeil. It was said that her great-great-great-aunt Oshannah was Queen Belcoeur's favorite handmaiden; she went with her everywhere, and for a time, was even granted access in and out of Sommeil when the world was first created. Belcoeur doted on Oshannah, like a sister or daughter—a companion in her desperate loneliness—and soon, Oshannah longed for freedom. The weight of Belcoeur's need was too much.

The queen relied on Oshannah for everything. And that was why she finally placed the faerie curse on her—not out of anger but out of love. The curse said that Wren's great-great-great-aunt would never be able to leave her side—would never be able to leave Sommeil. That if Oshannah ever tried to fly away from the queen, ever tried to sever her blood from her home, she'd turn to stone.

It was a warning shared by all the women in her family since before Wren could remember—a caution never to question the sanctity or the bounds of Sommeil. Never to disobey the queen's wishes and whims. Though Wren was never sure whether she should believe it or not, it was what made her wary when Heath tried to push on the truth, tried to seek escape. It wasn't that she didn't want to discover other worlds, didn't want to leave their dying one, but that she feared she couldn't.

And she was right.

Now it may be hopeless. It may be too late for her. Aurora's curse wasn't ever lifted—only amended. She explained it all to Wren during their journey to LaMorte, and despite Wren's attempts to keep her distance from the princess, she listened carefully.

She recalls that one faerie—a duchess in Deluce—had been able, if not to fix things, at least to help. She had altered the curse from one of death to one of gentle sleep.

And that faerie's name was Violette.

17

Isabelle

Against his better judgment, the messenger allowed Isbe to ride with him through the afternoon and into the night toward the war camp outside of La Faim. The rhythm of the horse is rough between her legs; her knees ache, her whole body is sore. She clings to the messenger's cloak—he rides faster than she has ever ridden on her own.

The density of the forest has given way to open fields loud with crickets on either side of the road. Urgency courses through Isbe's veins; her skin prickles with it. Rain has left the air cold, and she feels naked and exposed—even in the dark.

Isbe expects the camp to be quiet with sleep by the time they arrive, but a disturbing chorus of sounds greets her as they dismount at the edge of camp and move forward on foot: the injured whimpering, wives weeping over the dead, oxen shuffling, men awake all night digging fire pits, or latrines. Or maybe graves.

The smells too assault her: the swampy blend of sweat and stale meat, cattle and wet canvas, rust and waste. She's overwhelmed with a sense of ordered chaos, of death as an industry, as an art. The messenger helps her weave through the disarray, avoiding the makeshift shelters, wagons heaped with tentpoles and spare arms, cooking kettles and stores of supplies, narrating the terrain in his hoarse but practiced manner.

Finally they move toward higher ground; the muscles in her thighs twinge as they march uphill, to where the knights' tents are slightly wider spread. When the royal guards hold open the flaps of the royal tent, something lurches in Isabelle's chest.

She hears rustling movement, the quick intake of breath, the hiss of a flame consuming a lantern's wick, and she knows that William has not been sleeping.

"You shouldn't be here." His whispered voice reaches out to her, and suddenly she's in his arms, his lips urgent against her bare neck.

"I had to be sure. I heard the worst had happened," she says, emotion pushing up into her throat, tempting her to burst into tears of relief, even as her cloak falls back from her shoulders. She buries her face in his chest, feeling as he tenses his muscles, then relaxes into her.

It isn't until this moment, holding William hard against her, that she realizes how deeply she feared losing him. Some part of her was convinced that he might die or even disappear, smokelike. She has lost everyone she loves. Sometimes it seems inevitable that she will lose him too.

After a minute, he pulls back. "But really, you shouldn't have come. It's so unsafe." He touches her face. "And in the middle of the night?"

No matter that she's been riding for hours—she can't sleep now. "Tell me everything that happened."

And so he does, the terrible words muttered across her skin, even as he peels back her layers, his fingers fumbling with the strings on her muslin tunic. He tells her he would rather be dead than face his men now. She tries to kiss him, tries to take away what he is saying. His face is wet beneath her fingertips, from tears.

The new cannons—his special design—backfired. Literally. He tells her of the screams as men were devoured alive by the flames of their own weapon, how horses reared, throwing their riders. The mayhem; the bitter, choking black ash that clouded the air, causing confusion.

"William, you couldn't have known." She hesitates, almost afraid of him now, fearing that he too will somehow explode at her fingertips. She thinks of the model cannon he showed her back in the royal palace of Aubin—how she'd felt the crack in the marble and wondered at the beauty of his imagination, and the violence he'd been submitted to. Ever so gently, she touches her lips to the scar on his jaw. She tastes him, tastes ash.

"I could have—and I *should* have." The pain in his voice is so intense it makes her feel out of control, untethered. Stray tears streak salt into her lips. He kisses them.

"I'll never forget these horrors as long as I live." His voice shakes, comes at her low and powerful, like thunder. "I'll never forgive myself."

"You have to. Deluce needs you." He lowers her onto a pile of blankets on the floor. "*I* need you," she says, both hating the words and knowing they are true; they cut through her. She arches her back.

He holds on to her, shudders against her. His hands are at her lower back, then one on her leg, one on her hip. He moves over her, leaning in to her, kissing her neck again, even as he repeats that she shouldn't be here. She gasps. A sound comes out of her like a whimper, and she's not sure if it's one of pleasure or pain. She doesn't want to let go of him, imagines yet again that he will explode into dust just like the cannons, will disappear into thin air.

He cries into her hair.

They stay that way, striving for breath, kissing, moaning, gasping.

When it is over, she cries too.

———

And that wasn't even the worst of it, he tells her later, in and out of sleep.

Malfleur's Vultures are using magic against them. A kind of fire that eats right through iron in a breath, dissolving swords and shields and burning off their soldiers' skin, leaving screaming skeletons.

The image sends terror through Isbe, and she fears she will be sick.

"Retreat," she whispers, surprised at the word. "Come back with me." She kisses his jaw, right near the scar. Then his eyebrow. "We'll return to the palace together, where it's safe, come up with a strategy from there."

"Isabelle . . ."

"You need rest. You need a break. Come back with me." *I can't have you die on me*, she wants to say.

"I can't just leave, not now." And then, after a beat, "There's still a way. We'll find a way. You must return. I must think. The army needs me. *Deluce* needs me, like you said."

"But I want to help. *I* want to be needed."

"You *are* needed." He pauses, and she feels his chest rise with breath. "*I* need you," he says, an echo of what she whispered to him before. His hands find her tangled hair, and he's kissing her again, his mouth warm and hungry against hers. He pulls back. "I need you *alive*. You must go."

"No. I'm not leaving you." The promise feels uncertain on her tongue, a branch trembling under the weight of snow.

They sleep at last, but fitfully, the ground hard beneath them. She tosses and turns, her limbs entangled in his.

By morning, she knows how she can help Deluce. Despite

what she promised him, she *must* leave him. And she must hurry, before it's too late.

———

Deluce is losing the war. The reports have been flooding in, now that she's back at the palace.

A string of towns have fallen, there is no border protection to speak of.

Hurriedly, Isabelle stuffs her fur-lined capes and hooded coats—ermine and fox and marten—into a giant chest.

The king consort's cannon caused a blast that decimated some of his regiment's strongest men.

Thick underlayers. Leather boots with sable trim. She will need to stay warm.

If another wave of Aubin's reinforcements don't arrive soon, they'll have no hope of turning the tides.

In the midst of the frantic news, Isabelle is packing, preparing for a trip north, to the Îles de Glace, to seek conference with the Ice King. It's a rash, wild plan, of course. The Îles de Glace are notoriously neutral and have been for centuries. And no one has heard from Verglas in ages. Many think he, like the North Faerie, may be dead.

But after hearing of the horrible magic William told her about—Malfleur's deadly fire that can melt and destroy armor in seconds—she had felt helpless. Afraid. How could she possibly save her kingdom now? All she had were her words, and a useless symbol, a slipper made of winter glass. But then she thought of Binks, and how he'd wanted to trade men for the slipper—and then of Olivier, who'd expressed such a grave interest in it too. If the viscount is right, and the slipper is indeed made not of glass but of enchanted ice, then the person who must know more about it would be King Verglas. Malfleur's father. And possibly the only faerie whose power could match hers.

What Deluce's army needs, after all, is a kind of magical weapon that cannot break and cannot melt.

What their army needs is winter glass.

It's time to speak to Verglas. He may be the answer to how to win this war.

18

Aurora

Malfleur's magic fills Aurora like a heady wine; she imagines it rising up from her toes and knees to her hips and then her heart, then up her throat and into her head. She can call upon it but still cannot control it, cannot control when it will come or what it will do. But she feels it swirling inside her now, burning and bubbling in her ears as the sounds of the crowd through the closed doors greet her.

They are somewhere at the center of Blackthorn Castle, and Aurora can hear the murmuring and shuffling of spectators through the double doors ahead. She tenses her body, flexing her arms and legs, before releasing and shaking them out. She clenches and unclenches her fists, stretching her fingers. Her trainer pushes the doors open, and she follows him through, into the rush of wind and sound.

This is, she sees now, the same sky-lit stadium in which she had her initiation. Only now the cage is gone, and she can see in the shadows at the edges of the arena that there are risers and risers packed full with Vultures. Her muscles tremble with the reminder of the crows she was forced to fight off, but she shakes away the memory. The Vultures are just here to watch. The thought doesn't bring much relief. She doesn't know what they want—for her to live or die. It doesn't matter; suffering is their sport. They're in the middle of a war, and yet they find time to entertain themselves at her expense. It's brazen of Malfleur—and suggests that she has army to spare.

Aurora thinks of Isabelle and William. News of the war doesn't really reach Aurora here, and she has no idea how far the Vultures have advanced by now.

She scans the crowd until she finds the one unmasked face among them: the stark-white face of the queen, like a shattered plate, once perfect. Her gaze is intent and secretive. Nervous energy builds in Aurora's chest—What does Malfleur have planned? She must steel herself. There's nothing the queen can make her do that she won't do, now, for the sake of passing her test, living another day, stalling until she gets close enough to kill Malfleur. And surely there's nothing the queen can ask that's worse than hurting Wren.

But then she remembers: Wren escaped, and the queen must be angry.

She will want her vengeance.

She will want Aurora to pay.

A long chain wraps around Aurora's ankle, giving her enough length to traverse the arena but not enough to leap into the aisles above or escape.

The floor shines like a silver-black coin, and when Aurora steps forward, dragging the chain behind her, she finds out why—it is actually a shallow pool, no more than ankle deep, with gently sloped sides. As she steps into it, ripples move outward, reflecting the dim gray light in widening rings. The chain disappears beneath the surface like the water snakes that used to swim in the river by Nose Rock.

There is a second entrance on the opposite side of the arena, and fear creeps up Aurora's neck when she sees a hulking figure being dragged in by several Vultures. They are struggling to restrain the creature, whatever it is, or whoever it may be.

Aurora swallows. She has been given no weapons. Here she is, standing at the lip of the arena feeling like a complete and terrified fool.

They shove her opponent into the open. It is a man— not a beast. She heaves a sigh, but her relief is short-lived. Light catches on his broad shoulders, muscular beneath his black leather and metal armor. There's a bag over his head; he thrashes, splashing out onto the arena, causing water droplets to spark upward like flying diamonds. Through the sound of the water, she can hear a different sound: the man is snarling, like the wolf had been.

Another shudder of fear moves through her.

Two Vultures pull off the bag and nudge the man forward. His tangled, dirty blond hair sweeps down to his chin. When he shakes it out of his face, Aurora's breath catches in her throat. There is a kind of awakening in her body as she recognizes him . . . *him*. It's Heath. The same stubbled square jaw. The same arrogant face. But where his warm eyes had once kept him from looking too harsh, they now flash darkly, making his entire appearance seem sinister.

Her heart curls up like a scared hamster, clawing with tiny feet at the sides of its cage. Something occurs to her just as he tenses and sees her: she is going to feel all of this.

Of course. How very clever of Malfleur.

Before she has time to react, he lunges, his own chain dragging with a high squeal along the floor, then muted by the water. He grabs her from both sides with an intake of breath, almost as if he's lifting her into an embrace, and for a moment she feels the surge of his touch in every nerve ending. He throws her backward.

Water soaks her clothes as she catches herself on the floor with her elbows, preventing her head from cracking open, and she scrambles to stand before he is on her, pushing her down, one knee between her legs, pinning her shoulders, her head back in the water. The shallow water fills her ears, blunts the noise of his spitting and snarling. She's frantic, unthinking—she claws at his face with her nails and he snarls louder, rearing. She rips at his hair, yanking his head to the side. She spits in his eyes—those muddy green-brown eyes that now seem like twin pits of darkness.

What has happened to him to make him this way? Something rises in her to meet him, and she realizes he is feeling what she has been feeling: that same corrupting magic pulsing in both their veins. Another one of Malfleur's pets. Only he is much farther gone than she—he must be, because he seems to show no fear at all, no hesitance, only brute fury.

"Heath," she whispers, testing her voice with him. None of the Vultures will be able to hear her.

His hand moves to her cheek, and maybe she's broken through to him. She recalls in an instant his first caress, how it scared her in a whole other way, how she feared she might lose herself in it. And now his thumb finds her lips and tugs them apart, wrenches her face to the side so that she is forced to gulp and choke on the dirty water.

Everything in her shoots alive with excruciating hurt—her bloodied mouth, her banged head, her screaming wounds, the places where Heath has pressed against her to hold her down, the freezing water lapping at her face. Something in her splits apart then too—and that is a whole other kind of pain: the pain of betrayal, of powerlessness.

She struggles and flails, but he is heavy on top of her, holding her down, and he will drown her or bash her head into the ground, she's sure of it.

But still she bucks against him, bites at his hand, snorts out the water that has gone up her nose and manages to wrench one arm free. She flaps against the water, fruitlessly splashing, and then her hand finds something beneath the surface—a jagged object, slightly larger than her hand. She grabs it—a big stone—and swings it up, bashing it into the side of Heath's head. Blood comes out of his ear. He reels and pulls back—not far, but enough for her to squirm out from under him.

She is panting, heaving, crawling across the water away from him, dragging her chain by the ankle, but it's heavy, so heavy. She feels something else in the water and grabs for it, unseeing, even as she can sense his hot breath behind her. She pushes up to kneeling, her muscles crying out from the effort; she turns just as he plunges toward her again. The object in her hand splashes out of the water, and she discovers what it is by wielding it—a morning star club, black and barbed with metal.

The handle flies from her wet grip as she swings, the spiked ball rounding on Heath, smashing into his beautiful face before she has time to reconsider—not handsome, not heroic, but real and strong and so human, always, until now. Now it is twisted and inhuman and it hurts her to look even as he staggers backward, clutches at his bleeding cheek and mouth. The weapon falls into the water by his stumbling feet.

She doesn't waste any more time. She is all action. *There are weapons hidden under the water*, she realizes, shaking. She crawls around frantically, feeling with her hands. She had forgotten their audience until this moment. It occurs to her just how much effort was put into making this fight as entertaining as possible for the spectators. Of course. Because if there's one thing she has learned so far in her training, it is that violence is the food and the fuel of evil.

And the queen must keep her minions fed.

All of this is for them—and for her too, meant to drive her to the peak of her dark power. She will only survive, she sees now, if she allows the magic to inhabit her completely. Aurora will only live by eradicating herself. Even now, a kind of coldness has possessed her, numbing her emotions—all the shock and hurt and terror of seeing Heath seem coated in a blazing ring of anger. It would feel so good, so right, to burn away those feelings, to be free of them, to be pure. To be like him. Merciless.

He splashes toward her, just as she is reaching for another object in the water—she pulls up a knife, her fist around the blade, her hand a puddle of blood. She gasps from the shocking, searing pain of it, and the knife drops with a splash. She fumbles for the handle side, and is yanked backward just as she grabs hold. Heath is dragging her through the water. She pulls away and tries to stand. Falls to her knees. Tries to stand again but cannot. Why can't she stand? A new fear flaps inside her chest. She sits in the water, stares at her left leg, the one Heath grabbed, and sees that something is wrong. Her leg is mangled. Bloody. Standing above her, Heath is holding a bloody ax.

It takes a fraction of a moment for her to understand. To see what he has done. And then for the sensations to flood into her; the agony in her leg is debilitating. She's sick, swaying, about to faint. Will she ever walk again? Fresh rage rips through her throat in a roar only she and Heath can hear. She can no longer think, can only feel. Fire consumes her;

there's ash in her breath and blurring her eyes.

The ax comes down again and she rolls in a split second across the water, hearing the ax meet the hard stone floor with an ear-shattering clang. He is coming after her. With a speed she didn't know she possessed, she manages to get back to standing—leaning only on the right leg. She then flings herself at Heath, her drenched hair and clothes spraying water, her left leg dragging helplessly and bloodily at her side. She has grabbed him around the neck. She has the knife at his throat, but he drops the ax and grabs her around the waist. She swivels while still clinging to him, causing him to lose his balance. They both go down.

She only managed to nick his throat, and the knife has fallen, obscured again by the rippling water, which is now tinged with their blood. She is on top of him, but without a weapon. Something moves through her—the tiny kernel of almost-love buried deep within her is breathing new energy into her anger, her hatred, her desire for revenge. How dare he hurt her. How dare he become a monster. How dare he manifest everything she most fears becoming herself.

Around them, the water begins to harden toward ice. It is the cold of her dark magic, pulsing out of her. She reaches into the water and grabs a fistful of it—it becomes icicles as she pulls her hand out, and she flings them at his face.

But it is not enough. He manages to flip her, and now her back is submerged in the water, which is so cold, freezing all around her, about to seal her into its shallow coffin. Somehow he has gotten hold of one of the chains—his or hers, she can't tell—and thrusts it up under her chin, pinning her once again. She starts to gasp, to lose her breath. She chokes on icy water and saliva. He is strangling her.

She looks into Heath's eyes and sees no sign of the person he once was—the boy who dreamed of another world, who plotted and studied and mapped the Borderlands, who chased after the dwindling game and expertly brought home catch after catch to keep his extended family alive. All of that seems like another life ago—another world ago. And it was. A dream world. Her vision swirls. Behind Heath's sweating, dripping, bleeding face swim the masks of the Vultures.

Her breath is gone. Water fills her ears, hardening into ice inside her. She is so cold. Impossibly cold. And weak. She feels herself going limp. Blackness fills her vision.

Death comes.

———

But only for an instant.

Through the darkness and the muffled sound, a distant whistle pierces.

Suddenly the pressure on her throat is gone. The water softens and warms, though she is still shivering uncontrollably.

Hands wrap around her shoulders, pulling her backward and away.

She blinks, gasping. The skylight above, releasing a faint silver light, seems blinding. Where is Heath? She hears struggling and focuses, focuses. Across the arena, Heath is being dragged back by three Vultures. It takes a minute for her to comprehend that the fight has been called. Malfleur, it seems, saw that her favorite new pet was going to die, and saved Aurora. That can be the only explanation.

All the fury of the fight has seeped out of Aurora's body. She feels as though she'll never be able to lift herself out of the shallow water, as if it is mud clinging to her and weighing her down.

The Vultures haul her to her feet, but she still cannot stand. Her left leg doesn't hurt anymore—she lacks the sense of touch now that Heath is so far away—but something is very, very wrong with it. Two Vultures have their arms under her, helping to carry her away. She limps with them toward the exit but hears a commotion and turns her head.

At the opposite exit, Heath is struggling against his guards. He claws at them, trying to break free, swings with a hidden blade. There's a tearing sound as his knife meets the thick, tight leather of one of the vulture masks, slicing a hole in the side. Through it, bright red hair, slightly wavy, slightly curly, peeks out. The Vulture swings his head away from Heath and away from danger, momentarily locking eyes with Aurora.

She gasps and swallows, knowledge pulsing into her. Those are the eyes of the same trainer who brought her to Wren. The knowing eyes. The *known* eyes. She *does* recognize him. The foxlike hair is a dead giveaway. It cannot be coincidence. Can it?

Or maybe her mind is just desperately clutching again at

the hope of something familiar, some reminder of her old self.

As the guards pull her back through the doors and they swing shut behind her, she feels something shutting down within her too. A final narrowing. She has lost Heath—he is a monster. She has lost Wren, who believes Aurora is the monster. And the light of her old self is barely a glimmer in the distance now. If she focuses on it, it will wilt under the harshness of her glare. The faerie queen has taken everything from her, made her a pawn, just like she was when she was a helpless princess back in Deluce.

She has leaped from one form of imprisonment to another. At least here her imprisonment is obvious and not hidden under the delusion of being special. Even Isbe treated her like a child back home, someone who needed to be protected. She realizes, in a wild surge of despair, that Malfleur is the only one who has ever been honest with her.

The guards lead Aurora away through the dim-lit halls of Blackthorn, a weakened, bloodied shell. Everywhere her mind turns lie thoughts of bitterness and hate, ribbons and ribbons of darkness enfolding her, but between them, brief flashes of that pale, cruel face, intent and unsmiling: *Malfleur, Malfleur, Malfleur.*

She must have her revenge.

19

Wren,

Formerly a Maiden of Sommeil,
Indentured to the Mad Queen Belcoeur

She can't die. She is the last hope of Sommeil, of the refugees imprisoned in Malfleur's dungeon, stripped of their home, of everything they knew.

And she is only seventeen.

Wren is not ready to die.

But the stone gathers her skin into a hardness, cropping up everywhere now, the curse tightening its way across her shoulder blades, making her stiff, and moving from her ankles to her knees, so it gets harder and harder to limp along.

Still, at last, somehow, she has made it to Violette's mansion, which sits in a field of vibrant emerald grass, beside a vast and glimmering lake. The air is fresh, sparkling with moisture and the buzz of spring insects.

No wonder Violette loves to tithe human sight.

Wren knows, from the information she has gathered along the road, that she is right in the center of Deluce. She knows too that this is a kingdom at war, yet she has been helped at every turn by peasants seeking to do some good. And now, the vision of this grand estate moves her, makes her think that perhaps everything will be all right, that there will be spots the war won't touch, like this. That evil can spread everywhere, but may never take the heart.

As she makes her way on foot down a long private path toward the house, a carriage splashes past her. A man sneers down at her from the driver's spot—a wealthy gentleman, from the looks of his dapper clothing and upright posture, though it would be odd for a lord to drive his own carriage. He passes her, in the direction of the house.

So, she will not be Violette's only guest.

Only after she is let inside—with excessive caution, by a bizarrely coiffed and timid butler—does she learn who this other guest is. Another faerie—Lord Barnabé.

The two are seated side by side in a large ballroom full of mirrors. There are so many mirrors that the room feels not like a room at all but like an endless and terrifying world of repetitions.

The chairs seem like they've been hastily arranged in the middle of this otherwise empty room, with no other furniture around them, as though not only has Lady Violette rarely received guests but perhaps doesn't really understand what it means to receive a guest in the first place.

The lord looks down his nose at her. "I have *private* business with the lady of this house," he informs her.

Wren holds her ground. "So do I." She has not come this far only to be intimidated.

The lord bristles but turns to stare in a mirror and adjust his cravat.

Violette walks in, guided by the awkward, overly groomed butler, as well as a maid. They each hold an arm, as though the lady can't walk on her own.

Wren sits up straighter. Whatever she expected, this isn't it.

The woman looks, well, insane. She has flaming red hair stacked high on her head, huge lips like two halves of a purple butterfly, drawn-on eyebrows, and a bustle so high it's practically a hunchback. The sagging skin of her chin is literally pinned back by something like jeweled hairpins at the sides, giving the illusion of slenderness around the neck, stretching her mouth into something halfway between a smile and a grimace. It must hurt, but if it does, she must be used to it.

"To what do I owe this pleasure?" Violette asks, gazing not at either of her guests but at herself in a gilded mirror on the wall.

Wren shifts.

"My lady," Lord Barnabé says, sitting up straighter. "I must speak to you privately about a matter of mutual concern."

Violette looks startled—perhaps by his urgency, or perhaps by his presence, since she hasn't really acknowledged that either of them is even here. She is still staring at herself in a mirror.

"My lady," Wren jumps in. "It is *I* who must speak to you urgently."

"Me?" The lady looks almost, if Wren is not mistaken, *scared*. "But . . . but . . ."

"I have heard," Wren says, beginning to doubt herself before the words even come out—could Aurora have lied about the tale? "I've heard you have great power."

"Me?" Violette repeats. Behind the makeup and the elaborate clothing, she seems like a nervous girl. She is *still* staring at the same mirror.

"Yes," Wren goes on, less certainly. "I was told you have the power to amend a curse. You did so once before."

"Once before . . . ," Violette repeats.

Lord Barnabé turns to Wren. "You know about that?" His face has gone suspicious. "Who told you that tale?"

"I—it was—the Princess Aurora herself," Wren replies.

"So she knows, Binks," Violette says, almost to herself.

Wren juts out her chin. "Yes. I know you altered the curse on Aurora—a curse placed on her by Queen Malfleur—so that the princess would not die when she touched the enchanted spindle but would instead fall into a kind of trapped sleep."

Violette flinches but does not meet Wren's eyes, even in the reflection.

"I came to find out," Wren goes on, desperation pushing up against her ribs and into her throat, "if you can do so again. For . . . me."

Barnabé—*Binks*, as Violette called him—stares at Wren again, then lets out a startling laugh that sounds more like a small dog barking in the distance. "*You?* I haven't a clue who you even *are*, girl, but you must know the kingdom has more dire concerns than a cursed girl looking for a cure."

"A cursed girl," Violette repeats, playing with her skirts, aligning them so that the silk catches the light and shines. Wren is beginning to wonder if the woman can think for herself at all or only repeats words she hears aloud. But then, just as Wren experiences that thought, Violette catches her eyes in the mirror—for just a fleeting second. "I can't help you," she says, so quietly Wren almost missed it.

"Can't? Or won't?" she asks.

Violette stiffens. "Of course I *can*." She seems to consider what she has just said and as she thinks about it, she puffs up a little, shimmying her shoulders a tiny bit, as if to remove dust that has settled there.

Hope leaps in Wren's chest. "You'll help me?"

"*No*," Binks says, at the same time that Violette asks, "What is the curse?"

Wren stands up, but seeing how Violette flinches, she does not approach the woman, treating her instead like a deer that has frozen under the gaze of a hunter. She recalls the way Heath used to hold himself so still in the Borderlands before loosing his arrow through the silt-colored dawn.

Heath. Her brother in spirit, in practice, in action, in every way that matters. She hasn't seen his face in so long she is beginning to remember it only as a collection of fragmented feelings—confidence, patience, intensity, delight, and the perfect peace of spotting one's prey within the line of sight, just before the arrow's shot.

She glances cautiously to Binks, then back at Violette. And then she begins to explain her story. Slowly and carefully, so as not to leave out any details that could be important. How Belcoeur placed a curse on her great-great-great-aunt, and in turn on her entire bloodline, a curse limiting their ability to ever leave Sommeil, to leave *her*. The curse said if they ever tried to leave, they'd turn to stone. She tells the story of Malfleur appearing in Sommeil and killing her own sister, watching as Queen Belcoeur's blood became smoke and she writhed under her twin's touch. How the trees changed and the whole forest seemed to disappear, replaced by another forest altogether, and she came to realize that Sommeil was over, was gone, and now she was *here*, in Deluce. And the curse on her had come true.

Binks huffs. "Prove it."

With shame and nervousness, Wren lifts her skirt a few inches to reveal her stone ankle. She pulls at the shoulder of her dress to show a glimpse of the stone there as well.

Binks's eyebrows rise in shock. Then his face scrunches again in skepticism. "Don't trust her, Violette. There's a kink in your logic, my dear," he says to Wren.

"No—"

He holds up a hand to silence her. "If what you say is true . . . if Belcoeur has recently died, the curse she made should have died with her."

"But that's impossible. I saw her die. And yet the curse still holds," Wren says.

"Not *impossible*," Violette says, her voice worming its way creepily into their debate. Both of them turn to face her. She looks back at them, frozen, as if exchanging with them directly, instead of through a mirror, is overwhelming, like staring at the sun. "You said your bloodline was bound to hers. Well, perhaps someone else of Belcoeur's bloodline still lives."

"Someone . . . else?" Wren asks.

Binks looks between Wren and Violette. "A descendant," he says slowly. Confidence dawns on his face, and he nods. "A descendant," he repeats.

He stands up and begins to pace, his footsteps *click-clack*ing through the ballroom. Wren notices he is wearing heels. The fae seem to care a great deal about appearances—though the result is not that any of them are at all pleasing to behold.

"But—what does this mean for me? Can you amend the curse?" she asks, turning her attention back to Violette.

Violette plays with her hands. "I . . . I . . . Why, perhaps I can! Of course! I'm quite sure that I can!"

"Violette," Binks warns.

But thankfully, she doesn't heed him. Instead, she ruffles herself up taller, like a posturing bird. She seems to concentrate very hard and then, as if with great labor, she forms the words.

"To the blood of Belcoeur you will remain bound, never to fly free, your bond as firm as the stone you're already starting to become . . . *until* . . ." She pauses, and Wren isn't sure whether it's for flourish or to make up her mind about something. Violette scrunches her brow. "Until true love softens the stone back into flesh and bone."

A strange tingling sensation showers over Wren, making her dizzy.

She sits back down in her seat in the silence that follows Violette's pronouncement, but Binks shifts uncomfortably and pulls at his collar as though it's all he can do not to snort.

Until true love softens the stone back into flesh and bone.

A million thoughts swirl through Wren's head at once. She sinks farther back in her chair. *True love.* Does the woman even know of what she speaks? The amended curse is essentially the exact same one Violette performed for the baby Aurora sixteen years ago—and though it came to pass somewhat as she'd said it would, it certainly wasn't by any magic of her doing, or any awareness of her own. It hadn't even been *actual* true love that had awakened Aurora, but Charles Blackthorn's crown, affectionately dubbed True Love by the mad queen Belcoeur—a fact Violette couldn't possibly have known.

Does true love exist at all, or had the very lie of it been at the heart of Violette's words, and the reason they came about in such a strange and twisted fashion?

What could this possibly mean for Wren—and how can it save her?

Binks snickers.

Wren doesn't have the will even to glare at him. She is too heartbroken by the despair that has quickly settled in her heart. What if there truly is no way to save herself? Maybe she has come to the end of the road. Maybe . . .

"My man will see you out," Violette announces, turning back to the mirror.

With slumped shoulders, Wren begins to follow the butler out of the room and down the hall. With a *click-clack* of his shoes, Binks follows them both.

It is only once they are outside and the door has slammed at their backs that Binks suddenly grabs Wren's arm.

With a gasp, she turns to face him, sunlight dancing off the yellowed snags in his teeth, many of them, she can now see, filled with gold. His hands, though chubby and laden with an ostentatious amount of rings, are surprisingly strong.

"Let go of me."

"Perhaps we can help each other after all," Binks says. He lets go and she shudders, suddenly realizing something. . . .

"What were you doing here in the first place?" Wren asks. "You came when I did and now you're leaving with me and you didn't share your private business with Violette. Why?"

Binks grins. "After hearing your pitiful tale of woe, I

suppose I saw a better opportunity."

He pauses, but Wren only stares at him, waiting for him to explain. He leads her down the path and then across the yard into a dense cluster of trees. He looks cautiously over his shoulders as though even the young oaks might be listening. Then he whispers, "Have you ever heard the tale of the Hart Slayer?"

Wren stares at him.

He huffs impatiently. "The hunter who disobeyed the king and delivered his killings to the poor. No? Doesn't ring a bell?"

Wren shakes her head, wondering where this is going.

"Some of us fae had a little theory all these years."

"A theory," Wren repeats.

"Yes, yes. A theory."

"About the Hart Slayer?"

"Why, yes, obviously, about the Hart Slayer."

"Which is . . . ?" Now *she* is the one beginning to lose her patience.

"Well, you see, it was said the Hart Slayer had a gift. That everywhere he hunted, purple flowers would sprout up under his feet. The royal forest grew rich with the bright-petaled things. They were almost like his signature—a hint that he'd been lurking about, doing, you know, whatever it is he did. *Hunt* and all that." Binks waves a hand as though he has never quite been sure what hunting involves. "He liked the harts best."

"Hence the name," Wren says, desperately trying not to

roll her eyes. "What are you getting at?"

"Purple flowers. Purple *flowers*!"

She shakes her head. Whatever he's implying, it's not apparent to her.

"Well." He sighs. "Some of us—myself, Claudine, and Violette included—came to suspect the Hart Slayer might bear some relation to Belcoeur. After all, both were known for having a way with the natural world and, in particular, that type of flower. Don't you see?"

"The Hart Slayer is Belcoeur's descendant?" Wren says slowly.

"Why, yes, *obviously*, that's what I'm getting at!" Binks says.

"And this Hart Slayer could be the reason my curse is still active. . . . But why are you telling me this, and what did you come to Violette's for?"

"There's more to this theory," he explains. "More than one of the fae have heard Malfleur boast that she cannot be killed, except by one of her own blood. If it were true that Belcoeur had an heir to her magic and her bloodline, even an unknowing one, that descendant might be our only hope against Malfleur. 'Man's greatest foe,' as the myth of the Hart Slayer states."

"And you wanted Violette's help in finding the Hart Slayer to save Deluce?" Wren asks.

"Not exactly." Behind his foppish, aging handsomeness, she sees a true kind of ugliness in his features. "I was going to seek her help in winning over Malfleur. And now you've given me hope—you've given me a way. You must see how we may come to be aligned after all, you and I!"

Wren pauses, her mind turning. "No, I do not."

"The Hart Slayer was long thought to be dead. But some, like Claudine, insisted he was still out there. And now, you see, he *must* be alive—or some descendant of his, anyway. Your little curse is proof of it, isn't it? Belcoeur's blood still runs free in this world. The Hart Slayer must be found."

Wren stalls. "But how? When was he last seen?"

Binks shifts uncomfortably. "Well, that's the thing. The slight hiccup, you see, is that the Hart Slayer *was* never seen, except in glimpses. Around the time that the king became engaged to Queen Amélie, the infamous hunter quite simply disappeared, and no one knows what became of him."

"Queen Amélie . . . ," Wren says slowly, thinking about what Binks has said. "Princess Aurora's mother."

He nods. "Indeed."

"But the king and queen married and the Hart Slayer disappeared? And no one ever saw this famous hunter?" The answer seems so obvious to Wren that she cocks her head, surprised by Binks's blustery look of blank confusion. Now it's *her* turn to toy with him. "Isn't it obvious?"

"Obvious? What, girl, what's so obvious?"

"Queen Amélie. She was the Hart Slayer."

He stares at her as though she has just sprouted a mushroom from the top of her head. "What?"

"There's something you should know about me, Lord Barnabé. And that is that I am a very practical person."

"Then we have very little in common, but go on," he says.

"People don't usually just disappear."

He waits. "Well?"

"Is there any reason this hunter might not have been a *huntress*? Why couldn't the Hart Slayer have been a woman? It would certainly explain why she stopped hunting, and the flowers stopped blooming. I imagine it isn't very easy to run about hunting deer when you have recently wed a king."

He mulls over what she has just said. In the meantime, their minds seem to leap to the same conclusion. "With Amélie dead, that would mean Princess Aurora was the last descendant of Belcoeur."

"Aurora is destined to kill Malfleur." It feels right when she says it. It must be true.

"So are you with me? Will you help?" Binks asks.

"Help?"

He smiles, showing his sharp teeth. "Yes, help. Help kill the Hart Slayer's daughter."

Wren's jaw drops open. "You want to kill the one person who might be able to stop Malfleur's rise? Why in the world would you want to do *that*?"

The darkness moves into his eyes. "She's going to win the war, you know." Binks states it like a fact. "In the end, it won't matter what we tried to do to stop it, only that she has won, and she will get to decide what to do with the rest of us, you see."

"No, I don't see. I'd never agree to just clear the path for her to take over!"

Besides, he doesn't know what's hidden in Wren's heart. He doesn't know that she has met Aurora—not just met her, but cares for her. Might care for her more than she's been able to admit to anyone, including herself.

Binks raises his eyebrows. "Such patriotism in one so new to Deluce. But let me tell you, girl, in times of war, one must not think of flimsy principles like good and evil, but of one thing and one thing only: self-preservation. We must find a way to win Malfleur's favor before it's too late."

A chill moves through her as Wren realizes—in piecing together the theory that Aurora is Belcoeur's descendant, she has just put a target on the princess's back.

Could she consider killing Aurora? The thought fills her with horror and revulsion, but then she recalls the same sensations sweeping through her when Aurora nearly killed *her*. If her theory is right—and she can't be sure that it is—it would mean that Aurora's death would save Wren's life. It would lift the curse on Wren, and she'd no longer turn to stone. The idea seems too cruel to contemplate. Maybe there was never any hope of anything blooming between Wren and Aurora, but that one must die for the other to live seems like an added injustice Wren can hardly fathom.

And yet. It would also explain some things. What if Wren only felt close to Aurora because she was unconsciously bound to her by the curse?

"Will you help, then?" Binks asks, cutting into her thoughts. "Will you do it?"

She looks into his eyes, their unsettling flatness, as though there is no soul at all behind them. For a long time she says nothing.

And then at last, she says, "Yes."

PART

IV

AMONG ALL MEN AND
ACROSS ALL FAE

20

Isabelle

She remains belowdecks for the journey north, curled in a pile of furs, holding the slipper of ice in her hands, letting the delirious sway of the ship rock her. She thinks of Aurora—her steady and calming presence, the intimacy of her finger taps against Isbe's palms. When she closes her eyes and breathes slowly, she can almost imagine that she is lying next to her half sister the way they used to when they were little, especially during vicious storms, telling each other stories until Aurora's hands and Isbe's voice grew tired and they fell asleep like that, folded around each other protectively, like two halves of a whole.

Tell me a story. Maybe if she wishes it hard enough,

Aurora will appear beside her. *Tell me a story about two sisters.* But instead she recalls what Aurora told her about her journey to Sommeil, about the irreconcilable rift between Belcoeur and Malfleur. *If even the special bond of twins can be broken, nothing is safe,* Isbe thinks with a shudder. Nothing at all.

She clutches the slipper tighter to her chest and slips into a dreamless lull.

The journey across the North Sea to the Îles de Glace is shorter than the journey to the palace of Aubin, but once she and Byrne arrive, they must travel several miles over the glaciers to the ice palace.

In a small seaside village, they are equipped with a sled pulled by large dogs that Byrne says look like snowdrifts come to life, with black noses and fluffy tails. The yipping and howling stir Isbe; the animals are excited and eager to move, and so is she. They settle into their seat, and the sled driver stacks blankets over their legs, asking if they're here to take in the northern lights. Isbe has not heard of these, but explains that she cannot see, and that they are here for the king himself. She must speak to him.

The driver seems not to care in the end, so long as they're willing to pay what he's charging. The sled flies forward with a jolt, spraying snow up the sides and into Isbe's face. She almost laughs from the delight of it. The icy landscape refracts the sun and she can feel the glare of the islands, like massive white mirrors, warming the air, even as her breath crystalizes at her lips.

They pass through the seaside villages first, which smell of fish and damp wood and harsh sea air, then travel deeper inland, where the brine and salt give way to brisk icy winds, whisking across gaping swaths of uninhabitable frozen terrain. In the distance, huge glaciers rise up to meet the sky, making it look, according to Byrne, as though they are racing toward an endless white wall, a kind of blinding nothingness. "Almost heavenlike, Miss Isabelle," Byrne says, and it feels like how she's always imagined heaven: bright and impossible.

By the time they arrive at the palace gates many hours later, Isbe is no longer elated but freezing, her teeth chattering, her eyes nearly crusted shut with frost that has gathered on her eyelashes and brows. She imagines snowflakes crystalizing along her bones. The gates open onto an ice labyrinth; the palace sits in the middle. The driver refuses to take them any farther. They will have to find their way in by foot.

The dogs pant, exhausted from the day's run, and paw the snow anxiously, awaiting their driver's next instructions. He unseals a bucket full of sardines, and the dogs begin to whine as he tosses some in the snow. They gather immediately, snarling and snuffling.

"Buck up, Byrne," Isbe says as they dismount the sled, turning her chin down to block a blast of icy wind from hitting her neck. She pulls up her hood and shivers. "We've made it this far, haven't we?"

But she can sense Byrne's nervousness—after all, they are now winding through a labyrinth carved into hard, icy snow, and Isbe's of no use. There is no guide, no butler, no one to greet them. It's up to Byrne to lead her safely to the maze's center, and the palace doors.

When they hit the first dead end, Byrne's discomfort increases. He is fidgeting, causing his arms to shake as he ushers her forward, then tells her they must turn around and try a different route. "Wish we could see o'er the top a' these walls, miss," he says desperately, hoarse, the words almost immediately snatched away by the wind.

"Nothing ever came of wishing, Byrne," she replies automatically, trying to quell her own nerves. Her hands ache with cold, fingers clenched stiff even in her woolly gloves.

"What do you do when you're lost, then, miss?"

She thinks for a moment. "I reach out a hand, and try to feel what the world is telling me to feel. I suppose I always find something." So she reaches out now and steps forward until she touches one of the labyrinth walls through her glove. It makes a rough, scratchy sound, snow flaking off against leather. His question has given her an idea. "Let's not think about the path to the castle. Instead, let's think only of this wall, and what we can learn from it."

"How so, miss?" There's a rise of hope in his voice.

"We'll follow it."

And so they do, Isbe constantly keeping her left gloved hand to the wall, letting it graze along the icy surface, scuffing off snow dust. She doesn't let go, even as they follow the wall into several more dead ends and back out of them again. She doesn't let go until Byrne gasps.

214

"The palace, Your Highness."

"Byrne."

He clears his throat. "Miss Isabelle, I mean."

"Thank you."

———

The interior of the palace is warmer than Isbe expected; she is able to lower her hood after several minutes and allow her ears to thaw. They are led by a butler into a cozy parlor room. The massive hides of fanged white bears line the floors and walls, muffling the sounds of their steps and muting the echo of their voices.

Byrne has become a faithful narrator of the visual world, but there are times when Isabelle is glad she cannot see, and this is one of them—though she is curious about the castle, she imagines a whole forest of polar bears must have been massacred for the sake of such insulation. There is an unnerving roar trapped in the walls, the reverberation of ice melting, shifting and refreezing in tiny increments, though she can't help but think it is the roar of the slaughtered animals.

The palace staff is surprisingly animated. Servants bustle in and out of the room, making Isbe and Byrne comfortable, guiding them into ice chairs that are covered too in bushy pelts of soft fur, offering them thick, lined robes to wear over their clothes and formal slippers and insulated jugs of a syrupy drink that tastes both bitter and saccharine, like candied orange skins. Isbe's knees and toes are still throbbing from the cold, but she's heartened by the way the servants seem thrilled to have guests, and yet they are practiced and well trained for their arrival. Isbe wonders if they somehow knew in advance that she was coming.

As if in answer to her thought, a new maid enters, pauses to curtsy, then tells her, "The king has been expecting you."

A little rush of apprehension zips up Isbe's spine as she stands to follow her. How could the king possibly have known she was coming? Then again, who could guess what powers a faerie as ancient as he might possess?

"He'll see you in the library," the maid says.

The library is full of sleepy afternoon light; Isbe can feel it on her cheeks and dancing against the ice walls around her.

"Your Majesty," she says, bowing her head and listening for movement.

The king clears his throat, and she moves toward the sound. "It is a blessing, child, that you cannot see the wrinkled and overdressed pile of flesh to which you just bowed." His voice is ancient and dryly humorous. "What brings you to this icy realm?" he asks.

Isbe readies herself for an argument even as she takes a seat across from him. "You must know," she launches in, "that your daughter Malfleur is going to win the war against Deluce. The tides have turned in her favor. Evil will come for all of us—even you, eventually. Your precious neutrality will inevitably come under threat."

He is silent.

"So I've traveled all this way to ask for your help."

"*My* help?"

"I need a special kind of armor. Something strong enough to resist a deadly magic fire Malfleur's army has wielded against us."

He lets out a dry laugh. "I'm quite old, you know. Many people believe that I'm already dead, and sometimes I'm inclined to believe that too."

"Surely not too old to be of use." She opens the bag at her hip and holds out the magic slipper. "This is winter glass, is it not?"

He pauses. "It is."

"And do you know how it was made?"

"Of course. I made it myself."

Excitement leaps up inside her like a hungry flame. Isbe wants to whoop and cheer and throw her arms around the grizzled old king who, though she can't see him, must be like a bear himself, she imagines, covered in a white beard and gnarled white hair.

"And can you make more? I need a ship's worth of winter-glass shields."

He is quiet for a moment, and Isbe twitches nervously. Finally he says, "Do you know why winter glass is so resistant to destruction in the first place?" He waits a beat, then goes on. "Precisely because it is meant to *preserve*."

"Preserve what?" She fidgets. Despite the robe, she feels chilled. Even the air in this room is harsh with cold.

"Stories. Secrets. All ice is a transmutation of actual history, a physical record of what has happened. I simply use my tithe of knowledge to translate specific facts and events into frozen objects. It all started because I couldn't possibly carry all of the knowledge I had accrued on my own. The mind is a prison, you see. And it is limited in what it can contain. I had to find another way to store what I knew."

"You're saying that winter glass is made of . . . information?"

"Exactly. Only when it is melted will its story be known again. But it can *only* be melted when its true meaning is revealed. It's a paradox, you see. That is why it's such a safe method of storage."

"A paradox." She pauses, thinking for a minute. "So you wouldn't be able to tell me what information is stored in this slipper, then, without melting it first?"

"Exactly. But I can't melt it."

"Why not?"

"Only the person to whom the story belongs can release it."

"But how do we find out who the story belongs to?" she asks, growing frustrated.

"I don't have the answers, child. Only the slipper knows its own secrets. Our stories find us, not the other way around."

Another riddle. Isbe is starting to feel the effects of all her travel—she's exhausted, exasperated. "Never mind the slipper, then. Will you stand by Deluce, and make us more winter glass?"

He is quiet.

"Think of the suffering, if we should lose," she says. "The thought of Malfleur ruling over all the land is terrifying."

The king lets out a rattling breath and shifts his heavy robe. "Life *requires* suffering, my dear. Why should it be left to me to intervene?"

"Because it *matters*!" She has stood without realizing it. "Because if that doesn't matter, then nothing does."

"It is not up to any one god or faerie, man or woman, to decide what matters for other people, and what does not," he replies calmly. "But let's say I was to help you."

She sits back down.

"What might you give an old king in return for his assistance?"

"What might I give you?" she repeats. She puzzles for a moment, reminded of her very first conversation with Prince William, when she arrived in Aubin and begged him to take her side against Malfleur. At the time, she'd imagined he would agree simply because he believed in her cause, understood the rightness of it. But in the end, she'd been forced to strike a deal, offering Aubin what his country really needed—access to Deluce's oil. "Well, what is it you want?"

"All that winter glass . . . enough for a whole army?" he says, instead of answering. "It would require quite a bit of information, in order to make it. Information you don't mind locking away, possibly forever. The history of an entire nation, for example. It would be quite dangerous, don't you see?"

Another chill moves through her.

He goes on. "And no good faerie does his work without a price. Especially for something so perilous."

"But . . ."

"All of history," he says, "shows us how to forget. They say this glacier we stand on has been melting and continues to melt, even as we breathe, and that one day, thousands of years from now, the ice will be gone, and with it, the world's memory."

Now she is starting to feel scared. The idea of whole histories becoming locked away *does* seem risky. Is it worth the risk, though, to save her kingdom?

"Of course," he adds, "in addition to the information I would need to freeze into the armor, I would have to ask for a little extra something for myself, you see."

She takes a deep breath, bracing herself. "What else do I have that I could give you to make it a fair deal?"

"It has been a long time that I have lived up here alone," he says. "And my own past, unfortunately, is riddled with painful truths."

She begins to recoil from his words, but the old king laughs. "Don't worry, I am not asking for your company. *But* . . ." He shifts again, and if she's not mistaken, there's a wobble in his voice when he continues on. "I would ask for your memories. You are young. The experiences you've had, the joys you've felt, and the love you've shared with your sister, Aurora . . . these are pure memories, aren't they?

These are the kinds of things a person wants with him when he dies."

He wants . . . *her memories of Aurora?*

Isbe stands up again. "No." The word is out of her before she can think twice. "No. It is too much to ask. Without those memories, who would I even be anymore? I'd be split. Broken."

The king sighs. "You'd find new meanings, new memories. It's like I said, Isabelle. The mind is a prism. The light refracts through it and turns fractures into rainbows."

"You never said that," she says, stepping away from him. Edging toward the door. "You said the mind is a *prison*."

He laughs that dry laugh again, but makes no move to stop her from leaving. "Ah yes. Well, it is both."

———

She can't give King Verglas her memories—there's got to be another way to get the armor she needs.

The king, despite his strange ways, has offered her and Byrne rooms in the palace, but Isbe is far too upset to sleep. The king said he wouldn't help her, not without Isabelle relinquishing what's most precious to her. Her memories of Aurora.

And on top of it all, he has nothing new to tell her about the slipper, no light to shed on her own past, or how her mother came to possess the magical shoe in the first place. He says only the shoe knows—well, what good does *that* do? If only she could somehow read the shoe—or any of the ice secrets the king keeps—maybe then she could learn how he makes winter glass . . . or information with which to bribe him. Stories he doesn't want told.

The palace is enormous and mostly empty, making it extremely difficult to navigate as Isbe fumbles her way along its halls. She keeps expecting to run into a maid, and finally lands on a narrow door at the end of a hall that likely leads into servants' quarters. Perhaps there she'll at least locate someone who can help. She pushes through the door and is surprised to find herself, not in a corridor, but out in the open.

Icy winds nip at her skin.

She's outside. She's not sure how that happened, and takes a few steps forward, listening hard, trying to get her bearings. Is this a courtyard in the middle of the palace, or has she managed to find a secret exit in the outer wall?

Snow blasts down and around her like a blizzard. She isn't wearing gloves or a coat, and her whole body is already shaking. She needs to find her way inside, but when she swivels back toward the direction she came from, she hits . . . a wall. She turns and moves forward, only to hit another wall. How is this possible?

Her dinner somersaults in her stomach. Has she wandered into the mouth of the labyrinth?

With the sun almost down, that's the last place she'd want to be.

Panic rises. She darts again toward where the door should be, and finds, again, smooth wall. She tries her tactic of following the wall, fearing more and more by the second that this is not the wall of the palace itself but one of the many that make up the labyrinth.

Her fingertips are going numb, getting frostbitten. She lets go and tunnels frantically in a new direction. Wall after wall. Turn after turn. *No.* She is starting to cry and knows she mustn't—the tears are hardening and tightening against her face. She hears buzzing all around her, closing in on her. Is it the sound of the ice shifting? The wind's echo within the labyrinth?

She hits another wall and lets out a scream, stumbling backward onto the snowy ground.

The buzzing sound abruptly stops. She feels the silence of the snow.

She scrambles shakily to her feet and lurches forward—into something soft and thick and sturdy. Two hands fall on her shoulders.

"Miss. You should not be out here, and without a cloak." The voice is gravelly and unfamiliar. One of the palace servants, most likely.

She gasps with relief, clutching on to the stranger. Her teeth are chattering.

"You lost?" He clucks admonishingly. "Lucky I was doing last rounds." He throws a scratchy fur around her shoulders. "Let's get you out of here."

"Are—are you a g-guard?" she asks, trying to control the rapid tremor of her jaw. He laughs. "Groundskeeper. Name's Dariel. I keep the ice sculptures pristine with this," he explains, holding something up. It's whatever caused the buzzing earlier, Isbe guesses.

"There must . . . there must be a way," she bursts out, her voice still shaky.

"Yes, just follow me," Dariel says.

"No. *No*, that's not what I meant." She pulls against him, knowing that she's being irrational—that if she's left out here alone, she'll freeze. But it's like the ice is staring at her, waiting; she can feel the burn of anticipation, of its infinite crystal eyes.

"I'm sorry, miss?"

"To *read the ice*," she cries. "There must be a way."

Dariel pauses, as if thinking, and then responds matter-of-factly. "There is."

21

Aurora

S *ome kinds can heal, some can nourish, and others can kill.*
She hopes these are the right ones.

On her knees in the guest room of Blackthorn Castle,
Aurora tears off a corner of her sheet and slips it over her
hand like a mitten, then fingers the mushrooms she col-
lected, which have been drying beneath her bed. The
mushrooms crumble into a fine dust in her covered palm.
Aurora brushes this powder into an emptied clay vase. She
then carefully ties the piece of torn sheet over the vase to
keep its contents from spilling out. She puts the vase under
her bed. When the time is right, Malfleur will succumb.
Even the fae are made of flesh and blood.

She draws open the sashes, and the scarlet rays of a

smoky sunset spin through the window of her room. She had been consigned to a straw pallet during the first days of her training, which was still far nicer, she knew, than the terrible dungeon where the refugees from Sommeil are held. She can hardly think of them, writhing in fear and sadness, slowly starving—in fact she hasn't thought of them much since the dark magic began to consume her mind.

But recently—ever since her fight with Heath—Aurora has been given access to a bedroom with fine linens, as well as a small library and a sitting room where she meets with the queen. She has been moved up to these guest quarters ostensibly so that Malfleur can chart her recovery, though Aurora can't help but wonder if it's really that Malfleur gets a thrill from keeping dangerous things close.

Sometimes she can hear the queen pacing the halls. Last night, she heard Malfleur leaving her rooms for some unknown purpose, and several mornings ago she could have sworn she saw her return from an all-night sojourn before the sun had fully risen, wiping red from her lips. She couldn't stop thinking about it, wondering where the queen had gone, what that had been staining her mouth.

Aurora has been meeting with her every evening. The sitting room has a pair of thick-padded chairs, and a grandfather clock that stands in the corner, ominously ticking. The queen seems to enjoy playing with her experiment, asking Aurora to do petty tasks with her magic, like causing the candles to go out just by staring at them. She has even gifted Aurora with a pen and ink so that they can communicate.

Aurora can't help but admit to herself that their conversations have been fascinating. Her desire for vengeance is just as strong as ever, but it has become like a bejeweled dagger—something splendid to behold. She is tempted to take her time with it, to savor it.

But she has stalled too long.

Thirty days have passed since Aurora signed Malfleur's contract, and tomorrow the great hall at Blackthorn Castle will be clamorous with guests. The queen is having a ball, and even though there's a war on—or perhaps *because* of the war, and a frantic desire both for distraction and protection—it seems nearly everyone she invited has eagerly agreed to come.

Aurora is disgusted but not surprised. She thinks of the stadium with weapons hidden under a shallow layer of water. Malfleur's spectacles are rare, which make them even more highly anticipated. Her most recent spectacle, Aurora thinks with irony, was probably Aurora's own christening: the day Claudine took her voice in exchange for beauty, and Almandine took her sense of touch in exchange for kindness and grace. The day Malfleur tried to take her future.

In the days since her forced combat with Heath, the fight that almost ended in her death—or his—Aurora has stewed in tension, focusing on healing her body and honing her revenge. But in moments of solitude, when she can't sleep at night, she has thought about him, her muscles throbbing with the memory of their fight. She had already lost Heath once, had finally let go of what she felt toward him, let go of the hope that this feeling would turn into love. She thought she would have been prepared to see him again.

But not like this. She could never have been prepared for what he has become now—a kind of rabid beast, hungry for her blood, hateful and scarily strong. *Magically* strong. Malfleur's deadly pet. The idea brings a pain that makes her seethe with anger.

Is that what she has become too?

And what happened to Heath? Was he punished for nearly destroying her? Or sent to rooms similar to these? Is he close by, even now? At any moment, might he burst out of his cell and kill her? Or might she be forced to kill *him*?

And what of Wren? Aurora can't stop wondering what's become of her, if she has successfully escaped, whether she will ever forgive Aurora for nearly killing her. If Aurora succeeds in her plan to murder Malfleur, will Wren celebrate her as a hero or see only that she has become capable of horrors? And in the quietest, most fearful moments of all, she thinks about Wren's secret—the cool swath of stone stretched across her collarbone.

———

She slips on her gloves as one of her trainers lights a lantern and brings her down the darkening hall to the sitting room for another meeting with Malfleur. As the flame crackles in the lantern, the sound startles a memory from long ago: of Queen Amélie, before she got sick. Just a fraction of a memory, really. Her mother had been fickle, jealous—mean, even. But she'd also been lively and fun; she could fill a room with her brilliant and cutting observations. And she delighted herself by dressing Aurora up in the finest garments, weaving her hair into towering designs. Aurora didn't mind being treated like a doll—it was the closest thing to a mother's love she knew.

She is consumed now by that same sense of anticipation and dread. That same deep tremor of desire to be approved, admired, loved.

She nervously adjusts her gloves.

Malfleur's smile when Aurora enters the sitting room sends a shiver down her back. The room seems particularly dim—the clock in the corner overly loud, gonging out a warning in rhythm with her heart.

"I've seen you soften metal," the queen says before Aurora has even closed the door. "I've seen you freeze liquid." Aurora turns to face her, and Malfleur settles back in her seat, looking content—smug. "Tonight, I would like to see you shatter glass."

Aurora is startled. The task seems no more difficult or more special than any other she has been asked to do, but there is a gleam in Malfleur's eyes that makes Aurora wary. Whatever she has planned for the party, it must involve glass. Perhaps at tomorrow's ball, she will have Aurora shatter all of the crystal chandeliers, sending glimmering shards raining down on the heads of all her guests and putting out all their light at once.

Or maybe not. Maybe these are just the disturbing thoughts that twist effortlessly through Aurora's own mind now, drawing up visions that both disgust and delight her imagination.

Malfleur opens her palms. Inside them sits a small glass figurine, delicate and sweet, like a child's toy. It is cut from black-and-gray glass, or what looks like glass, in the shape of an animal—a fox, Aurora thinks.

For a moment, she turns her concentration to a window in the corner of the room, wondering whether it would be big enough to escape through if she were able to shatter it. But it's no larger than two hands, and the drop from here to the ground would be deadly.

She turns her attention back to the tiny fox, sending a wave of heat and fury toward not the object itself, which is too darling to look at, but at Malfleur's hands. Nothing happens. Frustrated, Aurora draws closer to the queen, feeling her own magic spike as she steps toward her, allowing the sickening excitement of it to fill her. She tries again, her eyes blazing hard, her pulse rising; the desire to destroy, to break things apart so that they no longer resemble what they once were, floods her mind in a black wave. She can hardly see. She feels the presence of the glass fox and something else too, a stubbornness—a protection, almost, like a shield around the animal. It feels almost like the wall separating the Borderlands from the Blackthorn of Sommeil. It feels like Queen Belcoeur's enchantment.

There is a screaming crack, and then the sound of a tiny explosion. Aurora's vision clears. The fox, strangely, remains intact, and Malfleur looks puzzled, her mouth twisted in a frown. In her peripheral vision, Aurora sees that it was not the figurine that broke, but the face of the grandfather clock, also made of glass.

The queen stands and paces, obviously upset, concentrating on the glass fox. Aurora wonders if Malfleur is trying to use her own magic to do the same thing, and discovering the impossibility of it.

In the split second that Malfleur is occupied with the figurine, Aurora spins toward the clock. She has been given no access to weapons, but the gong of midnight sounds, low and harsh in her ears, and as it does, she plunges her hand through the broken face and tears the iron hour hand right off the clock. Then, in a seamless movement, she turns, aims, and throws.

The clock hand skewers Malfleur in the throat.

Shock and victory freeze Aurora to the spot as the queen stumbles. Then Aurora snaps out of it and shakily removes her gloves, dusted in the poison of the dried mushrooms. *Run.* She should run. But instead she watches with horror as the wound begins to bubble with pus that turns white and then green as the poison takes hold. The queen clutches at her neck, a look of shock on her pale face. For a moment, all is stillness, all is silence, as the queen's eyes begin to roll back.

And then slowly, gradually, Malfleur removes her hand from her neck. The green ooze has gone. There is still a wound, bloodied at its edges, but not one deep enough to do serious harm. The queen looks at the blood on her hands, and then, to Aurora's surprise, licks her own wet hand like an animal. She catches Aurora's eyes. "Thank you, pet." Aurora stares, sickened, unable to move. "It has been too long since I've earned a scar from someone who matters to me."

Time seems to stand still as Aurora begins to understand that she has failed.

The queen considers. "Still, you will have to be restrained." She nods, and two guards race into the room, as though they've been watching all of this take place. Aurora had thought they were alone. The guards drag Aurora out of the room and through the darkened palace, Malfleur leading the way.

It takes a moment before Aurora realizes where they are taking her.

Back to the cage.

The metal door rattles shut with an ominous clang.

"My pet," the queen says to her through the bars, her head tilted slightly, as though she is curious, "you thought it would be that simple." Now her expression morphs into a crooked smile. "I am not so easily killed."

Aurora refuses to look her in the eye.

The queen carries on anyway. "My father put a curse on me that I would die by the hand of one who carries my blood. He didn't realize, I suppose, that this curse was more like a blessing. I became invincible. I have done away with my sister, and there are few living relatives left—if any—who might attempt it. I do not fear my father. He doesn't have it in him. And I certainly cannot fear you. You may be my pet.

My little protégé. But you are not my blood."

Aurora sinks to the floor of the cage as Malfleur walks away, her footsteps clicking down a long corridor. The queen stops and turns around. "Get some beauty sleep, Aurora. You'll need to look your best for the party."

Then she's gone.

Despair presses down on Aurora. Humiliation. Futility. And above all, anger—burning, flaming, making it hard for her to see or to think. How could she have come so close, only to fail?

No. She grabs the iron bars, pulling until her arm muscles feel as though they will tear from her skin. She channels her anger, wondering if she can bend the bars to the will of her magic—it floods through her, blacking out her vision. When she comes to, the bars are still there, though they now bear dents in the shape of her fingers, and the skin of her palm is sizzling and raw. She has burned herself, though she cannot feel it.

She paces her cage like a mountain lion, then kicks at the bars. Hurls herself at them. Lashes out as if her whole body were a silent scream. She knows she will injure herself, already has. She will become a bloodied mess, worse than after her fight with Heath.

Heath. Could he break her out of here? Could they kill Malfleur together? But how? She doesn't even know where he's kept.

She punches and pulls on the bars until her fists are bruised and dripping red, blood crusting underneath her fingernails. This is impossible. It was a waste—all of it. The journey to LaMorte. The covert break-in of the palace. The confrontation. The contract. The training. The careful preparation. All of it has led to this—another prison.

Has she really come anywhere at all from the scared girl she had been only a couple of months ago, alone in her tower room in Deluce, mocked by a starling?

Home. To go back. To start over again. That feels impossible too—because she *has* changed. She can't go back to that powerless person she used to be, waiting around in a flouncy dress for a prince to fall in love with her.

Still, she has nowhere else to go.

And even now, despite the ultimate failure, she's incapable of giving up. She wants what Malfleur has: Freedom. Power. Authority. Meaning.

The image of the queen wiping a scarlet smear from her mouth returns to Aurora now. It was blood.

She wants that: to taste life while its heart is still beating.

———

In the morning, a Vulture leaves her a secret stack of books, and she thumbs through them, dust rising from their pages, but cannot find the attention or the patience to read. That joy—one of her greatest and her few—has wilted. It seems to her that all the books she ever read until now were like lush flowers, distracting her from the real threats of the world.

"I'm sorry, Princess," he says, watching her toss one of the books aside.

She looks up at him, curious. An apology? *That's a first.*

He seems to shrug, though it's hard to tell in all his armor. She stares at the key worn on a chain around his neck. If she lunged quickly enough, could she grab hold of it through the bars? Would her injured leg hold up? Could she strangle him with the chain and then unlock the cage and run free?

He bends to one knee. It would be so easy now. She is poised.

She hesitates.

He slides a fresh book through the bars. "Perhaps you'll like this one better?"

And then he is standing, stepping back, as though he has just left raw meat inside the cage of a beast. Is that how they all see her? Is that what she has become? She has not seen herself in weeks. Even in the guest quarters she was given no mirror—nothing that could easily have become a weapon in her hands.

After he is gone, she glowers at the book.

But eventually curiosity takes over and she opens it, scans the title and contents. It's hardly even a book—more of a manual, really, about breeds of horses. She tosses it aside, and begins stalking again, restless. Why didn't she leap at him when she had the chance? Next time she'll be ready.

But it's as if all the Vultures sense her aggression— they're ready too, and keep their distance when they come again, each approaching only to deliver meager helpings of food and then quickly retreating.

The party is tomorrow.

What does Malfleur have planned?

Aurora goes back to the books, debating whether she can turn them into some sort of weapon. Stack and climb them, or pull one of the Vultures close to the bars, then bash his head in with them. She kicks the pile of them over.

The book of horses lands by her feet.

She stares at it. It suddenly reminds her of something. Of some*one*.

She thinks of that flash of red hair—of the knowing looks she has sometimes seen in one of the Vulture's eyes. Of her suspicion that she recognized him.

Gilbert.

It seems impossible, like so much else.

And even if she's right—what good would that information do? He's shown no mercy toward her before—none of them have. There's been a certain softness that she has detected, in moments here and there, from one of her trainers. Could it have been him? She might just as easily have imagined it, though, and he has never suggested he would actually help her.

Even if Gilbert *is* one of the Vultures, how will she find him again? And is he even Gilbert *enough* to want to help her? If it *is* him, he's a stern, vacant shadow of the boy who once tumbled around the fields and mucked the stables and dragged his hay scent in through Isbe's window throughout their childhood.

Hardly a spark remains of the flush-faced teen Aurora once caught leaving love notes in Isabelle's bedroom wall—

notes he must have dictated, since he couldn't write, and knowing too that Isbe couldn't read them. He really had loved her sister once. Aurora only realized the truth of it recently—in Sommeil. How the notes had not been a childish prank, but the act of a man who sensed his love was unrequited, yet still had to speak it, in some secret way.

The swirling magic, and the fury, that have been clouding Aurora's mind and tensing her body melt a little at this memory. She digs down, seizing on the tiny candlelight within her, wavering but not yet blown out: the real Aurora, beneath the stifling weight of the magic. She's still there.

Aurora imagines holding her palms cupped around that flame, protecting it from going out. There's a story in here, somewhere. Somewhere in here, there is hope.

Gilbert. Isabelle. True love. Secrets.

The love notes.

If only he were *more* Gilbert. If only he remembered.

What if that love for her sister still burns within him—a tiny flame, just like hers?

Quickly, an idea flashes into her, as though entering not through her mind but directly through her heart.

Hands shaking, she tears a page from the book, then bites her finger open until it bleeds.

With the blood and the tip of a fingernail, she scratches out a hasty note. She folds it, just like the love notes were folded into Isbe's wall, and pokes it out of the horse book. Then she props it through the bars, and waits. For the impossible to happen. For the right Vulture to return.

Several other guards come and go, seeming to ignore the pile of books altogether.

And then—and then—sometime late in the night, a vulture appears. He cannot have come to bring her food; it is too late for that. She waits, poised; she doesn't try to lunge for his neck. She tries, instead, to catch and hold his gaze. For a moment, it seems to work. She could swear the hardness in his eyes wavers, ripples like a stone thrown into a pond. And she's certain that her hunch is correct. It's him. It's really him.

But then he collects her books and walks away, not seeming to notice the note tucked within.

22

Isabelle

The basalt flame produces a faint smell, almost herbal, and a strange, gently undulating, blue-black heat. Isbe is back in the library of the ice palace, and it must be near dawn. She has not slept. Though the flame did not work on her slipper, she moves determinedly through the cavernous room, so different seeming in the dark—so much vaster and echoing.

For moments here and there, she has the most unusual sensation of being able to *see*—not literally, but abstractly, somehow. The absence of light, and shape, and form seems to be its own kind of substance. How can nothing be something? The air, even, dances around her, full of unfelt bodies. She shakes her head, trying to clear it, to make sense of what she's feeling. She wonders if the smoke from the torch is affecting her thinking.

She learned once from a palace chef that frogs will leap out of boiling water to save their own lives, but if the water's temperature is only gradually raised, the frog will not notice; it will remain in the water until it is cooked to death. She feels lulled by the flame's wavering heat, suspects she will succumb to something terrible in it. She fears the torch in her hand, and the icy whispers of the walls around her.

"My ancestors discovered the secret from the island's hot springs," Dariel had explained after she pressed him for answers about the ice. "The springs are thought to be healing, and our people frequently bathe in them to restore our spirits and release tension," he told her. "It is not uncommon to experience visions in the springs. Ecstasies. The steam comes from deep beneath the earth and seems to release the secrets held in the ice. Many believe there are real histories wafting through the steam and then dissipating in the air."

"So I have to go to a hot spring," Isbe replied.

"No," Dariel explained. "You do not. All you need is a basalt flame."

"A what?"

"It is a kind of torch made with bits of black rock from deep below the ice—the kind that heats the springs. But I must warn you—many men say these are the rocks of the underworld, the place of polar darkness, and that the visions they bring are not real but our fantasies come to haunt us."

A chill went through her. "I'm not afraid," she said,

though what she meant was, *I've come this far.* "But how will I find the story I'm looking for?"

Dariel thought for a moment. "You won't. You must trust the ice. The story will find you."

It's exactly what the king told her, and oddly, this reassures her. She would have to trust the ice.

She has no other choice.

Now she runs her bare fingers, chapped and blistered from the ice, against more ice. Searching, searching.

The flame makes the walls melt, but only a little, like beads of perspiration. Everything's slippery, and she has no idea where she is in the room. She has a sense of touching infinity. She shivers, hot and cold and hot again. The softening ice sends whispered words, phrases, even emotions that seem to reach out to her and wind their way inside her mind.

Where is the heart, the heart . . .

The phrase repeats and repeats, detangling itself into sense. *Where is all the hart?*

Isbe feels herself disappearing into the words and their story, becoming not herself and not a person at all but a kind of witness—she's all the figures in the tale and none of them at once.

There are woods. There is a mad clattering of hooves. A king's fury radiates between the tall trees striping the world all around him. This is *his* forest. The royal forest. The king is Isbe's father, King Henri. She is him and she is not him, but she can feel his righteous anger. All the hart are being driven from the woods, *his* wood and thus *his* game. No one is allowed to hunt the hart but him.

And yet someone has gone against the king's wishes. The Hart Slayer, that's what Henri has come to call this criminal—a mysterious hunter who is not only shooting his game but delivering his prizes to the doorsteps of random peasants throughout the area, making a mockery of the king and his laws.

The king is enraged. This hunter must be captured and hanged. An example must be made. Hunting is his chief joy, and now that joy has been ripped away, replaced with humiliation.

His royal guard has decorated the outskirts of the forest in posters declaring the king's offering of a massive reward for the head of the Hart Slayer. Sketches drawn from the brief glimpses of him by loyal villagers show a scrawny man of average height and unkempt hair. The hunter's only true identifying features are the special arrows he uses on the hunt. Some people have made a hobby of trying to find these arrows—all of them made of some sort of material that resembles clear glass, except that it does not break.

Winter glass, Isbe thinks, suddenly coming back to herself.

Her hands are shaking. She realizes they are drenched and numb, the icy water melting down along her out-stretched arm and trickling down her dress. But she must know more. She moves along the ice, seeking the voices again, that swishing of heavy cloaks against horses' backs and hooves on dense forest floor, that sense of galloping speed and that wondrously palpable feeling of anger.

On this day, the king is determined—more determined than ever—to catch a hart. He must have a win. He must feel the still-beating heart in the creature's warm chest before he drives in the final, killing wound. He will not stop until he has completed the hunt.

And then it happens, at last—a shift in the underbrush. The presence of an animal, lithe, skirting in the shadows, and tall. Fast but not fast enough. There is a clearing ahead; he knows these parts well, knows them better than he knows himself. Excitement and victory fly through his veins, nearly lighting him up from within, as he reaches for his bow and arrow, and aims, aims . . . *aims*.

He is a hair's breadth away from firing the shot, when something stops him, and the figure emerges, a scared look in its eyes.

No. Not *its*. Hers.

It is no deer, but a maiden.

There is no specific moment when the king, Isbe's father, falls in love with this maiden. It happens quickly, but in increments. He finds himself thinking of her all day and soon can dream of nothing but her at night—the maiden so poor she grew up not in a house or cottage but a hut built into the side of a tree, not in a village but on the outskirts of untamed land. Isbe's hands slide along the ice, and the torch burns hotter and hotter as the story of their chance meetings in the woods unfolds—once, twice, and three times, before Henri admits who he is: the king of Deluce. By then it is too late; the maiden has fallen in love with him, and he with her.

After some convincing, he persuades her at last to be his. She thinks she will be plucked from obscurity and brought into the royal family. It is what every young girl dreams will happen. To her credit, this maiden—Cassandra is her name—hopes that her love for the king will do some good for this world.

It will not, however.

It will do good only for the king himself. Cassandra will become his favorite mistress, because after he whisks her away to the palace and covers her in lavish dresses and tripled strands of sapphires, the Hart Slayer stops hunting in the royal forest. Cassandra, the king believes, has brought him good luck, and gradually he forgets his ire, forgets the affront to his ego the illegal hunter had caused. Even the people who were helped by the Hart Slayer—many as poor as Cassandra herself—go on about their lives and begin to forget their mysterious benefactor ever existed.

But Cassandra will never be queen and she will never be wife, and in two years' time, when she has only just given birth to the king's bastard daughter, she will be forced out and sent away, leaving her only worldly attachments behind: the child, whom she names Isabelle, and a small item given to her by her own mother—a tiny slipper made of unbreakable glass.

And as she flees the castle, a confidante—the minister of religion, a young woman named Hildegarde—shakes her head at the girl. "There is so much more you might have been, Cassandra."

Cassandra sets sail in a stolen fisherman's vessel, and finds, to her surprise, that a life at sea suits her. At first the life is not easy, and she struggles to survive by casting fishing nets woven of the silk veils she once wore at the palace, and tied with clove-hitch knots of her own hair. But the solitude soothes the pain of her past; the constant movement keeps her from ever having to be too still with her thoughts.

The singing voice she had once preserved for her younger days spent roaming the forest she now lets loose, and with it, she finds she is able to tame the wild beasts of the sea. Narwhals encircle her craft, drawn by her lilting songs. Fish frequently fly into her nets as if willingly—more than she could ever consume on her own. More than enough to gift. She finds a kind of calling again—a purpose. Over time, her past—everything she was and wanted to be—slips away into the dark and anonymous waves.

Years pass that way, bringing Isbe to what must have occurred only recently—no more than a year ago, maybe two: the day Cassandra herself slips away, her song swallowed by an angry storm, her ship sunk.

Isabelle experiences every writhing, startling pain as her mother lets go of the fight and allows herself to drown, and it is only in the final moment of letting go that Isbe comes to, gasping.

———

Isabelle staggers through the vast library, wanting only to lie down, but there's nowhere to lie that isn't cold and full of haunting whispers. She's awash in an unexpected sense of loss.

Shards of the story flash through her mind: the glass arrows and the glass slipper. Her mother's voice, the same one she has heard so many times in her mother dreams, singing her own version of the rose lullaby. The voice that made the seas friendly, drew fish straight into her nets.

Isbe recalls her own first journey at sea, when she and Gil stole across the Strait of Sorrow toward the shores of Aubin onboard a whaling vessel. She remembers that the sailors spoke of a mythic figure—the Balladeer—who sang to calm the waves, and who was known for leaving desperate villages with bounties of fresh-caught fish.

And now the truth feels so obvious she thinks she might drown in it: her mother *was* the Balladeer.

And she understands something that her father never could.

Cassandra wasn't lucky.

She didn't make the Hart Slayer stop hunting simply by falling in love with the king.

She made the Hart Slayer stop hunting because she *was* the Hart Slayer. Another anonymous hunter known for helping the poor. Isabelle's mother was the Hart Slayer, a figure about whom epic poems have been written. And she gave it all up to come to the palace. She gave up her calling for love.

But if she hadn't done that, Isbe never would have been born.

And now, Cassandra is dead—just as Isbe is discovering the truth. Too late.

Too late to ever know her.

The sudden grief is too much, and the notion of winter-glass armor now feels further away than ever—a fool's dream. A silly girl's wish.

How she hates the pain of wishes.

She feels more untethered and alone than ever before, and so very tired—more cold and more tired than when she crawled through half-frozen sewage to make her way into the palace of Aubin. She stumbles across the room and reaches out for something to steady her, somewhere to rest, and finds the ice desk where the king sat earlier, when they first spoke. She rests the torch down on the desk, its flame still burning.

———

Isbe dreams of the ocean's unlit depths. *One night so mild, before break of morn, amid the roses wild, all tangled in thorns, the shadow and the child together were born.* The words of the lullaby—her mother's version—weave through the darkness of her sleep and begin to take on a new meaning. It is no longer the tale of faerie twins Malfleur and Belcoeur and their infamous rivalry.

What the song is trying to say, her dream self sees now, is that innocence and darkness are inevitably threaded together in one tangled being. A paradox, like the fact that we are all born with the seed of fate inside our chests—that life itself is the gradual opening of death's red rose.

There are no longer two figures in the song, but one.

The shadow *is* the child, and the child is the shadow.

23

Verglas,
the Ice King

The king is startled to find his young visitor sleeping in the center of his library the next morning, and regrets that he did not refer to the room properly—that he did not tell her it was in fact a tomb.

And here she is, shaking and nearly frozen to death in half sleep, lying on top of the coffin of his former wife. The North Faerie.

He probably should have pointed out before that it was a coffin and not a desk.

He studies her in the morning light, oddly struck by the beauty of it.

He doesn't call for help. He wraps her in bearskins himself and places her gently beside a blazing fire. She shifts

in her sleep but does not wake, and he thinks, unexpect-
edly, of his daughter. Not Belcoeur, the one whose smile
used to play like a sad, lilting melody over a sun-drenched
field, the one everybody found easy ways to love. No, not
that daughter, but her twin, Malfleur. Though he cannot
be sure, he suspects that he once loved Malfleur best—loved
her in a fraught and difficult way. She had been his tiny
storm cloud, lined in silver. A tight, dark kernel of a faerie,
bursting inward.

He might have done a better job in those days. He didn't
anticipate his regret, however. One cannot. Now he sees it
is something we must grow into with age, like an overlarge
robe. He might have protected her from her mother, whom
she took after in all of the worst ways—the rages. It all
stemmed, he thought, not from an inherent anger, but from
the constant disappointment of a mind desperately seeking
absolutes: most beautiful. Most powerful. Most anything.

He pulls something from his pocket. It is a formal invitation that arrived recently by sleigh post. The penmanship
is left-slanting but otherwise perfect. He remembers that
handwriting. Malfleur must have penned each and every one
of the invitations herself.

It must be quite a party she's got planned.

And if he knows his daughter—he once thought he did,
anyway—she has no doubt convinced every important noble
in the known kingdoms to attend. But King Verglas will not
be going. He won't give her the pleasure of his curiosity. He
is beyond all that.

He returns to the library, paces the tomb of his second wife, the North Faerie. She had been with child when she was killed. He removes a velvet-lined box from the ice coffin. Inside it are all the figurines he once carved for the child who was never born. A collection of woodland creatures: raccoons and deer and mice. A fox went missing long ago. These, like Isabelle's slipper, were all made of winter glass, meant to last the ages. Now they are not toys but relics— reminders of a future that never came to be, a future that remained trapped in the past.

Because of Malfleur.

Perhaps it isn't all his fault, he thinks, the way Malfleur turned out—so murderous and hard. He believes she was in some way warped and jealous from the start, born dreamless, like a living shadow.

Is that really true, however? Perhaps it was only his *belief* that it was true that made it so. This is another thing he ought to have explained to the young princess. She might have found it interesting: that we sculpt truth out of the world's formlessness, and thus it is often precisely what we already believe that comes to pass. When it is decided that a person is broken, she may experience a life of sequential breaking. When it is suspected that a faerie may be black of heart, it is that very suspicion that begins to blacken it.

He checks on Isabelle. Her eyelids have begun to flutter.

She will want to leave, and he will soon only remember her visit as a spark across the arctic sameness. He will help. He will show Isabelle and Byrne the shortcut—the tunnel that leads right out of the palace kitchens and beneath the ice labyrinth. It's the path the North Faerie took many nights when she was his secret lover, before they married and grew tired of each other. Before his own daughter Malfleur jealously attacked her, practicing some new talent she called transference.

But that was all very long ago now, and the stories are kept safe in the walls, where he will never have to feel them.

When his guest has recovered some hours later, he waves and murmurs good-bye to her and her servant, Byrne, wondering if he will miss them, and whether any of us will ever find what we are searching for, or if it is simply the *searching for* that makes us who we are.

24

Malfleur,
the Last Faerie Queen

Malfleur arranges the sheer black veil over her eyes. She's standing behind a heavy brocade curtain, at the top of a staircase, preparing herself for her entrance. She can hear the milling guests in the grand ballroom below.

"Hand me the latest tally," she demands of one of her Vultures.

He passes a scroll to her.

"Hmm. Very well," she says after a quick scan. She gives it back.

She has checked, and checked again, but her father's name has not appeared on any of the guest lists. So, he is not coming to her party.

Just as well. She supposes he has not forgiven her for killing his flimsy wife, the North Faerie, all those years ago. Perhaps he knew, or has since discovered, the most disturbing part of that old debacle. The reason for all that blood, permanently dyeing the throne red.

The North Faerie had been with child when Malfleur killed her.

She hadn't *meant* to kill her, but that didn't really matter. In some ways, it was a kind of mercy. Perhaps another child by her father would have posed a threat to Malfleur's own safety. She might have had to kill that child, once it was born, anyway.

That the child's tithe was innocence seemed obvious to Malfleur. It was the unborn child that caused the problem with Malfleur's attempt at transference—and the North Faerie's death. A kind of unexpected magical interference. But there had been a surprising benefit, which was that Malfleur inherited not the unborn baby's innocence itself, so much as the ability to tithe it from others, to make others hard, and to make herself immune to feelings of guilt.

That immunity to guilt has come in handy. She's done a lot that one could feel guilty about.

At her nod, guards reel up the curtain, and the blazing glow of hundreds of chandeliers bearing thousands of glimmering crystals greets her eyes. As she steps out into the light, she thinks how solitary a life she has led these many years. It's been a long time since she's thrown a ball.

And, of course, this isn't just any ball.

It's a wedding.

———

Prince Edward smiles vacantly at her as she meets him at the top of the mezzanine. He is the least handsome of his brothers, has the same dark Aubinian complexion, the same high-ridged cheeks and square jaw that run in his family, though they seem a bit lopsided and harsh on his face, which matches the tenor of his personality. But never mind that—she's certainly not wedding him for either looks or charm.

They walk down the stairs arm in arm. Around them, nobles from across the land gather closer, their shining silk and velvet dresses and formal suits creating a vast sea of color. She hears a gasp ripple through the crowd as people begin to recognize Edward—the middle brother. It is like a resurrection. He and his brother Philip have been presumed dead since their carriage was ambushed on its way to deliver Prince Philip to the Delucian council, to marry Aurora.

Of course no one knew that the ambush had been staged by one of the brothers. Edward had resented Philip's intended alliance with Deluce and wanted to ally himself with someone even greater. Malfleur has never been interested in marriage, but she could not pass up the opportunity to thwart the Delucian council—and everyone's expectations.

She has been waiting to reveal her plans for Edward until she could secure her control over the Aubinian military.

But no one here knows that, and the looks of shock on their faces send a thrill of satisfaction through Malfleur's veins. She feels awake, alert, alive. Waiters dart through the room carrying silver trays of briar wine, a deep and sparkling burgundy. The room quiets as Malfleur lifts her veil and then raises her glass to make a toast.

"Thank you all for being here to celebrate this auspicious union between the great territories of LaMorte and the kingdom of Aubin."

Glasses clink and murmurs spread as her guests decide what to make of this news. She beams with pride. Edward has made a docile, if boring, puppet. But he cannot compare to her special pet, her grandest experiment yet. . . .

Briefly, she touches the side of her neck. The wound has already begun to heal nicely, and is mostly obscured by the veil. Still, its warmth fills her not with anger but excitement. When her feat is made public—when they all see how great her power is, that even Deluce's pride and joy, their golden-haired beauty, their innocent princess, has come under the spell of Malfleur's greatness—well, then she will have truly won.

This is not a war for land, but for hearts and minds. Revealing Aurora will be the final play, decimating any remaining support for the princess, or her wild half sister, or the pathetic and limping council.

"Ladies and gentlemen, I have something I would like to share with you all," Malfleur announces above the din of the crowd.

She signals to several Vultures standing guard by a back entrance. But they do not move to open the doors.

Frustrated, she marches over to them, and one tilts his head, silently suggesting they speak in private. She pushes him through the doors into a deserted stone atrium. "What's going on?" she spits.

"My apologies . . . your . . . Your Majesty. We have a problem."

The word sinks like a stone in her chest.

"The cage is . . . empty."

"Empty?" Malfleur practically roars, pushing past the Vulture and down the wide torch-lit hallway. Several other guards join them, each attempting to mutter an explanation or to stop her, but Malfleur marches all the way to the wing of the castle where Aurora's cage is kept. She can see before she gets there that it is indeed empty—and the door is swinging open.

Aurora did not escape, then. Someone freed her.

There's something on the ground inside the cage. "Retrieve that," she says, pointing.

One of the Vultures hurries to obey her command and hands her a piece of vellum, hastily written on in blood.

True love, is all it says.

25

Vulture

rue love. When he first saw the note, he didn't know what to make of it. It didn't immediately unleash a torrent of memories—that would come later. For now it simply tickled awake a minuscule *feeling*, like a new leaf unfolding. A dim recognition. The flap of vellum wavered in his big, clumsy hands like the flag of some forgotten country.

He doesn't know how to read, but it wasn't the words that caused a slow fissure in his consciousness, as though waking him up from a deep sleep. It was the letter itself, the way it was folded and left in the pages of the book. The feeling of receiving the note, knowing he would be unable to decipher it, but sensing that it meant something very important. . . .

He came to her cage. "Did you write this?" he said. It was perhaps the first question he had ever asked the girl. She seemed to *see* him, to know him, and this knowing was suddenly like a blade tearing through all of his heavy armor, shredding through the fabric of his existence. He shook, rooted to the floor, and in that moment of weakness, she lunged toward the bars, one of her thin, pale arms flying between them like a flash of lightning, and she had his cape in her grip before he knew what had happened.

Vulture was big, and strong. A trained fighter. And so too was that other person, that stableboy he had once been. But the man who didn't know what he was, the man caught between the two, was just that: caught.

She pulled him close, yanking hard at the chain around his neck and easily ripping the key from the metal with a little sizzle that suggested she'd used both strength and magic.

She was so fast, and he was too confused. He tried to stop her, but she easily moved to the cage door and unlocked it from the inside, freeing herself. As he moved to prevent her escape, she tackled him, sending him sprawling on his back on the floor.

His vision cleared. She was straddling him, her small but wiry, powerful hands around his neck.

He could fight her off. He started to, but froze again, realizing the quandary he was in: he could not kill the queen's pet, or he himself would be killed. But her magic had reached its heights, and she was desperate—he sensed he would not escape alive if he let her live. Which would it be?

Die without a fight, or die a slave?

He didn't have to choose. He felt her cool hands release their pressure from his neck and slide up, slowly . . . up toward his ears . . . and then, in a startling blur, she had yanked Vulture's mask off his head.

He lay there on his back, helpless, exposed as though in a glare of blinding light.

He rolled to his side and heaved, a tangle of his red, unkempt hair falling down around his eyes.

She let him recover for a moment, and he swiped the back of his mouth, rubbed his eyes, squinted, turned back to her.

There it was again, that look of profound knowing. Her eyes said, *I see you.* Her eyes said, *Gilbert.* Her eyes said, *We must hurry.*

And so they did. Numbly but with urgency, he led her through the tunnels of Blackthorn, secured them two steeds, and through the starlit night they flew down the side of Mount Briar, and he . . . Vulture . . . Gilbert . . . whoever he was, had the strangest impression that they were the only two people alive at that moment in all the world, the first two people to ever exist, and they were forming the world beneath them as their chargers' hooves met the earth—coloring it in and giving it shape as the sun, eventually, began to rise.

———

Now, as they race across gray mornings, the domed cupolas of the Delucian palace rising up through the mist to greet them, more and more memories begin to flood him. The tasseled pillows. The trellis outside the window.

Isabelle, her hair in a tangled knot behind her head, laughing, twisting her mouth up in frustration, reaching out to touch his shoulders, his face. . . .

And that's how it starts. It's not Gilbert, the former stableboy, who comes back to him first, but Isbe. It is only through remembering her that he begins to remember himself.

NO HEART CAN BE BRAVER

26

Aurora

"Women and children, into the keep!" Maximilien's shout swirls up into the wind and disappears into the chaos of the inner bailey.

Aurora has not seen the castle this alive since before the sleeping sickness killed off so many. Carts of food and supplies crisscross the green, mothers hold screaming babies to their chests, and boys are separated from their families, conscripted to fight. Aurora watches as one boy who can be no more than eleven or twelve reaches up to accept a set of armor twice his size from a grizzled old soldier who could be his grandfather.

Aurora has known that LaMorte and Deluce have been at war for some time, but she hasn't really *seen* it, hasn't been forced to understand it in literal terms. She has never actually witnessed a battle in all her life, despite having read about the great romantic heroes who've fought in them. Now, the anticipation in the air is palpable, even to one who cannot feel.

A tremor of guilt rattles her chest as she moves through the crowd, looking for Prince William. He had told her to stay in her tower room, but he needs to let her fight. She can't sit idly by—especially not when the imminence of battle is most likely her fault. Since separating herself from Blackthorn, she has tried to shake off the cloak of magic Malfleur gave her, but it is not gone entirely. She senses she may never be entirely free of it.

If she has power she never had before, she must use it.

And this isn't just an attack. This is vengeance. Shortly after she and Gilbert fled Blackthorn, Malfleur's forces began to march, trailing them like a dark tide. Now Aurora has brought the danger back to Deluce's palace, and everyone must prepare for siege.

Someone grabs her arm. She swings around, hoping to come face-to-face with Isbe, who has been missing from the palace for some time. According to William, she has gone north to try and secure support from the Ice King. But it's not her sister. It's one of the soldiers, his thick beard crusted with spit and sweat.

"Inta the keep for ya. You 'eard the general!"

Aurora cries out—or tries to, silently. She yanks her arm

out of the man's grip and runs, shoving into several other people.

Never mind finding the prince. She dashes past a cart full of unclaimed armor and manages to pull a breastplate and helmet from the stack. She doesn't slow down to think long about where this armor came from—it is not fresh. It was, perhaps, worn by another soldier, now dead.

Hastily, she stows away into her rooms to prepare—tucking her hair beneath the helmet and adding padding beneath the armor to better secure it, testing to make sure she can still move with ease.

A horn sounds from somewhere beyond the wall, and then another. Fear trills through her—and something else, something she doesn't want to name. She thinks of Malfleur, wiping blood from her mouth.

She grabs a sword.

Then she heaves a deep breath, swings open her door, and takes the stairs two at a time, flying downward in a swirl of angry metal and the burning need for action. This is the effect of Malfleur's dark magic still in her veins, she knows. She cannot help but need to move, to *do something*. Her blood is like a fire ravaging a field of dry weeds.

But before she reaches the next landing, a hooded figure slips from the shadows and reaches out to grip Aurora's wrist, startling her into losing her balance. The sword slips from her hand. The intruder quickly and expertly twists Aurora's arm, causing her to stumble to her knees. In the unlit stairwell she cannot see the person's face—a teen, not much older than her, judging by the figure's build, and he moves awkwardly, as though inexperienced in a fight. Whoever her attacker is, he has underestimated the princess's strength.

Anger laced with magic surges up in her blood, and Aurora manages to flip her opponent onto his stomach on the stairs. The figure pushes upward and back, bucking her off, and Aurora grabs one of his legs so that he cannot kick, then stiffens her other hand to swing at his neck. But he rears his covered head, causing both of them to lose their balance on the stairs and tumble, over and over each other, down to the next landing. Aurora fumbles for the extra blade hidden in her boot, but the figure—not very heavy at all, perhaps only a child?—is lying on top of her. She can feel his weight, feel bruises forming from the fall.

As she wriggles free, she yanks the hood off the figure.

Not a child. A woman.

Wren.

Aurora gasps, scrambling backward to the wall. "No," she murmurs. Then, realizing her voice is back, it comes more confidently. "No, Wren. I won't fight with you. Not again. I can't."

She sees now that Wren is heaving ragged breaths. Their tussle wore her out, and in the darkness, Aurora thinks she can see how flushed Wren's cheeks are from the exertion.

Her pulse leaps, no longer roused to defend herself but

because of Wren's nearness, the heat of her body where it clashed with hers. She can feel everything now. The pain in her back and knees. The tension in her shoulders, the twisting apprehension in her gut. The prickling along her skin. Wren's eyes look shocked and scared, but suddenly a smile tears across her face, in a flash of white teeth. "I'm not here to fight with you. I'm here to *stop* you from fighting."

"What?" Excitement, relief, and confusion battle for space in Aurora's head. "Why?"

"The kingdom needs you, Princess."

Aurora huffs. "Deluce needs every bit of muscle and blade it can get."

She doesn't know what Wren is doing here, how she made it back, or why the change of heart. She longs to reconnect with her, and even seeing her has caused some of that sinister magic pulsing within her to subside, and soften. But as the clamor outside only grows, Aurora's more certain than ever that she is needed, not here with Wren, but out there, where flaming arrows have begun to breech the parapets, where the foot soldiers have gathered behind the drawbridge, at the ready.

She stands up and attempts to push past Wren.

But Wren places her hands on Aurora's shoulders to stop her.

"You can't keep me from helping."

"Yes, I can," she says, with that quiet confidence Aurora has always found unnerving—and thrilling.

"I'm stronger than you are." The statement comes out like a dare. The return of her voice has gone to her head, and quickly.

"That may be so, but I know something you don't know. You may be the only person who can stop Malfleur."

Aurora stares at her, uncomprehending. "What do you mean?"

Wren swallows, and for the first time since accosting her in the stairwell, looks nervous. "I believe . . . I believe it is very possible that Queen Amélie was the Hart Slayer, and I have discovered that the Hart Slayer was a descendant of Belcoeur. If these things are true, it would mean that *you* are now the last living descendant of Belcoeur. As such, it must be your hand that deals the fatal blow to Malfleur. We have to protect you for that act, and that act alone. And besides . . ." She hesitates. "There are others who would see you dead before then. You must be careful."

"But . . ." Aurora squints at her, trying to take in this information. A shaft of light from a high window on the landing cuts across Wren's face, and Aurora can see the urgency written there. "But I already tried to kill her. I failed."

"I have a lot to tell you," Wren says simply.

"Does this mean . . ." Aurora's voice catches in her throat, and she struggles for a moment to speak. "Does this mean that you forgive me?"

Wren looks at her silently for a moment, studies her. Aurora feels pinned to the spot by Wren's dark eyes, which seem suddenly like portals into a dream Aurora can never know. For the first time in a long time, Aurora is afraid. Afraid that Wren cannot love her—not after all that she has done. How she tried to kill Wren, allowing the evil that had been gathering within her to take over, all in the desire to win, to hurt, to conquer. How she has failed her in almost every way.

Finally Wren lets out a breath and looks away, shaking her head. "I can't blame you for what you could not help."

It is not the outpouring of forgiveness Aurora had hoped for; nor is it the fear and hatred she might have expected. Aurora nods. "Tell me everything. I will listen."

She brings Wren back to her room, and as they settle onto her bed—not like old friends, exactly, but like how she imagines two soldiers must feel after they've fought side by side—she feels a zing of shock at how different this is from the last time the girl came to her room, stormy and cold, blaming her for the fall of Sommeil. Perhaps rightly.

Wren is usually right. That is one of the things Aurora has, in just a short time, grown to love about her. The word "love," just the thought of the word, sends warmth radiating through her.

But when Wren has finished her story, Aurora swallows hard, her joy at reconnecting suddenly plunged into ice water. "The curse . . . the stone . . ."

Wren nods. "Yes. It is you. It must be. You're the descendant of Belcoeur. You're the reason I'm dying."

Aurora gasps, still unwilling to believe it. "No. You can't

be dying. We've only just been reunited."

Suddenly she wants—needs—to touch her. To feel the stone, to understand. To feel the life behind and within it. Could she really be the cause of such a curse? It's too terrible to comprehend—the idea of Wren's life ending when it feels like everything is only just at the point of beginning.

There is so much still to share with Wren—so many stories, so many memories. She wants to tell it all with her mouth and her breath and when those are tired and wasted, she will tell it with her skin against Wren's.

But they may be out of time.

So instead, Aurora simply takes Wren's hand. There is a whole world between her palm and Wren's, she realizes—a world that feels bigger, full of more promise, than the real world and Sommeil put together.

She looks into Wren's eyes. "Let me fight, then. I can give my life to save yours." The words grate against her throat and she swallows hard, blinking down a sudden rise of emotion.

Wren lets go of her hand—a whoosh of coldness— mended, then, when her hand moves instead to Aurora's cheek. Aurora could swear she feels a flush of the dark magic given to her by Malfleur seeping out of her at that touch. Wren's breathing has become louder, labored, and Aurora suddenly wonders if it is because the stone has, already, begun to take over her lungs. Her lips are parted, just slightly. "Aurora," she whispers.

And though there is so much to say and everything

272

feels impossible, and though the castle is even now being bombarded from the outside, vibrations loudly thrumming through the walls, Aurora can think of nothing beyond this moment, beyond Wren's eyes, the seriousness in them, and something else too—something that matches what Aurora is feeling.

She meets Wren's lips with her own, sucks in a breath at the sudden rise of heat and pressure as Wren moves up against her, kissing her back. Aurora's hands become lost in Wren's hair, as though her hands are themselves two lovers running off into the woods.

When they pull apart, Wren carefully removes Aurora's armor, and Aurora shivers. An explosion ricochets outside the tower walls, and she feels it echo within her as Wren touches her bare skin. All the stories until now have failed her. She doesn't know what love is, or whether it is possible that it is anything other than the aching combination of touch and loss—but for the first time, she's convinced that she doesn't have to understand it.

———

They lie tangled together, the moment melting and seeping into a blur of moments, all of them urgent, until Aurora sits up with a rush of knowing.

She recalls the glass fox Malfleur commanded her to break. It was impossible—but why did Malfleur want to break it, and why couldn't she? Aurora had been so focused on her need to kill the evil queen that she hadn't thought much about it. But now the memory makes her think of the

Hart Slayer, who was said to have possessed magical glass objects. Arrowheads, if she's not mistaken.

"What is it?" Wren murmurs. There are tears at the corners of her eyes. Outside, the battle has still only just begun. It feels as though hours have passed when it can only have been minutes.

"The Hart Slayer may have been a woman, but she was not my mother," Aurora says. "I know it. Queen Amélie was many things, but she was not brave." An image comes back to her, of the queen in her dying days, lying in her bed, so cold and remote—how she failed to be everything Aurora hoped she'd be. "She had a weak constitution," Aurora says, "and preferred never to be outdoors."

Aurora knows the myth of the Hart Slayer. And by now she's heard too of the rumors of Isabelle's glass slipper.

"No, it was not *my* mother who was the Hart Slayer," Aurora repeats with more confidence. She begins to dress herself, putting her armor back on, knowing there is much to be done before they can consider giving up. "I'm not the descendant Deluce needs." Wren blinks at her in confusion, but for once, Aurora feels the strange kind of calm that comes with certainty. "But I think I know who is."

27

Gilbert

The castle yards are a swamp of mud that clings to the boots and weighs down soldiers already burdened under layers of steel and chain mail.

There is no need for cavalry, not in such close quarters. Malfleur's men have arrived at the walls, as Gilbert knew they would, on foot. As they thundered ever closer, archers have been picking apart their numbers. A wagon of supplies caught fire and spread among the opposition, stalling a large portion of the troops while the Delucian side scrambled to position and light the cannons. But the Vultures are fast. Even now, a faction have scaled the southernmost wall, and the sounds of high-pitched screaming, of metal meeting metal and flesh splitting, have grown only louder as the skirmish spreads.

Gilbert follows a small cohort in the direction of the breech, Prince William's battle cry ringing in his ears. *We do not go down without a fight.* The castle village is a maze of people running ammunition and supplies in zigzags, dodging flaming arrows, and sliding in the thick mud. *This is not a war of men, but a war of minds.* Already, aid workers are dragging the injured to safety, while fresh fighters launch out to meet their fate at the wall.

And Gilbert is one of these.

We fight not just for our land and our homes but for the freedom of our hearts and the liberty of our children.

The ground rattles with the release of another cannon—the blast resounding in Gilbert's ears, a black cloud of powder choking him, trapped and lingering in the humid air.

We fight because we believe in something better than this. Because the essence of good is to resist evil, or to die, over and over and over again, in the trying.

Gilbert coughs and stutters in the smoke and rain, wiping a smear of sweat from his eyes, trying to pick clear a path toward the violence. A wailing woman crashes into him, falling backward into the rain-soaked grass beside the forge. He helps her up and keeps running.

We die so that we may live.

He continues to dodge the onslaught of people moving in conflicting directions—those fleeing to safety, those flying toward the many-limbed mass of fighters on the ground, those racing to help support the men behind the barricades, the rain blurring all of it together. The palace has changed: there are more carts of weapons than trunks of silk, more soldiers than entertainers, no feast tables to crawl beneath but stores of precious rations stacked high inside the keep alongside a frantic gaggle of women and children.

Order governs among the trained soldiers, but only for a time. Untrained fighters join the fray, and everything becomes a weapon. Gilbert watches in mute horror as a red-faced baker, with a rolling pin in hand, races at a Vulture who has breached the wall. As the man swings, the Vulture—nearly a foot taller and, in his black mask, like the image of some unearthly demon—parries easily and, without a blink, takes off the baker's head with his broadsword. Blood sprays in all directions, like a firework.

Now that Gilbert is closer, he can see that part of the outer wall has actually *crumbled* and more Vultures are flowing over it like black tar. But before he can ponder the disaster, he is in it—bodies bashing into him, friend and foe alike. Shield lifted, he pushes through the combat to find a stance, easily taking down a Vulture with a kick to the knee and driving his blade at an angle just above the boot. One advantage to having *been* a Vulture is knowing all the strengths and weaknesses of their armor.

He swings backward into another Vulture and delivers an elbow to the neck, vulnerable just at the base of the mask, then uses his left-handed dagger to stab the man in the shoulder. A wasted move, as the soldier grimaces but launches himself on top of Gilbert.

Gil fights back, dirty, with his bare hands, which has always been his preferred style. He finds his way on top of the Vulture and rips off the man's mask. His startled face splatters with fresh pellets of rain as Gil's fist meets cheek-bone, nose, the bloody mass that was once an eye—over and over, hunched and sweating and drenched, deaf to the noise and movement around him, blind to everything but disgust at what he once was, and sees now in this man. A puppet. A mask. A soulless vessel for anger, for revenge.

He strikes the man for every time he delighted in Aurora's imprisonment. He strikes him again for every time he coveted the praise of Malfleur. And then, though the man has stopped breathing, he pulls the knife from the man's shoulder, with effort, and plunges it straight into the heart. That time was just for him, for the pain of everything he cannot even think, let alone say. For everything he has lost—and for everything he has *not* lost.

This is not his first kill. But it's his first as Gilbert, not a Vulture. And it leaves him aching all over, his ears ringing.

Someone grabs him by the arm and rips him off the dead, blood-soaked Vulture.

He turns, sword at the ready, full of righteous self-defense, only to realize that the person who lifted him up is none other than the prince of Aubin.

Defiance courses in Gil's veins, and all the hairs on his neck rise. This is the man who won Isbe's hand. Didn't he just lose the battle in La Faim? Didn't his cannon design backfire? If Deluce falls to Malfleur, it is Prince William who will be to blame, at least in the eyes of history.

But William is still holding him by the collar, and when their eyes meet, Gil sees something desperate and burning in them. William looks every bit the prince, with his impressive height and build, the proud cheekbones and thrust jaw, the gleaming dark skin and even blacker eyes. What is he doing here, on the ground? The prince should be keeping watch, somewhere safe. That is what royalty do, while it is the common folk who give all they have—their own bodies, their own sweat—to the fight. And a foreign prince, at that. He could be sitting on a cushy throne in Aubin if he wanted, far from the violence—but he is here, in the castle village, helping to stave off the most brutal and deadly attack in decades.

He is here to defend Deluce.

They both are.

Just then, another Vulture lunges at William from behind.

From the widening fear in Gil's eyes, William must sense the soldier's approach. He turns just in time, but the Vulture has slashed at the backs of his legs, and midspin, William falls to the mud.

Without thinking, Gil leaps over the prince in defense, staving off the Vulture's next blow while William gets to his knees.

"Can you stand?" Gil screams, unable to take his eyes off the Vulture to check on the prince. He ducks as the soldier swings feistily at him, and then Gil shoves his shield at the soldier, suddenly moved by the moment—moved by the need to protect the prince at all costs. His focus and drive have returned.

The Vulture is huge. He lumbers back with a growl that briefly unnerves Gil. Remembering the stunned reaction of the previous Vulture, Gil once again goes for the mask, knowing his advantage will be in revealing the man's face and making him vulnerable. Rain falls hard in his eyes, and Gil knows that one false move will leave him dead. It takes several tries, and he sustains a dizzying blow to the head and the gut, making him stumble and heave, before he slashes through the dense mask, tearing it off the man's face.

And then he realizes why the hulking figure is so terrifying.

He's the same man who was sent in to fight Aurora, gladiator style, in LaMorte—and almost killed her. The one the queen called off before he could finish the job. He is no Vulture at all, but another one of the queen's vicious pets. And Gilbert has witnessed his strength.

But the man, the monster, isn't after Gil—doesn't seem to recognize him, or if he does, to care. No, he is after William. The prince. The prize.

They all are. Gil takes in with horror the flood of soldiers—four more Vultures gathering around them now, surrounding him and the prince. They are outnumbered, and William has only just now limped to standing, but he looks like he's on the brink of collapse. Blood pours from his knees down into his boots, which look bloated with blood and rain. If those wounds fester, the prince will die. Gil feels like he's going to be sick, but there's no time to react.

Malfleur's monster tosses his wild, sand-colored hair and roars like an unleashed beast. Removing his mask doesn't seem to have softened him at all.

Gil thrusts his sword, terror becoming action, even as he sees from the corner of his eye that the prince has engaged one of the other approaching Vultures.

The man is powerful, and wild. Too wild. Gil thinks of Freckles, the mare no one could tame but Isbe. He realizes his opponent's wildness could be Gil's way in. He is disordered, has no real training. Like any wild animal, he might be skittish, hungry, and reactive. Gil feels that, even as the soldier lifts up his war hammer and swings.

Gil barely dodges, then leaps at him, ramming his shoulder into the man's side to unbalance him, then trying to drive a halberd up through the armpit opening in his armor—but he's not strong or fast enough, and the man throws him off into the mud. Gil scrambles, frantically scanning the mayhem for a distraction.

He sees the prince is down again, a Vulture on top of him, and Gil rolls to his side, dropping his sword and lunging on top of both men, grabbing the Vulture by his cape and flinging him off Prince William. But just as soon as he has that Vulture restrained, Malfleur's special soldier comes at him, grinning scarily. Gil is weaponless, but lifts up the struggling Vulture he grabbed, like a shield. The monster launches his weapon at the Vulture Gil is holding—straight at the Vulture's face—instantly killing one of his own. The man has no allegiance.

The Vulture slumps, his weight now yanking Gil off-balance. He shoves the dead man to the side as the prince leaps up and tackles the monstrous soldier from behind. The soldier roars again, swinging around as the prince's arms wrap around his throat.

And then time seems to slow as a word carries toward the men on the wind.

"Heath?" A woman's voice, somehow both soft and piercing.

A startled look comes over the monstrous man as he makes eye contact with whoever cried out his name.

And that pause is all it takes. Gil finds his sword in the mud and slashes it across Heath's middle.

Heath falls.

Gil throws himself on top of Heath, flipping Heath onto his back and holding him down while the prince pulls a dagger from his boot and plunges it through Heath's neck, sending a fountain of blood up onto the prince's mouth and chin, dripping down his chest, as though he has just coughed it up himself. Gil too is covered in Heath's blood, but there is no time to process, because the other three Vultures are flying at them at once.

And then something strange happens. Their grimaces

all seem to freeze on their faces as a flickering sound whizzes over Gil's head.

All at once, the three of them drop to the ground, and Gil sees a series of tiny darts—poisoned, presumably—sticking out of the necks of the Vultures.

There is a clearing. He turns to see a woman with long black hair and skin the color of new leather, bedecked in men's armor. It's the girl Aurora refused to kill for Malfleur. She runs to Heath's side, bending over his blood-drenched body, weeping. The prince is still kneeling nearby, looking dizzy. He is losing his own blood rapidly.

Through the thicket of bodies and blood spray, he sees Aurora, not far behind the girl.

"Aurora!" Gil cries out, and she runs to him. "Here, take his side." Then, "We need to get you out of here," Gil says to the prince.

Aurora and Gil grab the prince underneath his arms.

William shakes his head. "I am needed."

Gil looks into Aurora's silent eyes, then back at the prince. "You are not meant to die here. Come."

He and Aurora heave him up to standing. There is so much pain in the prince's eyes, Gil can hardly face him. The man looks broken.

"Wait," William says, staring at the spread of violence—the tangle of bodies, the shouts of men attacking, and the screams of men falling.

It seems hopeless, and Gil knows if they don't hurry,

they are going to die—and so will everyone in the castle village.

More Vultures pour over the wall on the south side.

Despair threatens to strangle Gil—images of his mother and father, his brother and his brother's children, flash before his eyes. All the faces he will never see again. Deluce is going to fall. It's over. It's all over.

And then the prince is gasping in his arms, and he turns his attention back to William and Aurora.

But the prince isn't gasping, he is shouting. The din has become so loud around them that Gil can hardly hear, and he leans closer.

"I have an idea," the prince says.

28

William,

Once Merely the Third Prince of Aubin,
Now Both Crown Prince of Aubin and King Consort of Deluce

He can't feel his legs. Men—Delucian men—fall from the walls, shot down by Malfleur's forces on the other side. All around him, men are dying. Technically, they are his men.

Someone is dragging him, a young man close to his age. And Princess Aurora, on his other side. Where has she come from? It is as though she has emerged from some storybook, but playing the role of a different character. Maybe he is dreaming.

Darkness clouds his vision, making him light-headed. The world goes mute and black.

He is a boy again, and his brother Edward has just smashed his latest model against a wall, putting a crack in the marble. Philip, the oldest, is off somewhere studying: removed, cold. There is no one to defend William. He runs to his father, the king, showing him the broken model. Not the cannon design—that would come later, and meet a similar fate—but an earlier model he'd molded to resemble a ship.

The fleet. *Where is the fleet? Has no one come to help him?*

"Will you tell Eddie he must fix it?" the young prince asks.

His father looks at the object and then at his son. "William. You will face many setbacks in your life. It is your job to see the victory in failure."

William forces his eyes open, forces his mind to focus and his breath to speak. "I have an idea," he says to the young man carrying him.

The cannons. The faulty cannons, of his own design. The ones that brought him so much shame just weeks ago because they backfired, exploding on his own men, decimating a huge fraction of his forces and causing them to have to retreat midbattle, even as Malfleur unleashed a wicked fire that melted their weapons at first touch.

He has several more of these cannons stored in the armory—the relics of his most epic failure yet.

See the victory in failure.

They need to staunch the flow of the offense—a wound leaking inward like an infection. What they need, in fact, is an explosion from within.

There is no time to lose.

He sounds the command.

29

Isabelle

By some miracle—and a series of explosions that left both sides devastated—the Delucian castle has fended off a siege, but scouts say more troops from LaMorte are on their way, camped less than a day's ride from the castle. If the castle falls to Malfleur, the war is as good as lost. The news reaches Isbe and Byrne even as they hasten back across the choppy waves of the North Sea. Everything adds to her remorse, from the angry thrashing of the waves to the barking of geese veering overhead as their ship makes port in one of the small, secret harbors amid the Delucian caves, known only to the military—and, of course, those who build their childhoods on eavesdropping, such as Isbe.

She berates herself every step of the way, as she and Byrne

disembark and find the treacherous switchback path up the side of the cliffs. She shouldn't have left William to defend the kingdom—*her* kingdom. She shouldn't have refused the Ice King's offer.

She did learn one thing: that her mother was the Hart Slayer. But that changes nothing. How she wishes that it mattered. How she wishes she could see Aurora one last time, before all of this is over. These wishes are so strong, she cannot resist them as she usually does, can't tamp down the feeling that rises within her, a burning all along her bones, painful almost to the brink of shattering.

She misses her sister. She is afraid.

———

They have hardly surmounted the bluffs when they are accosted by soldiers and dragged through the castle village. She has no will to protest, and they are not interested in listening anyway.

Isbe can hear and sense the devastation—the lingering smoke and the bitter taste of burnt oil in the air, and beneath that, the rotten stench of death. It's like the sleeping sickness all over again, but so much worse. There is an eerie quiet— not stillness, but movements that are deliberate and laden with sadness: the slow turn of cart wheels passing awkwardly around rubble. Unstable structures still in the final throes of collapse, dust lifting from crumbled stone.

And carried on the wind, the faint weeping of women and children, some in the keep, some tending to husbands and fathers, some scattered, disorganized, moaning, and lost.

Battles are brief, she knows, but the aftermath . . .

She and Byrne are brought before the prince.

"Do you not recognize your own princess? Let her go," William says when Isbe and Byrne enter his study.

Dimly, she registers Byrne's gasp as she rushes toward William, not caring what she may stumble over or bump into on the way. But to her surprise, Byrne stops her, gently taking her arms.

"Miss. *Highness.* He isn't well."

Isbe pauses. "What?" And then dread floods her. "What happened? William?"

"I'm fine," says the prince. His velvet voice is just a few feet away, and she reaches out to him, confused. "It's just . . ." He sighs, and she feels another tremor of uncertainty.

"What happened?" she repeats.

"My legs."

Isbe sucks in a breath and falls to her knees before him, resting her head on his lap. "No."

"It was them or me," he says, in that rustling way that suggests an almost laugh. He brushes hair out of her face and thumbs a tear she hadn't realized was there from the corner of her eye.

"What are we to do?" She is not asking about his recovery, but about Deluce.

"We drove them back, but the solution was only temporary. They will return to finish what they started. And . . . I received a letter." He clears his throat, his voice dropping low. "From my brother Edward."

Isbe startles. "But—"

William lets out a sigh. "He is alive. But as I've said before, my relationship with my brothers was always . . . complicated. I have only just learned that my middle brother, Edward, plotted the death of our elder brother, Philip. He staged his own death to make it look like a double murder, in part to stoke tensions between Deluce and Aubin. You see, he did it all . . ." He pauses, obviously having difficulty admitting the truth. "He did it all for the favor of Queen Malfleur."

Isbe shakes her head. It can't be true. She can't imagine anyone betraying his own brother, but especially not a brother like William.

"There is no fleet coming," William goes on. "Edward has commandeered the military and cut off the flow of supplies. Aubin is now cooperating with LaMorte."

Now anger replaces disbelief. "But we must write back to him, urge him to understand the grave mistake he has made—"

"Isabelle." Wiliam's voice sounds like it is going to break, and something in her snaps.

"No. No, William, this is not over." Now it's *her* voice that's breaking.

"At dawn, we evacuate everyone we can. There will be

several ships waiting to bring safe passage to Aubin. You will be on one of them, and so will I."

"So we're just giving up?"

"We're saving as many lives as possible."

A storm churns in her chest. "No."

"Isabelle," he says more gently. "We're at the end."

We're at the end. He said it to her once before, in the wine caves. The night he proposed to her for a second time. The night he touched her and awoke something in her that she thought wasn't possible. She hadn't ever allowed herself to love, or to want love—because she thought it would make the not having only more painful. She always hated that terrible wish—any wish at all. Wishes give her a physical pang, like a shock, a dizzying reminder of their futility, like the one she felt earlier, when she wished to see Aurora again.

And then . . . William cracked her open anyway; made a fine, nearly invisible fissure in her shell that would change everything. She let him. She let love in. She agreed to step up, to take on the mantle. To rule by his side.

And now, this is what it all comes to.

We are at the end. The last time he said it, they had really only just been at the very beginning. But this time it's different.

"I'm not leaving Deluce," she says, rising. "You may flee with the others if you wish. You may bring them to safety. But I will stay."

"I can't leave you behind," he protests.

"You can," she says, and when she says it, the fissure in

her heart grows deeper, and something even harder to get to begins to shake and crumble. Maybe something like her spirit, or her soul. She bends down to him in his chair, and takes his face in her hands. So strong, so determined, so stubborn. She loves every single thing about him. She kisses him, her lips taking in the salt of tears that have trickled down his face. "You can," she says again, pulling away. "And you will."

He is silent for a moment, and then says only, "Your sister needs to speak to you. She and Wren say it is urgent."

"My sister?" She feels a wave of shock and rocks backward, away from his touch. "Aurora is here?" She steps back, dizzy with the thought of it. "But she said—" Her voice drops off in William's silence. Realization splashes over her like hot water. Aurora never went off to make a life with Heath. "She lied."

In that moment, something else occurs, a kind of tingly pleasure pulsing through her. It's almost—*almost*—as though her desperate wish when she disembarked her ship has come true. Of course that's impossible. Nothing ever comes of wishing.

Does it?

William takes her hand and puts it to his face again, then kisses her open palm. "Go and see her," he says.

———

Aurora is in the library, which is now full of injured soldiers on makeshift cots. The contrast between the heroic tales shelved here and the reality of war at their fingertips is not lost on Isabelle, and she pauses for a moment, reconciling to it. She thinks too of the frozen library in King Verglas's palace, a room full of histories and ideas and contradictions, a room radiant with light and yet frigid with ice. Here, now, there are no ideas at all. Philosophies and pasts don't matter—it is all blood and bodies, needs and tasks and action.

Isbe stands out of the way and waits for Aurora to notice her. The old Isbe would have bashed through the busy room and made her presence undeniable, would have sought out Aurora the way she sought out everything in the world—arms first, then chest, then mind. But this Isbe is different. She hugs the wall with her back, feels herself becoming shadow. *The shadow is the child, and the child is the shadow.*

She clutches the ice slipper still in the inner pocket of her cloak. She doesn't feel reassured by it. She feels nothing. The world is upside down. Aurora, who she thought had run off to find love, to live her own life and her own story, is not who she thought she was. Aurora, who has always been the one solid thing she can hold on to in this world, has become yet another mystery. She was always Isbe's light—and what is a shadow without its light?

As she waits, Isbe feels more and more invisible, as though she is disappearing, or folding inward. All of her life, she has had to be strong, and somehow that made it easy to be so. Until now.

And then, gentle hands find her shoulders, sweep down

her arms, and wrap her in an embrace.

The crisp softness of Aurora that used to signify, in Isbe's mind, her beauty, is gone. She has grown firm and taut, muscular. She is still shorter than Isbe, but her long hair no longer smells of peaches and sun-drenched fields. Instead it carries the faint medicinal scent of the room, of bitter herbs used to cure and staunch wounds, of sweat and blood and metal.

Beneath those, there's a smell that is all her own, something that reminds Isbe of a warm summer evening.

Relief is a new current of breath in Isbe's chest. She *is* still Aurora—changed and yet not.

Isbe hugs her back.

And as she does, something inside her breaks open.

Isabelle, Aurora taps into her palms, but Isbe is shuddering, her face wet with tears. She's too overwhelmed to reply. She doesn't even know why she's crying—can't put words to it.

Aurora leads her out of the library in a huddle and takes her back to her old childhood room, the one she slept in for eighteen years before moving into the royal chambers with William.

Isabelle, what's wrong? Aurora taps again.

Isbe goes to her old window, the one where the garden trellis used to hang. The one through which she ran away a few short months ago.

Too many things are wrong. There is nowhere to start: that she only discovered her mother's identity after she was

294

already dead. That the war has come to this. That evil will win, despite everything. That she has spent all this time striving in vain to save Deluce—and so much time away from the one person who mattered the most to her in the world.

"You lied," is all she can finally muster.

Aurora takes her hand again. *I had to. You would have come after me otherwise. You would have tried to stop me from what I had to do. I had to try, Isbe. I had to try on my own to do the right thing—without you.*

"But what did you do? Where did you go?"

Aurora takes a breath, and then taps. *I went to see Malfleur. I tried to kill her.*

Isbe gasps, her emotion dipping to make space for shock. "But—but I could have come with you. We could have done it together." Why does saying this cause her so much hurt, so much embarrassment, that she wants to cry all over again?

You had much to do here, without me, Aurora points out. *And you would have wanted to protect me.*

Isbe realizes her mouth is gaping open, and clamps it shut. Because what can she say? Aurora is absolutely right. She would have gone after her. She would have stopped her. She would have tried to save her. Over and over and over again. Of course she would have. It was her job. Without that job, what good was Isbe? What good *is* she?

Anyway, Aurora taps on, *it didn't work*. She goes on to explain everything—what really became of Heath, and how the other prisoners remain trapped, still, in LaMorte, in Malfleur's dungeon. She tells Isbe of her contract with

Malfleur, and too of her feelings for Wren—fraught with confusion but realer than anything she has ever experienced before.

Isbe listens in a mix of fascination, awe, and something else—a raw sting in her throat that borders on resentment. Aurora has grown so brave, has come into herself, while Isbe has become a kind of shell.

She begins to pull her hands away. The story is too layered and too much. She needs to be alone.

But Aurora takes her hands more firmly than before, and taps again. *You must not despair, Isbe*, she insists. *We need you now more than ever.*

"Now more than ever? Haven't you heard, Aurora? War's over. Malfleur won. We leave at dawn."

"No," someone else says, coming into the room. "No, we don't leave. Not if Aurora's plan works."

It takes a second for Isbe to recognize the voice. The girl from Sommeil. Wren. "What plan?" she asks cautiously.

Aurora begins to tap an explanation, but she stumbles—there are not enough words in their secret language to say whatever it is she wants to say. *You are the heart*, she taps. *You are the hunter's daughter.*

"I don't understand."

Wren steps into the room and closes the door. "Your mother was the Hart Slayer."

"I know that now," Isbe says slowly.

"Some of the fae have reason to suspect the Hart Slayer

was a descendant of the faerie queen Belcoeur," Wren explains, her voice crystal and bell-like in Isbe's stunned silence. "And it is a descendant of Belcoeur who will save us all from Malfleur."

"But . . ." Isbe flounders. She wants to protest, but there's a tiny spark of hope in her chest that flares at these words, at a feeling of truth and possibility in them. *The shadow is the child, and the child is the shadow.* There is only one story, and it is every story, braided together into a single cord.

Still, how is it possible that *she* is destined to kill Malfleur? "I don't know. I don't know anything anymore," she says, pulling away from Aurora and sitting down on the edge of her old bed. "I don't even know myself." The words drag through her throat, and she is afraid she is going to cry. She doesn't want to cry again. Tomorrow may be her last day, and she doesn't want to die like this—weak and frightened.

But I know you, Aurora insists, taking her hand once again and sitting down beside her. *You are the brave and wild Isabelle. The one who always risks everything for the good of others, and never for herself. You have always sought your role in other people's stories, but when will you step into your role at the heart of yours?*

"But I *did*," Isbe counters. "I am queen of Deluce! I married Prince William. How much more central could I be? And still it's not enough."

Aurora taps gently. *Maybe that was just you playing my*

role. Maybe your story is different.

Isbe pulls away. "I need to be alone."

Aurora hugs her again, and then she and Wren step out of the room.

———

That night, Isbe lies awake, bereft, like a tiny ship floating out in the wide sea, with no land in sight. Just the vault of stars above and blackness all around. She reaches underneath her pillow, where she has stowed the slipper of winter glass. It's so tiny, she suddenly realizes it could have belonged to a child. She doesn't know why the thought has never occurred to her before.

The shadow is the child, and the child is the shadow. Her mother's voice moves through her mind, bringing strands of the lullaby—no words now, just the melody, both mournful and soothing.

She knows she doesn't need the slipper anymore. Doesn't need to know its secrets.

She needs to let go, to say good-bye.

But instead, she holds it close to her chest, feeling its iciness prick through her clothes to her skin. The slipper may not have any real story to tell her—but it is still her last connection to her mother.

Every story, she sees now, is different depending on who's telling it, anyway. Malfleur is the villain in Aurora's tale, but the hero in many others. Just like the two versions of the rose lullaby—the one everyone knows, in which

Malfleur kills Belcoeur, and the one she learned from her mother, Cassandra, who learned it, perhaps, from *her* mother, Isbe's grandmother, who was, maybe—if Aurora and Wren are right—the daughter of Belcoeur herself. In that other version, the sisters were friends, and played together until *darkness did win the light from the day.*

Isbe knows Aurora's right—she needs to stop chasing other people's stories. But what is her own? She recalls once again what it felt like when she first lost her vision—how she desperately needed a hand to pull her out of the darkness, needed someone to make her believe in the world again. She *is* that little girl now, lost and scared in the unknowable expanse, while Aurora, just a baby, cries silently, unaware of what has happened to Isbe, caught up in the bubble of her own world. From that day on, she has always thought it was up to her to keep Aurora safe.

But the day her sight was tithed—that was Aurora's christening. It was Aurora's day, the beginning of *her* story. Isbe's own tale had begun before then. She had been abandoned, left behind by her real mother, to run wild, abused and neglected by her father and stepmother, until Gil found her and became her first friend. *That* is Isbe's story. That is who she is.

She knows now: *she* must be the one to give herself a hand up and out.

She must step forward, blindly, into that darkness once more.

She must try.

To kill Malfleur.

Luckily, Aurora has a plan—the thought of it glows before Isbe, lighting up the night, crystal and pure, like ice. But it is not ice at all; it is a guiding star. And in its glow, she begins to see herself again.

30

Malfleur,
the Last Faerie Queen

Blackbirds take up the first chorus, swirling overhead in the remaining dark. Malfleur steps through the fields' tall, sparse weeds, all a predawn gray that pretends at silver.

For a moment, as dew vanishes at her fingertips, the faerie queen wonders if she is dreaming.

But that is impossible, because she does not dream. Her twin stole that power from her before either of them were born, sucked it out of her heart.

Malfleur has always wondered whether Belcoeur also absorbed some of Malfleur's magical gift; if that's why magic always flowed so easily through her fingertips, like the gold thread she spun.

For Malfleur, magic has always been so wrought, so

hard won. It is not a natural grace but an unholy gathering of everything unnatural, a knotted and dense thing, tangled and burning and immortal. It feeds on death.

Her father once told her of a theory that dying stars draw in the light from surrounding stars and become an ever-expanding hole of darkness that is both self-devouring and self-sustaining. That is exactly what Malfleur's magic is: desperate to destroy, and thus to thrive.

The morning's post-rain wet clings to her skirts, weighing them down, but still she feels intoxicated, immortal, as though she might take off soaring as she pushes away from the war camp, where her soldiers rest and plot and strengthen, awaiting the next round of supplies, readying themselves for another attack. This time, the castle will easily be theirs. They've put a stranglehold on Deluce's prize, and there is now no way out but into the mouth of death. Onto the waiting blades of her soldiers' lances.

The final siege will come. But first Malfleur must meet her pet eye to eye, must reclaim her. She gave Aurora a taste of her own magic, and now, no matter how far the princess runs or where she tries to hide, there's a thread that binds them together.

She clutches the message she received last night.

Meet me where dawn breaks on the cliffs.

Perhaps they will duel, or perhaps Aurora will simply beg for her forgiveness. Perhaps all of this—Aurora's escape and now her invitation—is part of an invisible dance. Malfleur can feel the thread between them thrumming with a faint vibration, tugging her onward, closer and closer to the palace of Deluce.

She hasn't been here, to her childhood home, in sixteen years. Not since Aurora's christening, when she cursed the baby princess in a way that now strikes Malfleur as almost whimsical. She had not foreseen then that by cursing Aurora with the promise of death, what would actually occur would be a kind of gift—that the princess would become *hers*.

Aurora was a far more successful experiment than her other human pet, the one called Heath. His mind had been too brutish, too masculine, too narrowly defined, whereas Aurora's was a wide-open landscape, fertile with possibility.

She will have her back, and soon. She longs to stroke her beautiful hair and teach her new things, to watch her talents blossom and her magic spark into magnificent flame all around them. She cannot be very upset with Aurora for breaking free—she designed her to be untamable, didn't she?

The palace rises up before her, piercing the still-dark sky. Fog wraps itself around the castle, smoke curling through it like a long-lost twin. For some reason, Malfleur thinks of that old lullaby, the one she created to spread the story of her dominance over her sister. *One night reviled, before break of morn . . . the shadow and the child together were born.*

The wooden barricades are splashed in scarlet, blackened from fire. Bodies lie everywhere, a massive blanket of masks and bloodstained iron shields. Malfleur must pick her way through them, even as a vulture flies overhead, tilting, ready to drop and scavenge.

This place has changed greatly since she lived in it—and nearly all of its secret passages have been blocked in with plaster. But a little plaster is nothing to her magic. When she reaches one of the secret entrances—known only to those familiar with the castle a hundred years ago, when it was at the height of its glory—she presses her hands against it and shuts her eyes.

The plaster crumbles under her touch. The past dissolves back into the present. She winds her way inside.

—————

Aurora is waiting for her at the exact spot along the cliffs that Malfleur expected—a narrow promontory on the north-eastern bluff. She's standing on the ledge looking out over the Strait of Sorrow, her pale gown and light hair billowing gracefully in the breeze; the first spark of sun outlines her silhouette in gold.

The princess turns at her approach, as if she has in fact sensed her coming, just as Malfleur has followed her senses here to find her. She can feel that the magic has lessened and faded in Aurora, but still it's there, a quiet pulse, battering and flapping like a fallen dove. She will scoop it up in her hands; she will fix it. She will get the formula right this time.

Queen, Aurora says with her mind, or her eyes, or her body—or perhaps with her magic. Malfleur isn't sure when she began to "hear" Aurora, who still cannot speak. It happened seamlessly.

"I'm here," Malfleur says soothingly.

You said you cannot be killed except by the hand of one of your own blood.

"That is true. I am protected. I cannot die."

I wonder, then, what would happen if I leaped over the edge, her eyes say. The wind gusts, lifting Aurora's hair, revealing her long, thin neck. It is a strange question.

"I would leap after you," Malfleur answers calmly.

And?

"And we would fly."

Something changes in the princess's face—at first, Malfleur believes it is a flicker of excitement, that the word "fly" has touched something in the princess's soul, has made her understand what they can be together, what Malfleur can *make* her. But then the queen sees that it is not excitement or joy. She could swear now that what she reads on Aurora's face is in fact sadness.

Or pity.

Fear seizes Malfleur's chest. She feels something radiating out of Aurora—it is magic, an offshoot of her own, but she has no control over it. It belongs to the princess, and it is icy cold, and powerful. It is like an invisible shield, and the queen suddenly realizes that perhaps all this time she has *not* been understanding Aurora's words, has not been speaking with her at all, but speaking instead with her own imagination. The real Aurora stands before her, but not the one Malfleur wants her to be. Not the projection of herself.

A princess. A stranger. Her hair gold and dancing

upward over the cliffs, like a flame.

And the queen knows, with a terrible suddenness, that this flame must be snuffed. She lunges toward her.

But Aurora ducks and rolls out of the way, revealing something—no, someone—who stood behind her like a shadow.

Malfleur halts, confused, as the shadow comes to life.

She squints between Aurora and the girl, realizing that she is the bastard daughter of the king. She has never laid eyes on Isabelle before, but has heard the rumors of how she has traveled Deluce, trying to rally the peasantry against Malfleur. Understanding dawns on the queen now—this is some kind of trap. Aurora lured her here with purpose.

But what purpose?

She looks at Isabelle's face, broad and angular and animated, and then she gives a quiet gasp. The eyes, unseeing, are familiar somehow. She could swear they are Belcoeur's eyes, except that they do not lock with her own in mutual recognition. The girl is blind.

Malfleur wants to laugh. If this is a trap, it is dismally disappointing. Without further thought, her dagger slides from its hilt at her belt and fits at home in her fist. She swirls toward Isabelle in one fluid motion, launching the knife toward the blind girl's heart. A look of uncertainty crosses Isabelle's face, and then she counters Malfleur's blow with something in her hand. Malfleur stumbles and sees that she has parried with a glass object. No. Ice?

It has been carved, if she's not mistaken, in the shape of a delicate shoe.

The queen nearly laughs as she swivels and lunges a second time with the dagger, but once again, Isabelle, without being able to see her, meets her blade with the glass slipper, which does not shatter. The third time, the queen puts her magic into it, and her thrust is too powerful for Isabelle to block. The shoe flies from the girl's hands and catches the light of the day that has burst open over the water. Malfleur, fixated with the need to know what it is, fumbles to catch the sparkling slipper, letting her own knife fall to the ground.

As the shoe meets the queen's open palms, it instantly begins to melt, and Malfleur finds herself frozen in its reflection, her own face disappearing, giving way to something else—a flurry of fractured images. Breathlessly, her whole body goes hot and cold as she is pulled into the ice, into the reflections, into a story of a different time and a different place, and some distant part of her understands with sudden clarity: this is winter glass.

Her father spoke of it once.

No, he is speaking of it now.

He is bending over her, and she is on her knees in snow, weeping. But she is not herself, she is Belcoeur, her sister, and younger, the age she was when she retreated forever into Sommeil.

She is her twin and she is sobbing into the snow, begging

her father to help her, to help *them*. It would be wrong to bring the child with her where she plans to go—it would be a kind of death. And besides, she cannot bear to look at the child, the little girl, her own daughter, who bears such a strong resemblance to Charles.

"Father, help me," she begs.

And so he does. The old, white-bearded king tells her about winter glass. "Take me to the child," he says, and she leads him back across the snowy woods to the little cottage. Hunting season has long passed, and the forest is quiet, empty of travelers.

Inside the cottage, a little girl is curled up in her bed in a nursery room, watched over by a maid called Oshannah. A candle flickers by the side of the bed. The girl is not even three years old, and has only just begun to speak.

"Mama," she says. "It is too cold to sleep. Read me a story."

She—Malfleur, who is Belcoeur, who is dead and yet not dead—reads her daughter a story. A tale she wrote herself, about a pair of sisters named Daisy and Marigold, who play in the tall fields until the sunlight is swallowed whole by the dark of night. The little girl yawns and flutters her eyes closed, beginning to sleep, to dream.

"Father," Belcoeur whispers to King Verglas. "She deserves to be free. She would never be free with me in Sommeil. But what can I do to keep her safe from Malfleur?"

The king tells her to go out and break the scrim of ice

over the well, then to draw a bucket of water.

When she returns, shivering from the cold, King Verglas takes the bucket and pours it, very slowly, almost tenderly, over the young girl's sleeping form. He mumbles to himself as he pours, and she can feel the magic of his words, of the story of this moment. The moment *becomes* the water, freezing it into a full-body armor of winter glass, including skirts and two dainty little slippers. He even fashions the child a satchel of unbreakable arrowheads, all while the girl remains asleep.

"As long as she is in possession of this armor," he says, "she will be safe. The ice holds the secret of her identity inside it—the memory of you as her mother. Now no one can know who she is—not even herself—and so she can never be found, except to be found by herself."

It is another riddle—King Verglas is fond of them, she knows, and a beat of fear passes through her, becoming regret on the other side. Has she made a mistake? It is too late to ask, and too late to ever know. She must leave, at once. Sommeil awaits her. A world where none of this pain exists. A world where Charles was never killed, where she never loved him to begin with. A world where her sister never broke her heart.

She kisses the girl on the forehead one last time, and in that kiss, Belcoeur, who is Malfleur, who is witnessing the entire history of the winter-glass armor in a single moment, feels the fluid and fleeting passage of time under her cold lips, and sees the daughter wake and step out of her armor, no longer remembering her own name. The girl has no recollection of Belcoeur, either. Still, the girl keeps the armor with her always, as a relic of a past she can't recall. The girl grows up to have her own daughter, whom she names Cassandra, and to whom she passes on what remains of the armor and arrows.

She raises Cassandra in obscurity, and Cassandra uses every single one of the ice arrowheads in her hunts, so that by the time she has met and fallen in love with King Henri, she knows not who she is or where she came from or that she is in fact part fae, and has given up almost every piece of winter glass that might reveal the secret. All she knows of her past is what she has left of her mother, and *her* mother before her: one tiny glass slipper, no bigger than a child's.

———

Though the knowledge contained in the winter glass has poured over her in an instant—an instant that felt like years—it was just enough time for Isabelle to seize the advantage. Malfleur's mind clears, her hands and arms drenched in melted ice, just as Isabelle pulls out a real sword hidden beneath her cloak, and plunges it through Malfleur's chest.

The blade meets her flesh, and in her last gasp, Malfleur feels the love that Belcoeur felt toward her, the love she felt toward the daughter she was forced to leave behind, the hope that Malfleur would one day forgive her, and above all, the heartbreak of knowing she would not.

Malfleur seizes, going stiff. Her eyes fly upward, and she sees only fog, only nothingness. There is no final wisdom, no final redemption, no final good-bye. There is no glory—a wellspring of beautiful magic dies with her.

Her breath goes, brilliantly and suddenly, like a light blown out.

She falls.

31

Isabelle

Timing is everything. Isbe, if anyone, should know that.

And still she wasn't prepared for the suddenness of Malfleur's death.

It was as though her dagger had cut a rent through time itself, and everything froze.

Even when the last remaining faerie queen fell to the ground, lifeless, and Isabelle was able to think clearly again, it still seemed as though time was moving more slowly than normal, like mist over water, twinning itself, every moment doubled and rippling.

The Vultures camped in the fields beyond the castle grounds were dismantled from whatever spell of magic the queen had forced over them, and awoke in a great confusion, removing their masks and scratching their heads, splashing cold stream water onto their faces and looking into it for some sign of who they were. Many could not recall their own names.

It was enough of a delay for William to rally one last bout of Delucian soldiers beyond the wall, but the day did not end in mass slaughter, for when the Delucian soldiers arrived at the site and took in the scene, they were struck by its innocence. Many of the unmasked enemy were revealed to be but young boys, lost and trying to find their way home—and those who were men, well, some of them were still full of directionless fury. The conflict was not without further bloodshed, but Deluce regained significant advantage and, in the end, drove off the last of Malfleur's former puppets. Her army was shown for what it had always been: one giant and dreadful enchantment.

It was an illusion that will leave many broken—for there are many who believed in Malfleur's message, who still thought she was going to make them all knights, going to restore a kind of power and privilege they could not access in this life. Many will not appreciate the return to reality, Isbe knows. The world is not a pleasant place for everyone in it. She learned that much, has seen it, even though she cannot see.

She recalls the stops she and William once made along the Veiled Road—servants willing to rally and support her mission even before she became queen. But she recalls too the many towns where she was unwelcome on her tour as their new queen, where she was accused of being an imposter—or worse, seen as just another aristocrat asking for more and more and more from people who had nothing left to give.

She had come for their men, and though huge numbers signed up willingly to fight for Deluce, many also lost their lives for a kingdom that has seldom if ever come around to earning that allegiance.

She doesn't know if she can fix it all, or even some of it. She doesn't know if anything she can do will ever be enough.

But she knows one thing with utter certainty: she can try.

———

And that is what she's going to tell William when she finds him to say good-bye.

He's packing a trunk, and she comes up behind his chair, puts her hand on his shoulder. He turns and pulls slightly away.

"I love you," she says. The words fly out of her like freed birds. It is perhaps the first and only time she has said it plainly.

Silence.

"Then why?" A question raw with hurt—it reopens the pain in her too.

Why? Does she really have an answer?

She *could* go with him, as he has begged her so many

times to do. Travel to Aubin and help him combat the rise of his brother Edward, attempt to prevent civil war from breaking out. She could leave Aurora here to run Deluce on her own, or perhaps with Wren's help.

"Because that's not my story," she says.

"But it could be."

"I love my sister. I love my kingdom. I love you too, but I don't want to have to choose."

"And yet you *have* chosen," he says. And then, "I will still love you, Isabelle. From afar. Not being beside you won't change that. I haven't given up."

"Good," she says. Then she takes his hand, and places it on her belly, where she feels a tiny stirring, perhaps nascent or perhaps only imagined. "Don't ever give up on us."

She puts her forehead against his, and they stay that way, breathing timidly, as if too violent a movement would separate them finally and forever. He does not kiss her, though she can feel his desire to, the heat of him, his intense gaze and his serious chin and his careful hands and the hurt that has chiseled him into the man she has fallen in love with. And she understands why he doesn't. It would be too much. Already this moment is too much—it contains its own ending, as every moment does.

———

But this is not, she understands now, the ending of *her* story. It is evening. She stands on the parapets of the palace— where until recently she and Aurora used to seek escape and spy on the council meetings—listening to the roar and rage of the strait below, the rustle and slap of sails as the prince's ship sets off for Aubin.

That—her ending—is something that must still be discovered and created, cut and polished and sized and honed just like the Delucian sapphires that, she once learned, came out of the ground rough and dark and covered in dirt. Mined by the very people who fought and bled for this kingdom.

And though Isabelle has vowed to stop positioning herself in anyone else's story, a question still remains that keeps her awake at night. If she *is* Belcoeur's descendant, doesn't that mean that she's part fae, and capable of ruling in her own right? The fae all have magic that is specific somehow to who they are, but if Isbe has any special power, she doesn't know what it is. She wishes she knew for sure. But nothing ever comes of wishing.

Or does it?

She recalls how hard she wished to see her sister again when she returned from the Îles de Glace, and how that wish swept through her with a physical agony that resulted in, seemingly, its coming true.

What if wishing is what caused her own miraculous survival throughout all of the adventures she's had?

Gilbert is back and alive. She has not seen him yet, but she knows that he saved the prince in battle.

Maybe he lived because she wished it so.

Maybe William loved her for that reason too.

Maybe the deepest wish of all—to matter, to help—is

what killed Malfleur, and not simply the recipe of Belcoeur's bloodline in Isbe's veins.

She thinks of what Dariel told her about winter glass—how our stories find us, and not the other way around. Aurora said something similar, and perhaps she's right. Isbe has spent so much of her life searching, striving. What if the answer was sitting in her heart, plainly, all this time?

There is only one way to find out.

To know for certain, she must make a wish. Just one wish, not enough to turn her mad with greed like so many of the fae. Just enough to prove to herself that she's right, that the magic in her is real and alive. That her power is wishing.

Just enough to finally know herself.

She doesn't have to think for even a moment—it's as if the wish has lived inside her forever. Or at least, since Aurora was born, since the day Isbe was given a sister, and a purpose. The wish has been curled and dormant through everything the sisters have experienced together: through the years of coded messages tapped into Isbe's palms, through the constructing of snow statues and whole worlds unto themselves. Through summer evenings full of eavesdropping and bartered gossip. Through cold nights haunted by fits of coughing and even colder mornings coated in the frost of unfathomable loss—first one parent, then the other.

Even in her isolation, in her journey away from Aurora, away from all she thought she knew about herself and her sister.

Yes, the wish has always been there; it is there, still, waiting to be wished, and it is the truest form of love that Isabelle knows.

So she closes her eyes, and wishes it.

EPILOGUE

Violette,

a Faerie Duchess of Remarkable Bearing,

According to Her Selves

The young maiden of Sommeil—Wren is her name— awoke the very next day, the day after Queen Isabelle's secret wish, to discover that the stone that had begun to usurp her body had vanished with the night, and in its place, flesh had returned, spotted in places like a new leaf, tender and soft and alive. Belcoeur's curse on her had been lifted.

Or so the rumor goes. Trade routes have reopened, and with them the flow of gossip has returned. Not that Violette prefers the rancid breath of messengers to her own curious thoughts, but occasionally she does take interest in the goings-on of the kingdom, especially when they reflect so highly upon *her.*

After all, was it not she who amended Wren's curse in the first place, just like she did Aurora's? *To the blood of Belcoeur you will remain bound, never to fly free, your bond as firm as the stone you're already starting to become . . . until true love softens the stone back into flesh and bone.*

The maiden and the princess had clearly found true love, and that was why the curse was broken. All exactly according to Violette's own words.

She smiles smugly at the reflection in her billiard table, which is, of course, constructed entirely out of mirrors, except for the velvet-lined pockets. Sometimes she likes to linger in the billiards room, playing games with herself. She *almost* always lets herself win.

But just as pride surges within her—surely it's not too presumptuous to assert that *she* is the real hero of this tale?—she experiences a most discomforting tremor of doubt. The doubt rapidly succumbs to panic, as she recalls a slight snag in her own rationale.

She had not thought true love existed.

It had all been a twisted, painted, yet delightful fiction, presented to impress, like a rouge or fancy hairdo.

And there is a second piece to the gossip, which doesn't fit with the first.

Soon after the maiden from Sommeil discovered that her curse had been lifted, she told the princess that she longed to fly free. Wren had, after all, spent her whole life trapped—in a world of dreams—and now she saw that she could only be happy if she knew no confines and no bounds, or so the rumors say. There was a great world beyond the palace of Deluce to explore.

But if the stories *are* true, if Wren left Aurora, then this cannot signify true love. Can it? Indeed the story seems, as the old Ice King, Uncle Verglas, might once have said, like a paradox.

And Violette dislikes paradoxes almost as much as she dislikes insects, visitors, and expectations. Fears them, actually, nearly as much as she fears being alone in the dark.

She sinks the winning ball—or is it the losing shot?—into a corner pocket. Or is it a socket? Her hand begins to tremble. She begins to contemplate terrible, demonic things. Like what people would think if they found her hanging by her neck from one of her chandeliers, and whether the chandelier would hold her weight, and at what angle her head ought to be cocked so as to appear the most tragic—the left or the right.

She begins to cry quietly, because dying that way seems awful and yet she knows she deserves it, for all of the innocent people whose sight she has tithed over the years. For her willingness to side with Binks and, in turn, Malfleur.

Now even the great and powerful Malfleur is dead, and so is Belcoeur, and even Claudine. Their cousin Almandine is but an addled and vacant-eyed living corpse. What is to become of Violette? What is to become of any of them?

Despite their propensity for long lives, the fae have been rapidly vanishing from this world, and she knows it. Who will save them? Are they meant to be saved at all?

Perhaps there is some other curse at work, one she does not know about. Perhaps there is time yet to amend it, to undo it. After all, no one knows exactly how a faerie curse works—a curse is almost always more powerful than the faerie who uttered it.

Yes, surely it is not too sentimental to hold the view that the future of all the fae lies in Violette's own delicate hands.

But then, saving her kind would mean risking a lot of things, like exposure to sunlight and other people's opinions. She shivers and stares down at the billiard table. In addition to the surface, the playing balls are also made of mirrors. In them she sees a series of reflected eyes, all of them rolling this way and that. All of them judging her.

With the butt of her cue, she shatters the table.

In the cracks between the shards, she has a momentary revelation. She sees the truth, the real tragedy, so clearly it might have shattered *her*—except that, thankfully, the sun angles through her window and catches the light of the broken mirror, now become mirrors plural, many-angled, and in them all, she is haloed and safe.

Violette heaves a sigh of relief, and fixes a stray hair.

What was it she had been worrying herself over? Something to do with true love. A quaint thing, really. A good story, anyway, if she does say so herself.

One of the best kinds.

EPILOGUE

(the Real One)

Gilbert

A giant, steaming manure pile.

That is the state of Deluce. Who knew winning a war could look so much like losing one?

Roul was killed when his village was overtaken by enemy forces.

His children are, even now, on their way here, accompanied by a local milkmaid—a young widow who will be entrusted with their care. This young widow is said to be as pretty as she is kind.

Gil knows what will be expected of him. It is understood, without anyone ever saying so, that he will marry the beautiful stranger.

And perhaps he will. He is no faerie, after all; he certainly cannot predict the future, and it's unlikely he has much power over it whatsoever. The future, he has always thought, is like an untamed colt. It will trample anything that comes underfoot.

It only wants to be free.

It breaks Gil's heart that he has lost a brother, and that Aalis and Piers are orphaned. And yet he knows that his own losses are nothing compared to what others have seen. Everywhere, there is devastation, disorganization, bitterness, and death.

In fact, next to all that, actual manure looks rather inviting.

Gil finishes mucking the last stall, his arm muscles singing with the bend and lift of it. The familiar stable smells fill him with a kind of homesick joy. Thrushes dust through the shimmering, sunlit mist outside, and the horses shuffle their hooves, sniffing the arrival of spring, soothed by it, or by Gil's return, or just by the stillness of the morning.

And that is where Isabelle finds him, brushing Cobalt's coat, which gleams so black it's almost blue. Cobalt gives a low whicker at her arrival, and Gil turns to see her there, framed by the open stable doors, as he has seen her so many times before, though this is the first time since his return.

The sun has grown so bright behind her that it takes a few seconds for his eyes to adjust to her. She steps forward, and he can see her face. For a moment, she is Isbe at twelve, come to harass him out of boredom and dare him to abandon his chores for the fields. Then his eyes focus, and she is *this* Isbe, in possession of her full height, her cheekbones wide, and for the first time, in his eyes, *regal*. She has changed, irrevocably, he sees. She is no longer the wild-haired, crooked-grinned child, nor the fierce-lit young woman he'd fallen hopelessly and secretly in love with.

He finds that his jaw has dropped open, and though she wouldn't know it, he sheepishly clamps his mouth shut. He finds too that he is shivering slightly, despite the heat of the day breaking out, pushing back the cool shadows of dawn.

"Gil," she whispers, as though speaking in the language of the horses. "Is it really you?"

He can't find a reply—his tongue has gone to straw dust.

"Say something so I know you aren't a ghost."

"I'm not a ghost," he says—because at least that much he's fairly sure of.

She nods, a mixture of emotions chasing across her face. She rests her hand on the door of an empty stall.

"I miss her," she says quietly.

It takes him a second. "Freckles?"

Isabelle nods again.

"Cobalt will be foaling soon," he tells her, feeling sheepish all over again. Hasn't he anything more impressive to say than that? After all this time?

But she smiles, suddenly lit up. "I hope she will have a mare," she says, and he grins, happy that he has made her happy.

"I will let you know when the foal safely comes." A

promise that means more than what it says. *I will be here. I will always be right here.*

There's a sudden ache in his arms and hands. He goes back to brushing Cobalt, muttering softly to her, in order to keep his hands occupied, in order to keep his mind from running his fingers through Isabelle's hair, tracing her jaw, reminding himself of the way her lips taste. He has not allowed himself to hope for anything—he never has. Not even as he watched the prince's vessel set sail for Aubin.

And he can't start hoping now, or it will break him.

But still she draws closer—carefully, like she doesn't want to startle him.

"Gil," she says again. "I want to thank you."

He turns again to face her. She is now only a few feet from him. Another step, and he could reach out to touch her. He would no longer be touching the wild girl she was, but the princess she has become.

He never dreamed, not really, that she'd be his. But he didn't anticipate, either, the sting of the day she'd end up someone else's. In his mind, she could never belong to any man, or anyone at all.

But what does he know? He's just a stableboy.

"Thank me?" he asks.

She clears her throat, and he sees a brief storm of feeling there. "For saving William's life." She pauses. He nods, though she can't see it. "And for rescuing Aurora. For . . . remembering."

He swallows a small lump in his throat. Guilt strikes him

hard at the thought that there was a time, however brief, that he'd truly forgotten.

She draws in a deep breath. "And for me. Thank you for saving *me*—again and again and again." She steps toward him, reaching out, her hand seeking his face.

Unable to exhale, he leans in closer, so that she may run her fingers lightly across his cheeks and eyes and mouth. He tries to smile but another, far more humiliating urge possesses him, and it's all he can do not to break into tears. Her touch feels like rain, washing away that urge but bringing more of it.

"I—" He ought to tell her that he loves her and always has. That would be the noble and right thing to do. To lay it bare, bravely and boldly, no matter the consequences, no matter the impossibility of it.

No matter whether she will ever say it back.

And yet the words are caught somewhere deep within, turning themselves over, like the unborn foal inside Cobalt, still finding their way into being.

But she must know already, because she puts her hand on his cheek, and then she stands on her tiptoes and briefly—like the heartbeat of a tiny creature—brushes her lips against his.

He feels as though *she* is the one who's a ghost, as though his last breath has been stolen, and he doesn't mind; he never wanted to breathe, never wanted to live except for this—except for her.

"There is much left to do," she says now, already backing

away from him, and he wants to reach after her, but he mustn't, and he doesn't.

He lets her go. He will always let her go. He will be content to know only his side of it, only his side of love.

———

"Isabelle," he says suddenly, finding his breath again, just before she exits the stable. "What did you wish for?"

The story has traveled around and abroad, growing grander by the whisper. That Isabelle is part fae, that she possesses the power of wishing but has vowed only to use that power once. Her way of assuring the people that they can trust her.

She tilts her head, and then she does something that surprises him. She blushes. "It might seem silly if I told you," she says.

He is flooded with happiness. It is just the glimpse of the old Isbe that he needed. "Just tell me," he says, partly because he wants this moment to go on just a second longer, and partly because if he can possess one last secret of hers, it will sustain him, perhaps forever.

"Gil, do you believe in true love?" she asks.

"Yes."

She pauses. "Good."

And then she is gone.

———

Isabelle never answers his question; not now and not in the years to come. Not when all of Deluce goes into an uproar after Isabelle and Aurora grant the territories of LaMorte to a crazy old nun by the name of Hildegarde. Not after Gil marries the pretty widow, Editha, and becomes a good father to his niece and nephew. Not after Isbe's daughter by William is born: a tiny, gangly, part-fae child with long limbs and a voice as loud as a rooster's.

She doesn't have to say. He has figured it out on his own. Because Gil knows her—knows her heart, and what it wants most in all the world.

The answer has always seemed plain to him:

Isabelle wished for Aurora to find true love.

———

And perhaps, after all, she did.

Acknowledgments

I thought the sequel to *Spindle Fire* would be easier to write than the first book. I was wrong! At many times this book seemed instead like the winter glass itself—an impenetrable paradox. No matter how I held it to the light, it refused to reveal its secrets to me. I think that's why the theme of storytelling emerged—how do you know what your story is, and how do you let its message find you, instead of the other way around? That's the miracle of writing: the moment the story discovers and claims you.

I have many people to thank for supporting me in this process. I will start with Kamilla Benko, Alexa Wejko, and Tara Sonin, who all contributed, at various times, from helping to brainstorm Aurora's dark journey to untangling the logistics of all the curses. Kamilla, the hour hand inside the clock was a stroke (pun intended!) of pure, Cinderella-inspired genius! As always, I have Lauren Oliver to thank as well, who talked me through my own low moments with this book, and reminded me of the simple fact that the true self is uncluttered; it's always there, at the center of everything—this was, in a way, what Isabelle needed to remember too.

Then there are Jess Rothenberg and Rebecca Serle, who spent many hours beside me, type-type-typing away, in addition to the other members of the Type A Writers' Retreat.

A super-powered thank you to the SPINDLE SQUAD (who deserve ALL CAPS!) for cheering me on and supporting the series from the start. You. Are. Amazing. Huuuuge thanks are due to Adam Silvera too, the brains *and* brawn behind so much that goes on to get both books into the hands of readers and fans, and to Emily Berge, who swooped in late in the game like an unexpected faerie to help out!

Thanks are, as ever, due to my wonderful editor, Rosemary Brosnan, who helped to bring clarity to every muddled moment. And thank you as well to Stephen Barbara: literary agent, venting partner, savviest suit wearer, and lifelong champion.

I'm incredibly grateful to everyone at HarperCollins and Epic Reads, including the indomitable Kate Jackson and Suzanne Murphy, as well as Andrea Pappenheimer, Jessica MacLeish, Courtney Stevenson, Erin Fitzsimmons, Barb Fitzsimmons, Kate Engbring, Bess Braswell, Olivia Russo, Sabrina Abballe, Bethany Reis, Laaren Brown, and everyone else. (There are just *so many* people whose hands and hearts touch these books!)

Same goes to the team at Inkwell Management, including Lindsay Blessing and Claire Draper. And to artist Lisa Perrin for making the covers of my dreams! Thanks as well to glorious Diana Sousa for her awesome graphics and incredible world map. And thank you to Howie Sanders and Jason Richman at UTA, for all their efforts on behalf of *Spindle Fire* on the West Coast.

Thank you to my family and family-in-law—I can't list all the names here, there's just not enough room! But in the theme of sibling love, I'd like to give a shout-out to my sisters and brother—Shira Hillyer, Megan Schulz, and Adam Schulz—and to my grandmother, Ellen Friedlander, who passed away during the writing of this book, but who reminded me, a month before she died, that I should chill out a little. With any luck, our greatest work is still ahead of us.

Finally, thank you to my husband, Charlie, for the countless ways he supports me, and to my Minna Freya, who is, I'm beginning to think, part faerie after all.

LEXA HILLYER is Founder and President of Publishing at Glasstown Entertainment, a creative development and production company located in New York and Los Angeles. She is also the author of *Spindle Fire* and *Proof of Forever*, as well as the multiple-award-winning poetry collection *Acquainted with the Cold*. Her work has been featured in a variety of journals and collections, including *Best New Poets*, and she has received several honors for poetry. Lexa earned her BA in English from Vassar College and her MFA in poetry from Stonecoast at the University of Southern Maine. She worked as an editor at both HarperCollins and Penguin before founding Glasstown Entertainment along with *New York Times* bestselling author Lauren Oliver. She lives in Brooklyn with her husband and daughter and their very skinny orange tree.

www.lexahillyer.com

A PRINCESS SLEEPS,
BUT THIS IS NO FAIRY TALE.

READ THEM NOW!

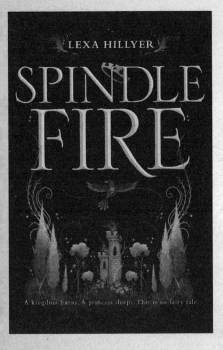

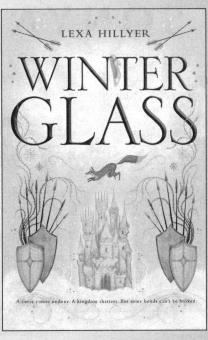

"The writing is lovely, the sisters indomitable,
and as the truths behind the faerie legends were revealed,
I couldn't turn the pages fast enough."

—Kendare Blake, author of *New York Times*
bestselling novel *Three Dark Crowns*

HARPER TEEN
An Imprint of HarperCollinsPublishers

www.epicreads.com

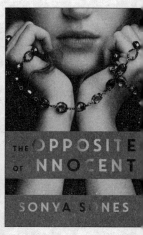

JOIN THE
Epic Reads
COMMUNITY

THE ULTIMATE YA DESTINATION

◄ **DISCOVER** ►
your next favorite read

◄ **MEET** ►
new authors to love

◄ **WIN** ►
free books

◄ **SHARE** ►
infographics, playlists, quizzes, and more

◄ **WATCH** ►
the latest videos